DAVID T LADUKE

The Smell of Rubber

The Tamari Banks Terroristic Thriller Series, Volume 1

I0680494

Published by LaDuke Communications, 2019
Pittsburgh, Pennsylvania

Tamari Banks

https://tamaribanks.com

Cover design by Rebecacovers

THE SMELL OF RUBBER

First edition. March 15, 2019.

Copyright © 2019 David T LaDuke.

ISBN: 978-1-7329115-2-9

Written by David T LaDuke.

David T LaDuke
Author+Believer+Communicator

The Tamari Banks Terroristic Thriller Series

Eyes Wide[1] (Prequel)

The Smell of Rubber

Watch for more at David T LaDuke's site:

http://dladuke.com

---

1. https://books2read.com/u/md0ekR

Dedication

To my wife for her love and support, my son Josiah for all the talks, my family, and the Lord Jesus Christ for life.

To the readers who helped iron things out - Judy, Mike, Tanya, Roger, and others. I cannot thank you enough.

To the Christians in the Middle East who have suffered tremendous loss, persecution, and even death for remaining faithful to Christ.

Foreward

There is a tremendous clash of cultures ensuing not only in America, but around the world. Western Civilization, and the tenets that have historically defined and upheld it are increasingly under attack from various quarters. In this fictional work, some of these sources of friction throw off sparks through the course of its story arc. While it is a thriller, and hopefully entertaining enough to keep the reader engaged, it is also intended to provoke a deeper discussion. To say that some in modern society will be offended by this is a given. But it is not the author's intent to just poke a stick in the eye. There are certain things that simply will not improve if left ignored.

Tamari Banks has her head in the game. She is striving to take on the terroristic destruction that is blazing through her city, threatening the citizens she has vowed to protect. And what of this great upheaval? In this instance it comes from a source that has been troublesome not only to the United States, but many other nations around the world – Islamism.

This is certainly not to impugn all Muslims, particularly those who generally desire to live in peace with neighbors of different religious and philosophical perspectives than their own. Rather it is to point to the threat of those radical groups that now exist, holding fanatically to a belief that they must by any means, violent or otherwise, conquer and subjugate the world for their religion.

The unremorseful violence and suffering Islamists wreak upon others is not a reasonable sharing of their beliefs. It is not an open debate, or discussion in a free society. Rather, it is the fusion of tyranny and terrorism, of fascism and faith set to force itself upon humanity.

At the writing of this book there are multiple thousands in the Middle East who are suffering persecution, displacement, sex slavery, torture, and execution. Often, for various political, monetary, and cultural considerations little is said about the plight of these unfortunates by news media outlets in the US. Christians, Yazidis, and even other Muslims in the path of radical Islamists are tormented by the violence and oppression brought upon them.

But how shall a nation, such as America, stand against this aggression if it is too politically correct to even call it out for what it is? Will its people be kept safe from the violence forever? What if it comes forcefully to this land? And while The United States has been painfully touched in the past by such radicalism, are its people prepared to stand against it now? Will its citizens be wise enough to discern between those that are merely "different," and those that are truly "destructive?" Perhaps only time will tell.

These thoughts and more are woven into this novel. And so, it is left to the reader to wend their way through these pages and decide if the topics of terrorism, clashing faiths and philosophies, and a strong hero striving to defend the innocent have been worth their time. The author hopes it to be so.

DTL 2019

Chapter 1

In the dark corner of a filthy cage, in a violent compound, outside a city of turmoil and upheaval he sat. He crossed his arms over his knees, then rocked, and rocked. No longer speaking, no longer responding, he neither cared, nor cried. Burning thirst and a swollen tongue ceased to torment the broken thing. To himself he was no longer a man, no more living than death, no more mortal than the dead. He did not exist.

There was no season, no light pressing into the sky, or the return of its dark, eternal foil. *Now*, *then*, and *is to come* held no relevance. Time flowed like concrete, oozing, slowly pouring into one place and hardening, settling down like rock.

They had taken him, interrogated him, tortured and beaten him nearly every day. He had been broken. Merciless, ruthless, beyond gathering information or cowed submission, they dragged him into the vicious, godless realm of sick sadism and bloodlust. There were no creeds, codes, or anything found by them in their faith that had voice to constrain. They were at liberty to wound until he sat, emaciated, arms around swollen legs, head bald and scarred and battered.

Dead to this world he was beyond all help. None could deliver him, none tried. Amidst the fetid stench he moved to and fro, an autonomic pendulum arcing from nothing, to nowhere, and back again. He rocked, and rocked, and mindlessly rocked.

Yet, he dreamed.

Chapter 2

Away from the pain, the darkness and sorrow he groped through the chimerical mists, escaping from the broken world and battered frame in which he physically existed. The ground, wet and cold beneath him, stung his bare feet. Coming to a hedge he spied the slightest gap and pushed toward it. At the mouth he paused, gazing into a warm light pulsing beyond the swirling haze.

He heard a feminine voice. It was soft, happy, and free.

Looking back, he saw nothing but moor and fog. A reeking stench fumed from black, bubbling puddles and bracken. Scattered on the mottled, patchy fen were pieces – human pieces.

His pieces.

Giant hands had taken him in effigy, twisted 'til the joints popped and fastenings sheared, then carelessly strewn the shattered parts about. He saw his crushed head. Cracked and weeping red from several fissures, the eyes on it lay open, fixed and staring back at him. Shuddering he turned again to the light, the voice, and the promise of escape. He rushed through the branches and brambles, out onto the sands.

Rich and full the summer sun beat through his skin, into his chest, out of his pores. He ran. From a thick wood, sweet with the heavy air of late July he flew down the flowering hair of the bank and out across the field of waving, downy fronds and wild tufts.

He was laughing.

So was she.

The girl was never more than ten yards in front of him, but as light and swift as the seed-laden breeze. Brown, curling, and long, her hair fell about smooth, supple shoulders, down from an elegant, curving neck. She ran, just out of his reach. Turning, the young fille flashed her vibrant green eyes and laughed again, louder, not to scorn, but of love, and light, and the passionate vigor of her age.

She was winsome.

She was maddening.

Joyfully, he roared with the lion of youth, absorbed in the hunt. Rising up the steep turf of a violet studded sweep they flew with great strength and will. He was gaining. She crested the mound and dropped from his sight. Following with thunder he leapt and came down heavily on the long sweeping descent to the lovely, azure sea. Heaving with blood-pounding breaths he searched about in vain.

She was gone.

Gone.

Chapter 3

"Bro, you up?" Rick Mata asked.

"Yessss," Dane grumbled sleepily. "I'm up," voice thick as paste.

"Okay, are you *vertical*?" Rick's voice pitched up with the question.

Mumbling, Dane pulled the sheet over his head. He let the cell slip.

"Dane!" shouted Rick. "Dane!"

The lethargic man didn't respond.

"That's it, dude," the voice on the phone said playfully. "Dane, pick it up, bro."

"Whaaaaat?" Sharply irritated, he put the cell to his head.

A shrill whistle blew into the tired man's ear. Dane shot upright.

"You freak! That hurt!" He swore, lunged out of bed and ended the call. Pulling on sweats and a Red Wings hoodie Dane stumped to the small, cluttered kitchen.

The phone buzzed. He answered.

"Hellooooo," Rick, obnoxiously cheerful.

"Jerk! I am *so* gonna pay you back!" Dane was smiling, only half as angry as his words.

" 'Shove a little love, bro. Shove a little love my way,' " Rick sang the lyrics to a popular tune.

"I'll shove something!" Dane let out a salvo of choice interjections, adjectives, and not a few invectives.

The only effect was to make his friend chuckle.

"Eh, hombré. Is that Español?" Rick asked. "Es no Inglés." He colored the words with his natural Hispanic flavor. His family had moved to Detroit from Puerto Rico in the late sixties, renting one of the small homes put up to service the influx of auto workers. Second generation from the island, he grew up speaking Spanish at home, English in the neighborhood and at school.

"Okay, estúpido," Dane said through a yawn, "this is the part of the show where you tell me WHY you called me at seven A.M. on a Saturday?!"

Rick started laughing. "You have your head stuck in code, dude."

"Wuzzaaaaah!" Dane fired the private arrow.

9

"Uh…" Rick breathed out quickly. "You insult your best friend?" pretending to be offended.

"Wuzza, wuzza mata u?" Dane said in a sing-song, childish chant.

"Insulting my family name?" Rick, sounding indignant. "You know how tender I am about that. I have feelings too."

"You're as tender as jerky." Laughing with mocking tones, Dane put the phone on speaker.

"Look, Daney, I hate to bodder u little bit, but today is da rally."

Dane swore. "Rally? Today?!" He cursed again. "Next week, dude. I've got a date tonight-"

Rick cut him off, laughing. "Both of those happen, like, uh, only once, mmmm…maybe twice a year."

"Oh, you're hysterical. A FREAK!" Dane shouted into the cell. "Hysterical freak!"

"Look, my dateless friend," Rick said, "meet me at Dingo's in one hour. We'll hook up with a few other compadres and then off to da races. I'm out!" He disconnected.

Dane grunted. He pressed his eyes.

"Great! GREAT! *Now* what am I gonna do?" He shook his hands and shuffled bare feet on the kitchen tile to the coffee press. Mixing, pouring, dumping, switching, he stood over the machine letting its gurgling sound, and warm, steamy smells wake him up.

Just over six feet, long limbed, and somewhat athletic, Dane cut an energetic figure of a man, quick in both wit and movement. His brown, mildly curly hair, was kept short and neatly trimmed, the same as his slight, thin mustache. White and even teeth smiled easily behind his moderate lips. He was attractive to many women, particularly those who adored his deep, chocolate colored eyes, set as a print on the naturally pale wall paper of his skin. But lately none had been able to get close enough to pursue a relationship.

"So much for dating," Dane sighed.

He poured coffee, hit the shower, pushed open the door, and was off.

Chapter 4

Dane and Rick had just left Dingo's, parting company with two other men and a woman. They had all agreed to meet at the rally at noon, wearing protest buttons and carrying signs. Leaving the warm restaurant, with its rich, inviting smells they took to the frigid streets. Rick and Dane both shivered. The wind was fitful, and at times unkind in her temperamental coldness. Early Spring in Michigan was simply a prolonged reminder of a prolonged Winter, who being an ignorant tenant, was unwilling to leave. Old, dirty scraps of paper and blue shopping bags tumbled across the hard, grey sidewalk gathering at poles, curbs, and the small, tired bus stop with its dirty windows, tarnished frame, and faded poster of the Channel Seven News Hour. It was an earlier attempt at a cosmetic renovation of an old, beat-up neighborhood, wearily hiding in a worn-out city.

"Still thinking' about her, man?" Rick looked straight ahead. This was "guy contact" not eye contact.

"Yeah. Can't help it." Dane's gaze instinctively fell to the ground.

Rick glanced at him. "How-"

"Two years, three months, a day and a half, and a handful of minutes." The words came out of Dane's mouth like a memorized answer to a test.

"Sorry, bro." That's all Rick could think of saying.

"I know. I'm sorry, you're sorry, her mom, brother, sisters, Aunt Z are sorry, and so are all my 'social media friends'." He said this last with a funny, lisping sound.

Rick laughed. It was that easy sound shared between lifelong buddies, full of the miles of understanding that grow between boys who went to school together, played hard, fought worse, and came to manhood three doors down. On in the silence, trolling the frigid air like two northbound ships fuming steam they ate up the pavement.

Dane's friend slipped more glances at him. Rick's dark brown eyes looked out several times from under thick brows. The curve of his tanned, Latin features contracted in thought. Unless it was something smart, Rick seldom had anything to say. It was even worse when it came to consolation. But this man was his like his brother. He groped for words.

"Micka," Rick started awkwardly, "Micka was a good girl. No one would blame you for missing her."

Dane nodded, exhaled, and put his hands in his coat pockets. Hunching his shoulders forward he dug deeper into the long, black garment.

"A good girl..." Dane's voice grew quiet, heavy. He felt he would never shake his love for Micka.

Lamicka Latour was a tall, curvy, black girl, with supermodel face and a superhero smile (so said Dane). He also teasingly said her name sounded like someone selling El Dorados with cheezy, late night commercials on old channel twenty. In response she reminded him that she had a habit of dating "skinny, friendless, computer geek, white boys" because she pitied them.

He adored her for that – her smart mouth.

Like a red, undying coal he loved her passionately, deep in his gut in a way that worried and burned him nervously when she was around, and worse when gone. He had "it" bad. And he loved "it", and her.

"Mz. Latour," as Dane often referred to her when he wasn't calling her Micka, or some other romantically queasy name, was a brilliant, radiant soul whose sense of humor was famous in school and neighborhood. She possessed a mental sharpness that made her the stuff of praise, and the promise of a bright, well-educated future. This was good for her and her family, whose struggling neighborhood of Ravendale, a suburb of Detroit, would hardly seem to be the launching point for a future matron of the sciences.

At seventeen Micka graduated high school with top honors, finished her bachelors the class salutatorian, and was striving through a rigorous master's program at U of M with an eye on her doctorate. That's when Dane met her. While she was working for a local lab analyzing "swill", as he called it, she also picked up hours at Gabe's, a campy little bar and restaurant combination on the far East side, just north of downtown. Dane was working for Astertech at the time, making a small killing as a young, up-and-coming computer programmer. At random he stopped in one humid, summer evening, sat at a table, and lost his heart.

He never recalled his order. The old, grease-stained wall paper and chipped, formica table top completely escaped his notice. Bitter, stale, brown coffee and day old half and half swirled by a cheap, tin-stamped spoon went past his lips without a thought. He didn't know what time it was when he came or left. All he remembered was those eyes, warm, brown with the little flecks of gold that fascinated him. That's when he knew that he knew.

Dane came in the next day, and they talked. The next, and they flirted. Six days later he asked her out and Micka wondered what took him so long. Off they went, and the rest was a fuzzy blend of incredible moments, stretching into weeks, then months, then a year.

Tuesday.

She got sick on a Tuesday.

It was the Tuesday before the weekend he was going to propose. He had the ring, a gorgeous, sparkling, chocolate diamond, (Micka's favorite), thronged by a host of brilliant, white-fired stones, exquisitely cut. They all thought she had the flu. Then it got worse. To the ER, her PCP, the hospital, the oncologist, to the unsuccessful chemo and radiation appointments.

He watched her wither.

Helpless.

It was the first time Dane ever really hated himself, his impotence to fix this, to do something. She was a healthy tree, laden with Spring blossoms, the green, glossy leaves, turning fatal grey. He mournfully followed behind her on the slow, painful march down to an open grave at the end of a terrible hill. A thousand times, through tears and bitter anguish he said goodbye and clutched at her for life. But death gripped harder. Her breathing slacked. The smile faded. Her heart slowed, and those beautiful, passionate eyes narrowed, the gold turning silver, then copper, gently dilating, becoming cold as stones.

Micka was so loved. She was so cherished by those who knew her. The small tribe of her blood and friends wept for the passing of its star, its angel. Staying by her side, he held her hand as the warmth slowly left her body. He could not say goodbye. Pitiful sobs of loss and despondent silence were the seasons he wavered through. The large blur of memories was a scattered album in his mind. There were some murky traces of plans, a funeral director, a church, a casket, sliding the ring on her finger – all of them snapshots in the fog. As a helpless wraith, half gone from this present world, he was shuffled to and fro by kind hands, a hollow, pitiful being. Three days, three long days of this darkness he wandered from her grave side. He had loved Micka, oh, how deeply he had loved.

"Dude," Rick broke into the mist, "I am so sorry about your date." He smiled that teasing hook that always found a way to sit irritatingly on his face.

Dane suddenly came back to the present. "What?" looking blankly at him. "Oh, Sheila. Yeah, Sheila, she's a nice girl."

"Cute chica!" Rick smiled

"Yeah, cute. I like her family, but-"

"But?" he smirked at Dane.

"But, uh..." Dane adjusted his hat, moving a stray curl out of his face. "I guess I'm still in love."

"Dude-" Rick shook his head.

"I know, Rick, I know – 'she would want you to move on,' 'she's not coming back,' 'you should get on with your life,' and 'she's in a better place.' I've heard it all."

"No, man," Rick corrected him, "I was gonna say 'Sheila is sweet lookin'.'"

Dane laughed, swore at Rick, and rammed him with his shoulder. Rick let it go after that. He never saw anyone so stuck on a girl. Rick, on the other hand, "loved" a different girl every week. He never got too hung up on anyone.

They went on in silence passing row after row of boarded-up buildings, stubbled with weeds, covered with old posters and graffiti. These were the gutted, long depressed lanes of Detroit, clinging to shadows of the past, now haunted with poverty, hopelessness, drugs, and crime.

Dane and Rick headed toward Woodward Avenue, hoping to join in the protest for the city bus drivers and their union. Like so many others he often reacted emotionally to the decayed tooth of their hometown. Seldom did anyone think through these problems with practical, rational, or economic faculties. In this instance the workers were railing against the powers in charge because of layoffs, and a reduction in both hours and routes. These aggrieved had a hard go of coming to the facts – there were fewer people, at least those who would pay, and a dwindling number of pick-up points and destinations worth stopping at.

For decades the population of this sagging city, this erstwhile "Paris of the Midwest" had been steadily declining. It had suffered a decrease in jobs, particularly in the automobile industry and related manufacturing, an increase in crime, illicit trafficking of all kinds, and a general ignorance among the youth of good work ethic and such morals as would stabilize neighborhoods and grow healthy families. Added to all that was a culture of political corruption that seemed a perennial plague. With so much lost, devastation and hopelessness were easily sown amongst its alleys and within its chain link fences.

"Over there, dude," Rick pointed. They hustled toward a growing mass of people gathered around a truck with protest materials in the bed.

"Here," Dane turned, handing a sign with a slogan to Rick. "Even if you can't read it, just hold it like this." He lifted the placard over his head and bobbed it up and down.

"Just like you couldn't read the name tag on that speed dating chick," Rick smiled. "What was it, Agnus-"

"Angie. An-jee," Dane repeated, phonetically.

"Dude, you called her 'An-Gee.'" Rick laughed. "Sounds like an old Scottish guy with hairy legs."

"And a kilt." Dane added.

"She wore a kilt?" Rick sounding pained.

"No, *she* had hairy legs." Dane laughed.

"Oh, dude," Rick looked sad in a painful, gassy sort of way. Hoisting up the sign he began to dance around Dane and shout, "An-Gee, An-Gee, hairy-legged An-Gee!"

"Shut the mouth, Ricardo," Dane said, laughing.

A woman looked at them, aghast.

"He just got out of rehab," Dane, apologetically. "He's still acclimating."

The woman rushed past.

"You think I should ask her out?" Rick, sign frozen in the air.

"Nah, she ain't interested in *you*, Ricky."

"Hey, beggars can't be choosy."

"She didn't look like a beggar." Dane noted.

"I was talkin' about me." Rick pleaded.

"You're *always* talking about you."

"Not when I'm talkin' 'bout Sheila," Rick spread his arms wide, a broad smile on his handsome face.

"Hey, you want her number, Ricky?"

"Yeah, I-"

A squawking bullhorn cut across Rick's words.

"Attention! Attention! Everyone here for the bus union protest, make sure you have a sign, and put your email down at one of the registration tables. We will begin in five minutes and march toward the bus depot."

"Five minutes! Five minutes!" Rick danced around. "How do I look, seriously, I mean, we're gonna be on camera, maybe on the news." He danced again.

"You look like a moron," pausing, Dane looked him up and down, "*and* a socially conscious protestor."

"Ha, baby!" Rick shook the sign. "My Aunt Sofía said I'd never amount to anything."

"Dude...look at you now!" Dane swung his arms out.

"That's what I'm talkin' about." Rick snapped his fingers. "A papi like me – I look good from *every* angle." He flashed his devilish smile and stuck out his chin.

"Ah, Princesa Bonita." Dane gave a mocking bow.

Rick gasped. "There you go again, mano, hurting my sensitive feelings!" He dropped the sign and pouted.

Dane laughed and shook his head. He turned to stand in the loosely formed ranks of the crowd.

"Alrighty," the bullhorn, "it's four blocks to the depot. Remember, keep it orderly, and loud!"

A few cheers went up. The thirty or so that had gathered moved down the patched pavement bordered on each side by old, rusting cars. The sky turned the color of dirty sidewalk. A cutting wind picked up.

Dane swore. "It's cold out here," rubbing his arms briskly.

"Thanks, Captain Obvious. I knew I marched with you for a reason." Rick pulled his jacket tighter around him, puffing out a long strand of vapor.

The group came to the desired spot, formed up a line and began marching in a long oval, handling their signs, shouting their slogans. Other small crowds were gathered, yelling catchy phrases, calling for justice, fairness, and promising a general peace in the cosmos if the obdurate bosses would but listen. A mocking chorus of "the wheels on the bus go 'round and 'round" began rolling up and down in front of the depot.

All the hub of activity was at the main entrance to the bus garage. Across from its dull, yellow brick face was a large, vacant building, sadly downcast with weeds and vile graffiti. The narrow, two lane road was easily choked with the fifty or so people rallying in the bitter air. At both ends of the milling protestors a patrol car was stationed, each with two officers.

Standing up on a crate the bullhorn spoke. "Thank you all-" the speaker squealed. The controls were hastily adjusted. "Sorry...as I was saying, thank you all for coming. We are here to support the bus union's efforts to keep its people working. We all know the drivers, dispatchers, mechanics, and others need these jobs!" Shouts, and a few whistles flew up from the crowd.

Dane looked around. This was his thing. He felt a certain contentment, a sort of social high when he joined in. And he was serious about it too. Some just liked to smoke weed – an occasion to party. Others came to hook up, or to cause trouble. But he really believed in making a difference. Yeah, this was his thing.

At his company, some of his co-workers poked good-naturedly and called him "bled-heart lib." Others supported him, and his causes. It didn't matter either way to Dane. He had a sense of humor, fairly thick skin, and broad shoulders. Whatever side they were on, he was going to be who he was. He was all about current issues, and big government as the solution to society's problems. Whoever tooted that horn had his ear.

Another man stood and spoke passionately. Looking around Dane noted that things were generally peaceful. He didn't like violence and was glad this group could make their voices heard without injury.

"Thank you, Tim. Your service is-"

The speaker was suddenly cut off. Someone screamed. Behind the cops to the north of the bus garage entrance a hooded, crouching figure had crept up behind a young patrolman and gave him a stunning blow on the head. The policeman staggered but didn't fall. He reached for his gun. Pulling a pistol the man aimed at a random protestor and shot. He fled, leaving the young cop holding his head, and his weapon.

At the same instant a man to the south jumped up on a car hood.

"Filthy pigs!!" he shouted, throwing a brick at a nearby cop. It hit the officer's head, knocking him to the ground. His partner pulled her piece but the assailant had already ducked and ran. Screams and chaos blew out the order, sending protestors flying in every direction.

Dane and Rick backed up toward the overhang at the front doors of the bus depot.

"Free speech!" someone screamed from above and threw down a concrete block. Dane, keeping nervous eyes moving around the street, reached back for Rick. He wasn't there. Turning, he saw him lying near a curb, the block tumbling away. Blood was spurting from a deep gash in his scalp. He lay, making a grunting, snoring sound.

"Rick! Rick!" Dane ran to him, falling at his side. "Help! Help me!" he looked around frantically. "Someone help! He's been hurt!"

The police, though taken off guard, were quick to move and recover. One helped their partner, another the shot protestor. A third grabbed the radio mic at her collar, calling for back up and an ambulance. She headed toward Dane.

"Don't move him!" she commanded. "That's a head injury. His neck could be hurt too."

Dane got out of the officer's way and sat back on a step. Stunned, he sat shaking, a bloody smear on his cheek. He couldn't do this. Rick couldn't die. He couldn't lose anyone else.

Chapter 5

"**W**ho left that body? That...dead woman?" the old man's voice rumbled from his desk in the dusty office with fatherly authority.

"Sir?" Tamari Banks unfolded her arms and stopped leaning on the wall. Her partner was at a small table to the left, attempting to get a cup of coffee.

"Aimes, Banks" the Director called to the agents, "both of you come here."

Glancing at her partner she sighed, a wry grin pulling at her mouth. "Orville Aimes," she laughed to herself, "what evil parent named their child Orville in the late nineteen sixties?"

Aimes was blowing into a styrofoam cup. He insisted they were loaded with chemical dust. The hot liquid poured in, dancing with steam.

"Aimes," the seated man called more firmly.

"Yes?" Orville turned, knocking a stack of napkins off the table.

Tamari put an index finger across her mouth.

Both agents approached the large, walnut desk.

"I said 'who left the body?'" Director Marz looked up at them through thick, smudged glasses.

"Uh," Tamari turned to Aimes.

"We don't know," Aimes replied, cautiously sipping his coffee. He studied the surface of the liquid for a telltale sheen. "Well, that is, sir, we are looking into it but haven't made discovery yet."

"The feelers are out, sir," Banks added.

"Look at us," the Director pulled off the eyepiece, "we're the stinkin' Office of Internal Security and not only have we failed to identify a corpse on our front steps, we don't have a clue as to who put it there!"

"Perhaps a wild moggy, sir?" Aimes looked innocently over the top of his drink.

"Whuuuut?" Tamari said, rolling her eyes toward her partner.

"Funny," the Director's lids half closed. "A regular stand up. Good thing I know what that means, you old bull." The older man tossed the glasses on the desktop. He wiped both hands across his face and left them for a moment on his temples.

"We *are* pursuing it, Director." Aimes said without humor.

"I know, I know," Marz softened his voice. "Just a bit tired, I suppose. And uptight." These last words seemed to hang in the air, reinforcing what Tamari had been feeling for the last two weeks.

Everyone was in fact tense these days. All the government agencies were so overloaded with information traffic it left them spitting like cats, backs arched, hair stiff as wire brush. What should they aim at? Which targets were material, which ones were ghosts? Which ones were deadly?

The OIS, the latest manifestation of bureaucratic terrorism angst, was designed as a small, highly mobile band of elite investigators meant to act quickly on the latest intel. Marz put his glasses back on and focused on the two agents. He gave a little chuckle. Having watched Aimes eyeball brown pools of liquid for styrene residue made the Director rethink the concept of "elite".

"Sir," Orville said, "the entire intelligence community is a purée-"

"You don't have to tell me, Aimes." The Director swore and stood up. He smoothed a wrinkled hand over his thin, silver hair, exhaling slowly. "Every department is concerned – and little wonder. We are absolutely flooded. Flooded!" He threw a file down emphasizing the last word.

Tamari stood by the desk, arms crossed. As the Director extemporized on the "rat's nest" state of affairs she listed off into memories. Good, church-going parents, inner city upbringing, neighborhood generally safe though rough at times, gymnastics, basketball scholarship, state college with high honors, Army Officer, helicopter pilot, served with distinction, out in six, then recruited by the OIS.

Then saddled to Aimes.

That smile danced on her full, rounded lips. The Director went on.

She and Aimes - what an odd, yet strangely functional partnership. Never in her life would she forget the day they were assigned to each other, okay, *chained* to each other. Tamari thought her life was over. Seriously, glue her to Mr. Cueball?! What was she, mini-him?!! Was this a divine comedy, a cosmic snicker after all her hard work?

When she first joined the OIS they took her training to a whole other level. If she was a stretchy doll, her limbs would have been grabbed by Navy Seals, spooks, CIA handlers, and other dark specimens of humanity falling under the general heading "very dangerous, but very useful people." They pulled and pulled until they could check off each of the appropriate boxes. Her head was left for the techie gremlins who yanked her hair and pounded her brain with utter geeky glee – numbers and codes and operating systems and lock picks and hacks.

She endured it all. She excelled. She was some sweet juju.

And as a reward for her efforts they hitched her to Gru wannabe. Oh, he was polite and all that, but homely as his mama's dog. His contemplative, slightly wispy voice had just a touch of British inflection. You were never sure if everything he said was really smart, or really Creeptown. Weird – that was the word; well, the *main* word among many.

It all went down in this very office. The Director had been moved from some other hush-hush position to head up the Northern Mid-West Division, headquartered in Detroit. He did the honors. His grim, straight-up-business face didn't even twitch when he introduced them to each other. She figured he was saving it for drinks and laughs with a few of his inner circle.

But Tamari soon learned that when it came to Aimes no one in the agency laughed. The older ones seemed to purse their lips or lower their eyes in thought. A few younger operatives actually looked scared. "Scared?" she thought then, "of ping-pong head?"

As they began to work together her whole perspective changed. He wasn't much to look at, but in truth he was strong and in great physical condition. Beneath his plain and unassuming ways was a hard and vicious soldier imbued with a genius in his profession. Just when you thought he wasn't paying attention, lost in some nearly autistic distraction, he would unravel an impossible knot, or explode into action with impressive outcomes.

Results – he always got them. The agents knew that, the big suits knew it, and the Director knew it more than anyone. He had a long, murky past with Aimes. That's all Tamari was told. The few times she had tried to ask for more only earned her one of those odd, toothy smiles from her partner. She decided it was something she didn't need to know.

"White noise," Aimes interrupted the Director's musings. Tamari turned towards him.

"Go on," the older man motioned, clasping his hands behind his back.

"It will rain manure soon, sir, tons of it. I don't know the game yet. But this," he paused, finger on lips, "this is only a warm up. It's a flood of static. The next will be a sortie, skirmishers probing, and, I think, feinting. But the real items are up and coming."

"So, what do you suggest?" the Director said quietly.

Tamari raised her eyebrows and looked towards her partner.

Aimes head was dropped. His eyes wore a dark, deadly look as he brought up his face. "I say we make some noise of our own."

Chapter 6

He sat staring. Staring. Long moments passed while he sat motionless, looking at, but not seeing, lost to the office noise, lost to the empty screen in front of him. Burning through three vacation days had done little to stem his anxiety. Rick was in a coma. He was intubated, not breathing on his own...yet.

Hopeful?

Never.

Reality.

He's spent enough hope for a lifetime walking down hospital corridors with Micka at times talking and laughing through their stupid, funny memories. At other times he let sorrow flow, head bowed, not praying, really, just talking, thinking to the air.

He cried out now in pitiful whispers – "Help...not again."

The hospital atmosphere was an endless loop of the same beeps, the same rhythm of the ventilator, the same soft rustle of nurses. Rick's family in and out, a couple of ex-girlfriends, two co-workers – all were at a loss. Dane thought going to work would help him get back in the groove. It just sunk him farther into another hole.

"Why?" he asked the empty screen. "Why?"

No answer.

He moved his hand. The flat panel jumped to life, displaying everything in sharp, crisp colors. Dane's life was a tattered grey. Somewhere in the machine things were in order. You could fix things in there. Out here, out where there was pain, and loss, you could only suck up and move...somewhere. There was no back-up system here. There was no play from the start, no respawn. What happened, happened and you had to live with it, or through it, or die by it, or something. Dane laughed to himself. He sat in the mud puddle of his hapless, broken state, envisioning H.R. taking him bodily to the corporate shrink.

Spotting someone moving toward him from the offices he ducked his head. "Oh, no," sarcastically, "the school nurse." Dane was a valuable asset here, and a good friend to many. He knew they worried, especially his boss.

Fluid, articulate, and successful in his niche, Dane wrote code like a seasoned composer wrote music.

"Dane?" It was Sharon. "Sickie Sharon" they called her, not because she was a pervert, but because she was the health counselor. And it was funny. She was a cross between an RN and a hypnotist. Her eyes were that freaky sort, like an E.T., the iris dark and indistinguishable from the pupil.

"We don't seem to be doing well today." She was a kind woman, but never got a clue about how irritating her condescending, pre-school voice could be. Harry Dunstin liked it. Then again, Harry still lived with his mother.

Dane sighed. "No, we don't," dryly, a dash of sarcasm.

"Now, how about we take off the rest of today and tomorrow, and maybe get a fresh start on Monday?" She laid her hand gently on his shoulder. His emotions reacted to the touch involuntarily. He felt alone. So alone.

"Thanks," dropping his head, "I...I think I will."

With a card swipe he logged out, stood, and put on his coat.

Sharon gently saw him down the elevator and to the door.

Chapter 7

Dane walked the empty blocks to the bus, then took the hollow, creaking transport to his stop. It was eleven in the morning and traffic was light. Standing on the hard pavement he watched the bus pull away, belching a stream of black exhaust. Dialing the hospital his mood spiraled downward. The nurses station gave him nothing new. Rick was still unresponsive. The swelling in his head was putting pressure on the brain, more than was safe. The doctor would be there at seven AM.

"Thanks," Dane said to the nurse. "I'll be up sometime in the morning."

He put his phone to sleep, shoved his hands into his coat pockets, and pressed for home. The sky was sullen, the sidewalk dirty chalk. His heart filled with fog and troubled musing.

Coming to his front steps he looked up. He stopped. There was a small envelope taped to the door. What now? Without knowing why, he kicked at a small, scrubby bush in the pathetic landscaping in front of his apartment. Dane cursed quietly. Nothing more, he wanted nothing more to deal with, no surprises, no problems, and no stupid, unexplained things stuck on his stupid door! Standing there for half a minute he blinked and stared at the thing. Was this more trouble? Who would...? He walked up and stood. Stared.

Suddenly he grabbed it. On the outside it read "Hunky." Now Dane knew where it was from. Now he was even more afraid to open it. Turning back towards the sidewalk he swore louder this time and let out a long stream of breath. He gripped the side of his head, pulling up a shank of curls.

"How did she?" Dane never finished the thought out loud. A firm set came to his jaw, teeth grinding together. His eyes wandered around the outside of his house. "Why me?" cursing at the sky.

Pushing into the warm apartment he closed the door and leaned against the back of the living room couch. He sighed heavily. Tearing open the envelope he read the sparse, printed words:

STUPID

MY PLACE

FRIDAY AT 6

403 WASHBURN
REAR
UPSTAIRS
DRAGON LADY
XOXO

"Jia," he said flatly.

In spite of the sorrows on his mind he chuckled a little. She was such a drama freak. Exhaling, he stood. Maybe, in all this madness, she would be the distraction he needed. He also considered letting a bus run over his foot, just for giggles.

"Friday," he grumbled, flicking the little three by five back and forth. He moved around the end of the sofa, dropped headlong on its cushions, and fell into a fitful, dreamless sleep.

Chapter 8

Staring out the old, dirty window around the cracks, Michael Pearce sighed and watched the street. His dark face reflected on part of the pane.

"Too serious," he said to himself, laughing quietly. His wide smile brightened the picture.

Michael lived in this neighborhood once, not right on this block, but not too far either. There were better neighborhoods in the late seventies, there were worse. He tapped the cold glass where his breath fogged, tracing a cross in the vapor. Cars, were there more or less then? They rolled by, ignoring him, not seeing him. Warren was a long highway traveling through the sad, forgotten neighborhoods of Detroit's far east side. On this lonely little block, the boarded-up stretch between Nottingham and Beaconsfield he stood inside the front part of what used to be a bar off a small bowling alley.

He remembered riding his bike down this way. He wanted to bowl. He was just a kid. It sounded fun. He went in. The owner glared at him. A few patrons stopped at their drinks and looked. Most paid no attention. They couldn't really *keep* him from the pins, but they could keep him from wanting to be there. Michael was black. The owner reminded him he was black. His neighbors reminded him. Other blacks reminded him.

Even his grandparents reminded him.

Only, they drilled it into him that it was a fact never wed to shame. Others may try to make it so, but the older folks made it known that no one could hold him back, except himself. They ground into him that he must take responsibility for the fruit of his life. *His* life. No one else's, save for God. His. There was no one left to blame for his choices. They too were his.

The heroes they introduced to Michael were Frederick Douglas, Harriet Tubman, Booker T Washington, Jackie Robinson, and King. People who made no excuses but made a difference. People to whom "the content of character" meant more than the color of their skin. He despised race baiters. He intrinsically mistrusted politicians and all their airy promises. His trust was in God, and the everyday man and woman.

It was his passion to hold forth the Word of Life, lifting up God's king-dom to humanity, to bring hope and a future to all America, and to the world. Black, white, red – Michael didn't care about their color because God didn't judge people on their color. Even more, Michael reaffirmed time and again that the Lord was the one who *created* the diverse human pallet. It was only our human failings that found a place for prejudice in the heart.

Many hated him. Ironically, most of those hated Michael for not hating others. Even some of his own family accused him of being a turncoat, a trai-tor. Hating, they told him he was full of hate. Prejudiced, they falsely accused him of being a mouthpiece for his "white masters", and a host of other choice insults and invectives. All because he spoke the truth, because he called his own ethnos to reflect upon their heart's choices, their actions before blindly screaming for justice, before picking up a brick to throw.

He believed in the tenets of King for non-violence, for examining the virtues *and* failings of one's self and community. Too, his tenacity and pas-sion inspired him. He loved his people. He believed in them. Their capacity for greatness he never doubted. But how do you change hearts and minds? How do you wade through years of depression, violence, drugs, poverty, and dependency on government? The Doobie Brother's song Takin' It to the Streets sickened him because he was tired of the lie that the answer was in waiting for someone to show up and rescue them. They were a powerful, beautiful people, convinced that someone else was responsible to make them rise. This thinking, in great part artily cultivated by political forces, was a sub-tle, insidious form of velvet slavery. He despised every inch of it.

"Reverend Pearce," the young, warm voice nudged his reverie.

"Yes?" Turning to Andrew he greeted the handsome, ebony face with a satisfied smile. Pearce had met him at an outdoor rally in one of the worst neighborhoods of Chicago. He offered him hope. He spoke of a future.

Andrew responded, pulled by the gravity of a gracious, merciful God, grasping hold of the slender, yet unbreakable rope lowered down into the hell of his world. He was never given orders, but a choice – life or death, ghetto or better. Michael couldn't change the past; he was no genius at turning the tide of all social ills on a dime. He couldn't believe any country, people, or government would ever be perfect. Only God owned that description. But he knew, that not only for eternity, but for time, changing even *one* life could make all the difference.

The Gospel was the everlasting starting point, the foundation and the mortar for the bricks of choices in a solid life. But he had learned, oh, Pearce had painfully learned on mission in southern India, it was hard to preach the bread of life to an empty stomach. The eternal realities, by far the real value, could not be de-coupled from feeding the starving masses. The "loaves and fishes" being dispensed, the common people heard the message of Christ gladly. God cared about souls. He cared about people. He cared about the starving, the poor, as well as the rich and powerful. His arm was not too short to save any of them.

"Reverend, here are the reports from the Life Project."

Andrew handed him an impressive document, columned, full of graphics, tucked into a smoky-clear binder.

"Thank you, Andrew. Nice work, son, nice work."

"Thanks." Smiling, Andrew flashed his perfect row of teeth and armed his "lady-killing" dimples - the one's that made Pearce's niece flutter her eyes, and his brother grumble and growl. He thought it would be nice to see Andrew married. All in good time.

Andrew turned and walked back to the small office behind where the bar counter used to be. "How far had he come?" Pearce wondered. The young man had met his father only once. His mother was too tired, too broken, and too strung out on prescription drugs to really care. Pearce was building him up for more – so much more.

The Life Project was Pearce's efforts to reach out with The Bible and the "bread" of hope. He organized rallies, pulled together volunteers, and was making a difference in the lives of hundreds. He prayed and worked to make it thousands. Detroit was hurting, the country was pulling farther and farther away from God; the people of this nation were tearing at each other. You could cry about the state of affairs, or you could see it as an opportunity. And to Michael, this opportunity was *his* mission field.

He walked back to the window. There would be people out there who despised him, utterly, completely, and with a profound hatred. Others would love what he had to say. Sadly too many, far too many would simply turn their face away and go about their lives indifferent to the hurt of humanity.

"Father give me Grace to do your will. Yours," he tapped the glass, watching the cars drift by, "and yours alone."

Chapter 9

The restaurant hummed with voices. Plates clinked, cups rattled, and the constant sound of sizzling mingled with the rich, homey smells of eggs and hash.

"I have a little finch," Aimes said.

"Oh?" Tamari sipped and put her cup down.

"He's a smart, little bird," her partner looked up, "black and yellow, quite pretty. I love the way he ruffles his feathers, sort of shakes all over, settles down, then chirps most delightfully."

The bald man looked out the window, thumbing the handle of his mug. He absently picked up a piece of toast, munching at the edge.

"You got any other birds?" Banks smiled in a familiar, devious manner. These two were quite used to each other, dissimilar as they were. In contrast to the pale, tired-eyed, quizzical man, Tamari was dark and attractive – an African princess, tall, muscular, and lithe.

"There is a fellow, more of a hummingbird, really, who visited my sill recently." Aimes reached for his tea. "He never landed, but did that curious hovering just outside my window. Ah, but the tales he told, ever so softly from his jeweled throat."

"And what, pray tell, did he say?" Tamari prodded.

"Many are the hands rowing a certain, disturbing ship into our harbor. Shall I be more pointed?" Orville smiled enigmatically. For him it was all part of the game called conversation.

"Please," she motioned with her fork, a chunk of home fries dangling from it.

"Ah, the young tire so easily." Her partner's mouth pulled crookedly, exposing a few yellowed teeth. "We will suffer many attacks, soon, it seems. A number of our, how shall I say it, *non-allies* appear to be egging on some grumpy zealots in the Middle East. Perhaps they should take up yoga?"

Banks shook her head. "It still sounds vague."

"It is, because it is." He nodded over his cup. "We know only threads, but I am weaving, ever weaving."

31

Tamari leaned forward. "We have to ferret this out! How many are going to die-"

The man held up his hand. "Let's go for a walk," he mouthed. A small wad of cash fluttered to the table. Jingling their way through the door they stepped out into the late morning sunshine. She walked the concrete sidewalk with a certain graceful harmony. Stumping along beside her was the lithic, heavy footed fellow-agent who seemed to be perpetually pounding the world back into place.

He turned to her. "Banks, everything I know, all the people that need to know have it as well. But I have the feeling this is too well planned to head it all off."

"You sayin' we ignore it?" Raising her eyebrows.

"No," Aimes shook his head, "yet it's all reactionary. Our job, our function is to get ahead of things. We can't afford to get tied up in the immediate. Leave that race to other horses in the stable. The OIS was created to be at the point of the spear, not the haft. There's something bigger, farther reaching that's coming – that's the target."

"And what's the clever plan for that?" Tamari asked.

"That, my dear, is the day's question," Aimes responded.

"So?" She looked sideways at Orville, then point-by-point scanned their surroundings.

"So, for now we let our birds fly." His soft, refined voice trailed off as he walked beside Tamari, arms clasped behind his back. Pursing his lips he looked up at the baby blue sky laced with thin ribbons of cloud.

Banks walked next to him, gaining distance from the grill. They were both deep in thought.

"You ever tried on yoga pants?" Tamari broke the silence.

Aimes smiled. "My dear, I never stretch and tell."

Her laugh floated off into the air.

Chapter 10

Dane stood at the bottom of the long line of rusty steps. This place was dingy, dirty, a creepy back alley boxed in by old, weary, brick buildings. The graffiti was faded. Even punks didn't come here anymore. The trash, the top layer of it anyhow, was the newest thing around. He was not looking forward to seeing her again.

Sighing, he put his foot on the first rung and let habit take it from there. Each step rang hollow, shaking the iron treads. He stood in front of the old, battered door. A three by five was stuck to it.

STUPID

KNOCK TWICE, PAUSE

TWICE MORE

"Oh, Jia." Slumping his shoulders forward he shook his head. This was *really* not going to be fun.

He knocked.

He knocked again.

A small metallic click sprung the old door open and it slowly creaked wider. The room seemed unusually dark. He hesitated to go in.

Dane cleared his throat and almost whispered. "Hel-"

"You gonna stand there all day?" a hidden, feminine voice asked.

"Charming," he whispered sarcastically and stepped forward. "Jia, I can't see anything." He strained his eyes and looked around. "Jia – okaaaaaaay!"

The door slammed behind him. He swore and about fell over. She was beside him.

"You came. I can't believe you actually came," lightly patting her hands together.

"You didn't add serial killer to your list of weird hobbies, did you?" asked Dane.

"Not yet," Jia hissed wickedly.

Dane turned towards her. "By the way, how did you find me? I-"

Without warning she launched herself at him, arms grasping around his neck. Her sweet warm face pressed against his in a sort of desperation, the clutching grip of the lonely.

What a clash of emotions struggled in Dane. He smelled her cheap per-fume, the kind she wore since fourteen, the brand he nicknamed "Prom Rot". Micka sat quietly in his mind, his memory. But in his need for love, for real, physical touch he thought of how he felt here and now. She snuggled deeper. He also thought of Jia and her effervescent brand of insanity. His common sense kicked in. It always talked to him so practically, with such understand-ing, reasonable tones. He began to pull away. Their faces were across from each other.

"The 'kiss zone'!" he said to himself. "Must get out of the 'kiss zone'!"

With a little effort he separated from her. Jia breathed heavily, forehead bunched, lips slightly parted. She blinked rapidly. With a sense of embar-rassment, she reached into her jeans and pulled out a set of glasses. They were black, almost industrial, with thick, heavy lenses. Dane always thought it made her eyes look like two marble shaped fish flitting around their optic bowls.

"H-how have you been," Jia said, staring down at the ground. "I-"

"It's good to see you, Jia." Dane said softly.

Looking up with expectancy she met his eyes. How she hated those Nutella things. They unglued her. She could keep everyone else in the world at arm's length, but not him.

"It really hurt-" she began.

"Jia, don't start," he gently pleaded.

She walked past him and brushed the wall. A set of lights slowly rose to visibility, flooding her crowded, but neat apartment. It was really more like the upper storage area of what was once a small factory. She had moved in and made it her own eclectic hodge-podge of secondhand outcasts, campy chic, and cutting-edge tech.

"You're probably wondering why I invited you here," she said.

"I guess to say 'hi'?" Dane replied.

"Sure," she twisted her lips, " 'hi' works. I'm," looking awkward, "I'm sor-ry, would you like something to, ah, drink?"

"Water would be sweet," he nodded.

"Nothing harder?" Preferring him fuzzy.

"No, thanks," he said, preferring things clear. Very clear.

She sniffed, tilted her head and handed him a bottle.

"You can take off your coat and sit down," Jia motioned to the couch.

"Shoes too?" Dane brought up the old joke.

"Of course, I'm Asian," she said sarcastically. "What else does one do in Asian houses but take off their shoes?"

Dane shook his head, looking at her from the tops of his eyes. Unscrewing the cap he sat on a tweedy, thrift store refugee. She sat opposite him on a bar stool, a low, black table between them. Taking a gulp of some amber liquid she pulled off her glasses.

Drawing in breath the young man sighed heavily. He felt a "something-Jia-this-way- comes" moment approaching.

"Yeah, yeah," Jia said, filling the empty glass, "that's right I'm the Asian girl - that hot, brilliant, and incredibly solitary Chinese chick that all the guys look at and yet strangely give a *wiiiiiide berth*." She said these last two while sucking in her breath.

"Jia, sto-"

"I mean," continuing, her pitch rising, "I know I could start a camp fire with these goggles," flailing the glasses, "but I'm a freakin' wall crawler without them." Taking another heavy swish, she pointed at Dane and stood.

"Oh, dear," he exhaled, looking at his clear, plastic drink. It had a label with a gushing spring falling from a snow-capped mountain. At this moment Dane wished he was there – *anywhere* but here.

"I think you said...you," Jia pointed erratically at Dane, "and it *was* funny, that these lenses were military grade, or something."

"BCGs" he responded without expression.

"Whatever." She swore at him in Mandarin, one of the six languages she spoke fluently. He had never learned what that word meant, exactly. But when she first spit it out at school, and her sister, then visiting the campus, turned pale, then red, then burst out laughing he knew it was some tasty, little epithet. He suddenly wondered what the pictogram looked like.

"Jia, why are you doing this?" Dane said flatly.

"You mean, why I act so loopy?" She pointed at her head.

"Well..." Dane hesitated, "uh, yeah."

Jia started pacing the length of the table and began one of her typical tirades.

" 'Miss Cao Hong Jia,' my shrink, Dr. Feldman would say..." She stopped and faced Dane. "You know, I really hated the way he butchered my family name. It sounds like the mating call of some Australian bush bird."

Despite that she said all in earnest, Dane had to hide a laugh behind his hand. He looked up at her through the fingers.

She fumed at him and continued pacing. " 'Yes, Dr. Feldman?' I would sweetly ask."

"To which the good doctor would reply, 'You, Miss Konk-a-wee-a-da-bang-bang, are verbally abusive and quite histrionic.' "

"I, in turn, would respond to my rather enlightened shrinky dink, 'Why thank you, Dr. Feldman for your scintillating analysis, which, of course, makes me conclude that you, sir, are a MORON!!' " Jia's shout spewed out with surprising fury, the cords on her neck quivering. " 'And lends resounding confirmation that when you get home at night your fat and psychopathic wife thrashes you to within inches of your life. All of which suddenly inspires me to do THIS!' " She snatched up a pillow and violently hurled it at Dane, soundly hitting the side of his head.

"Jia!" Dane spat.

She stood there frozen, worried fingers to trembling lips. Looking at the glass she gently set it down.

"I'm sorry," her voice small, whimpering.

Dane stared at her, squeezing and crinkling the clear plastic.

"It's alright," he said evenly. He twisted his mouth, breathing long and slow through his nose. "Nice slipping Floyd in your rant."

"Th-thanks." Jia's eyes began blinking, two little wrinkles dancing above the bridge of her nose. Pink, but dry, her lips turned down at the corners. She fumbled about nervously with her hands, not quite sure what to do with them.

Dane stood up and motioned for them to sit down at her small, eating counter.

Theirs was such a complicated relationship. There was no "simple" to have, or to do. They met at college, or more precisely Dane saw her first in the cafeteria and watched with that Freshman "oh, look – it's a girl!" curiosity. She had that beautiful eastern elegance of frame, dark, thick, straight hair, and the deepest black eyes shrouded by that slight fold, upturned at the ends.

Her high, graceful cheeks and oval face were covered with a flawless, pale, almond skin. With an almost clinical fascination he studied this bombastic character from afar, like, *way* afar.

Over that fall several young men had approached Jia, for she *was* quite attractive (even with the fishbowls on). They stood dumb and amorous in front of her like so many mute stacks of hay until she torched them, crisp and smoking with her flamethrower mouth. Other girls? Lost cause. She hissed and sputtered, burning every bridge possible. Faculty? Now that was a touchy one. Some loved her, some were irritated by her, at least one banned her from their classes, but *all* of them respected The Brain (as Dane called it).

Jia was simply, with no exaggeration, a genius, possessing an intelesque capacity to cogitate, assimilate, calculate, and regurgitate every piece of information in any and every academic discipline known to man. Yet, Dane saw quite early that The Brain itself, which he jokingly considered a separate, yet symbiotic, inter-dimensional being, resided within a horribly insecure, friendless, tactless girl.

On a beautiful, Mid-West, Autumn afternoon, Dane saw her sitting by herself in the university commons. She looked so fragile, and so very alone. He walked up, set down his backpack, and took a seat across from her. If he expected her ire, he found none. She brushed the doll black hair over a petite, graceful ear and looked at him shyly. Jia's eyes were wet with tears.

"Hi, my name's Dane."

"Dane-Dane-Dane!" exploded in her head. He put out his hand. She took it. Little fireworks went off around her temples, the fishbowls got cloudy. She smiled and held on to his grip. Dane smiled back nervously. She didn't let go. He pulled a little. She still didn't let go.

"So, what's your name?" He flashed his perfect teeth and leaned in. A faint smell, cologne maybe, filled up Jia's senses. She looked into those eyes, those deep, hazel-nut-n'-chocolate eyes. Those gorgeous, captivating-

"You do have a name, right?" Dane half laughed.

"Uh," the fishbowls cleared. "Jia." She grinned stupidly. "*Say something,*" lectured her head, "*he thinks you're a dork.*"

"Well, uh," Dane looked at his hand.

"Oh, right," she blushed quantum red and pulled her's back, slowly.

There are some souls that have enough native material allowing for water to be absorbed and held. Provided they get the occasional shower of attention they will exist sufficiently, if not altogether happily, and make a go at life with relative success. There are others, however, that are but desert sand – parched and longing, they instantly spring to the bloom at even the very first sprinkles of affection. This was Jia.

No one really understood her. In truth, Jia scarcely understood herself. She was a motley, emotional combination of several odd, fracted parts of one person, and each noisily clashing with the other. Like a house of martins, her inner world was one box with multiple cubbies, and all filled with squawking, flittering tenants, vying for attention. A prodigy, for certain, but never a familial paragon, she alternately clashed with parents and siblings, or withdrew into the chaotic, yet sad and anxious world of her isolation.

Her mental acuity was aggravation itself, spewing condescension and impatience which produced an apparent rejection from her brother and sisters. As she was also extremely self-conscious and sensitive, she angrily abandoned their society retreating into a sort of hostile miasma. Other children shunned her. She was like the nasty, little dog one's grandmother has - no one likes the cur but her.

Her parents loved her, and as good parents do, they tried to comprehend their brilliant, misanthropic offspring. Jia was a middle child, born into a period of relative peace and financial prosperity in her industrious, tight-woven family. How proud they were of her early development and the sharpness of capacity to learn. Her father's father was a diplomat at different points to France, and Italy. Thus, he taught his son to be fluent in both languages, along with a primer on Spanish. Jia's father passed all these arts to his brood with discipline and strictness of intent. However, his children, intelligent and capable in their own right, were eclipsed by The Brain. This funny, little, myopic, volatile girl took to language as a fish sucks water. Every tongue she heard became natural, an engrafted Lingua Franca. Mathematics was unchallenging. Books, particularly encyclopedias, became her silent, unjudging friends. Science, philosophy, logic, they were all the play toys, the childish building blocks of this weird, caustic wunderkind.

By twelve she was utterly bored with school, a misfit, friendless, playing four simultaneous games of solitaire in her head, and, to be quite frank, hating every minute of it. She was listless, longing for identity. No one could think, or speak, on her level. In truth, she ached for friends – a friend, one, perhaps; some other clique pariah who might at least *try* to understand her. And a boyfriend? "Ha!" she would bitterly laugh to herself, "fat chance and dreaming on that one."

Then one day it happened.

IT happened.

No, not a boyfriend, or a friend, or an android (though she *had* thought of building one), or a cosmic craft piloted by large-headed, empathetic travelers.

It was a computer.

A desktop computer.

A new, gearphillic, massive processor, humming, clicking, beautiful piece of silicone-infused Nirvana having fallen to Earth landed neatly on her study desk.

Trudging home from school, Jia carried her backpack with the world and its weight inside. Slowly climbing the stairs, she made it down the hall to her bedroom door. With a sigh she turned the solid brass knob and pushed it open.

In the shadowy backdrop of the sun gushing through the window by her bed the technological savant sat. "Hummm," it called, throwing kisses her way.

Beside this sat her father. He had been waiting for her. Of all people on Earth she tugged at the strength of his love as someone rappelling a cliff holds to their rope.

"Sit, my daughter," he said in his smooth, gentle Mandarin. She did, laying her backpack carefully on the floor. "You, my child, are a deep well that is hard to see to the bottom of. But I love you and understand you enough to know that you are struggling," he paused, swallowing, "hurting. I thought that this may occupy you, perhaps give you someone who can keep up with you." He tilted his head, a slight, compassionate smile brushed his face. She looked into his kind, handsome eyes, a blur of tears clouding the view.

"I am your daddy," using the most endearing of terms, "and I am to guard and guide my family in all things." He leaned toward her taking both slender hands in his. Jia loved him beyond comprehension. In her chaos and pain, the interminable estrangement from humanity, he was that slender, powerful shaft of light in her darkness.

At his touch the deeply hidden heart suddenly burst within her and she began to cry. He tenderly pulled the thick glasses off and embraced her. How marvelous are the arms of a father, a fortress, a stronghold, the assurance that you can meet anything, overcome everything, so long as that man loved you, believed in you. She did not know then that he would die suddenly, four years later. What that added to her isolation was an unendurable hole, a hurt-filled, inconsolable hunger, a longing for the wellspring of love.

"Mercí, Papa," she sobbed in French. How that tickled him. "Mercí." He dried her eyes and turned to the flat panel monitor. Jia touched the mouse. The screen came to life.

And so did she.

However complicated it would be, however volatile, having a relationship with Dane was the first real crack in the shell surrounding her turbulent, secluded existence. He became her all, her everything, her love.

Chapter 11

"There's one thing I have to know," Jia turned shining eyes to Dane. They sat next to each other on the bar stools. "Did you – Dane, please...please look at me. Please..." her voice softening.

He pulled his heavy eyes up and sighed.

She continued slowly, emphatically. "Did you love me?"

Dropping his head, the young man carefully weighed his words. Which way the lesser pain? He looked again into those desperate, beautiful eyes. Turning, he squared toward her.

"Yes." The word came out audible, though weak; though weak, powerful.

Jia blinked. She pressed her hand to her chest and breathed in quickly. Small, painful shots of air gasped from her. These turned into sharp, muffled cries of relief, of hurt, of long delayed, troublesome thoughts resolving on yet more troublesome questions.

"Jia, please...I" Dane reached out his hand to comfort her. She brushed it away. "Please don't cry."

The trembling girl bolted up, knocking over the stool. "Don't," heaving, "don't cry!? Oh, sure," wiping her eyes, "I'm the walking calculator, the modern Maschinenmensch. I don't cry when it hurts, when someone," she gasped loudly and groaned, rubbing the sides of her eyes, "when someone leaves me."

"Jia!" Dane stood.

She backed up, so vulnerable and hurt, yet so afraid of losing him. He was so close to her. He was here.

"Don't...don't hate me," her lungs surged in and out. "You left me, switched your number, moved away – not a word, nothing! I have feelings too," she spat some crude names at him.

"Jia," Dane softened his voice, "you burned my life to the ground."

"I know I was, I was so..." she trailed off.

"You became the ultimate control freak-" Dane said firmly.

"I couldn't help it," she pleaded.

"-after we kissed." He finished.

"It was nice," Jia brightened, running the heel of her hand up a slippery cheek. "In anticipation of growing intimacy, I studied the kissing habits of five distinct cultures. I know exactly-"

"Jia," he interrupted, "stop!" Dane's voice growing hard. "For once in your freakishly incendiary life stop raving and hear what someone has to say!"

She sniffed and listened, truly listened, her hands nervously folding and unfolding in front of her.

"We were friends. You were so smart, waaaay smarter than me. But I saw how sad you were, a pretty, little island surrounded by angry surf."

"That's...poetical." She blushed.

"Don't interrupt." He said firmly.

"Sorry," her hands rubbing together.

"I felt badly for you," he continued. "It was easy enough to see you needed someone to be kind, to understand you. But girl, you really could be nasty."

"I know-" quietly.

"Shhhh!" He cut her off.

"Sorry." Hands.

"And you earned how mad you made people. Dumping hot macaroni in someone's lap? Red pop? Lab frog?" Dane ran his hand up his forehead and into his hair.

"Frog? I forgot about that," she said quietly.

"But I stood by you." Dane shifted towards the door then pivoted back to face her. "I really liked you. Oh, Jia, I loved you. I did love you. Once you let someone in you're a sweet girl. But Jia!" he threw his hands up and turned away, took two steps and turned back.

"Don't go," softly, pleadingly.

"I'm not going anywhere!" he said with heat. "We either lay it all out or I'm done," he swirled his finger in front of him, "*we're* done - for good!"

"Both barrels, Captain. Aye, aye," she said weakly.

"Jia," Dane dropped his head, standing firmly in place, "you followed me, spied on me, watched me."

"I wasn't that bad." She took a step forward.

"You put a camera outside my dorm room," Dane looked up at her.

"Okay, I-" her brows bunched, "how did you know that?"

"Who cares!" Dane nearly shouted. "That was way over the top. You were nuts!"

"Still am," looking down, wringing her fingers, "just a little less peanut, more cashew."

"That's reassuring." He moved closer to her. "Jia, you made everyone hate me. You poisoned my friends. You were a jealous mean chick, or...or something."

"I couldn't help it. I – I loved you, stupid," her voice cracking.

"Girl, you choked the life out of me. And," he breathed heavily, his jaw set, "you hurt some people. You-"

"Hey!" Jia folder her arms. "Her hair grew back. Can I help it if I had an anti-skank policy?"

"She was my *friend*," Dane said more softly.

"*I* was your friend!" Jia's arms shot straight out to her sides, fists balled.

"No, Jia, *they* were my friends. You, I loved." He said this tenderly, taking another two steps toward the scabby, metal exit. "But you tried to take over every part of my life."

"What was so wrong with that?!" heat rising in her high, curving cheeks. "Isn't that what love is?"

Dame shook his head. "It's not love to mess people up. And it wasn't love to burn me like you did."

"Like *I* did?!" she searched, wondering what he meant. "You left me because I was too possessive?"

"Obsessive. I left because I had to." He laced his fingers behind his head and looked to the floor.

"Had to?" Jia's voice thin and breathy. "Had to?" She put her palms on the crown of her head, perplexed and in pain.

"Remember, Professor Reiner?" Dane asked.

"Reiner Whiner!?" Throwing her hands down.

"Yeah," laughing a bitter, little sound. "Remember the Junior year final he gave?"

"Pfff," she flicked her fingers.

"Okay, it was a blow off for you, but – hey," his eyes squinting, "why *were* you in that class?"

"You, stupid." Jia said. "It's also the reason I stayed at the university. Well, that and my parents always said that higher ed would do wonders for my socialization skills."

He grunted. "Epic fail."

"No. I met you," her voice breaking. "I met you..."

Dane wrapped his arms around himself, braced his feet and continued. "Jia," with gentleness, "you hacked into his files."

She blinked several times. "Maybe," squeezing her lips, looking sideways at the ceiling. "Okay."

"You messed with my score," Dane said flatly.

She nodded her head sideways.

Dane continued. "Reiner checked the hard copy against the spreadsheet and saw it was changed. He not only printed it out but took snaps with his cell. Then he called his IT buddy."

"That waddling dude, uh, Lemmy, or something?" Jia snarked.

"Yeah," Dane agreed. "I don't think he actually found anything."

"Duh! The only thing Waddles could find was the cafeteria. And I *never* leave anything behind!" Jia's pride flamed. She pushed up her glasses and sat on the back of the couch.

Dane walked over softly and eased himself down beside her. He folded his arms, staring straight ahead. His voice was soft, little more than a gentle whisper.

"The bottom line, girl, is that he blamed me?"

"You?" Jia looked at him, concern bunching her face.

"I know, right," Dane laughed. "Though I am rather good at hacking-"

"In a paint-by-numbers, sort of way." Jia blurted it out before thinking. She put both hands on her head.

Dane stared at her.

"Sorry," she whispered.

"Okay, Jia, I'm not the artiste you are. Still, I could burn through their firewall without any trouble. Only thing is, I didn't." He looked at her again letting the meaning of his words soak in. He stood up and moved across the room. "It's funny," leaning against the wall opposite the couch, "but the A-gave me just enough points to pass."

"I couldn't let you fail." Jia's eyes blinked at him through the lenses.

"That wasn't up to you, Jia. My mom just died. That was the worst time of my life. She was the only one I had."

"Not the only one." Her voice took an earnest, pleading tone. She shifted off the couch and stepped closer to him.

"Jia, they accused me behind closed doors. They didn't want everyone to know how easily it had been done. I went before a disciplinary board. I couldn't tell them it was you – I couldn't snitch. And frankly, the mood I was in, I guess I didn't care. I just gave up. They, how did they put it, 'summarily dismissed me.'"

"Dane!" She swore.

"So, yes," he continued, "I loved you, but you ruined everything around me, clung to my ankles, tracked my every move, and then got me kicked out of school! I had to leave. If I told you where I lived, you'd follow me and do the same thing again. You were a freak about everything, and it really hurt. I'm sorry I didn't turn to you, but you lost me. I moved to save my sanity...and to grieve."

By now Jia's hands were covering her mouth. Tears in thick, heated streams ran over her sculpted face. Small sobs and moans of the bitterest regret beat against her palms, little, dark birds flailing against the bars. Holding out a hand she pleaded with Dane.

"Please, please...forgive me. I didn't mean to hurt you. Oh, no! No, no, no! I am so sorry. Dane," her voice hoarse, "please." Face in hands she sunk to her knees, overwhelmed, dismayed. The truth burned her like glowing metal – he didn't leave her, she shoved him out of her life.

The young, empty man was lost. He stood helplessly silent, too scared to move in any direction. He still had feelings for Micka. But wasn't it time to love her memory and not her ghost? Jia? That was a carnival of concern. Yet, he too was so lonely, his heart so troubled about Rick, about life. And it had been so long since he held anyone.

Jia sobbed uncontrollably. She had changed a lot, matured, grown out of the rashness, the imprudence of her clutching, grasping ways. She would never be normal, as normal goes, but she knew how to love – deeply, passionately, loyally. What a mess...what a nine-day mess it all was.

The sides of her hands squeezed salty water from her eyes and she looked toward Dane. Somewhere along the way she ditched the coke bottles but was close enough to see him. He was kneeling in front of her. A broken toy, he slumped limply at hands and head. She closed the gap between them and lay her arms around his neck.

Chapter 12

Thin, pale light fell on the blue, graceful minaret rising from the mosque. The structure was not glorious or large, as at other, more affluent locations, but was still a personal triumph for the cleric. Though his people were located in this poor area of Detroit he wanted to raise up a symbol, a focus above their modest, old building. He could not afford to spend funds on a structure with platforms, nor did he have the help to man it with a muezzin. So, he settled for a set of tastefully hidden speakers. Ringing out across the dirty, boarded-up streets, the adhan lifted its lilting cant, calling the faithful to prayer.

Sipping his tea, the elegant, bespectacled man leaned back in his chair. His pristine, white cap, a tribute to his wife's industrious care, clung tightly to his scalp, offset by the thick flow of a greying beard.

The wind beat at the sash, rattling against the worn, weathered frame. He smiled. Sighing, he shook his head. Offering a short prayer of thanks, he drifted through the thin, sweet clouds of memory. "Prince of Sands" was his grandmother's pet name for him. Yes, sand he could take. Heat he liked. Even the swirling winds did not bother him. But cold? Ice? Snow? This place was filled with it. Sighing, he took another sip. The drink was hot, and so comforting in the frigid, northern clime. He was ever glad that Spring had finally come, though the weather was far from warm. Looking up he spotted someone in the doorway.

"Ah, Yusef," he rose, addressing him in Arabic.

"Don't get up, don't get up," the man waved him back.

"Salaam," the holy man greeted.

"Salaam," Yusef returned.

Both men sat down.

"So, tell me, Aalam," Yusef, pouring out some tea from the tray, "how are my sister, my niece and nephew?"

"Well, thank Allah." The cleric kept his eyes fixed on the tapestry hanging on the wall to Yusef's right. He aimlessly followed the patterns.

"So, any news?" Yusef asked.

"Nothing new," Aalam looked at his brother-in-law and corrected, "oh, other than the usual message – 'plan in place, all going well.' "

"Ah, such detail," Yusef smirked. "I suppose that was encrypted."

They laughed.

"I, my friend," Aalam said plainly, "am a man of religious studies, not espionage." The cleric picked up the fragile teacup, running his fingers over the faint, grey design. "So beautiful," he thought, "so exquisitely made." He was a refined man of much learning and erudition. These meetings with Yusef were not entirely comfortable. There was much they agreed on, and as much tacit disapproval that flowed between them. Aalam was committed to his faith, and to his mission. He was, however, not overzealous. Content to do his part, he had boundaries he would not cross, improprieties he deemed unbreachable. He would only get his fingers so dirty.

Yusef, on the other hand, was entirely mercenary, and everything else fell in lock step behind. Though little educated he was in all things cunning and expertly pragmatic in supplying the cause, and in lining his pockets.

Aalam sipped again and looked at his guest. "Robespierre," the French name he jokingly, privately called him. He was a lion of revolution now, but in time he knew those in power above them both would consider him a liability, a reprobate. He would need to be crushed under judgment's hand. The handsome man was useful for now but would be an embarrassment later on. They were well aware of the BMW, the tailored Giorgio suits, trysts with unclean women, and the little side deals he hustled with some of the movement's supplies. Aalam laughed to himself. Yes, they let Yusef play his part as the successful, high tech salesman with powerful connections and lucrative government contracts. But he was too immoral, *and* he knew too much.

That is why the cleric, indeed a functionary in the scheme of things, was content to play a small part. He was but a diminutive, though solid gear, only familiar with those he immediately meshed. Keeping out of Yusef's intrigues, asking no probing questions of anyone, at any time, meant that when the current plan ripened, when things broke loose, he would simply fade into the background of his quiet, simple life. He would love his wife and children. He would fulfill his duties to the Mosque and its people. While those above him may send a quiet, subtle message of thanks, he looked to Allah for his reward.

The men talked their small talk, finished the pot of tea and Yusef left as unceremoniously as he came.

"Yes," Aalam said to himself, "it is all coming together."

The blue minaret sounded.

Chapter 13

"Aimes?" Tamari called from the hallway. His apartment door was slightly open.

"Entrez, dearest, I have some tea on." Her partner's voice floated from the kitchen. "So glad you've come."

Orville sounded unusually cheerful. That might not be a good sign, considering what sort of things perked him up. She stepped into his comfortable apartment and threw her light coat on one of his unique armchairs. The small, cozy living room was truly exquisite, but not to her taste. Many an evening they had passed the time carefully sipping extractions from his collection of Cortado sherry, the red flowering fireplace pushing out the Michigan chill. For all the more she first thought of him as the stalest biscuit in the tin, she had learned to enjoy his sincerity, his kindness, and the intellectual passion he brought to any topic he bothered to engage in.

The décor of his place, particularly this room, was an omâge to nineteen sixties interior design. How readily he emphasized that his tastes, even his very life was hopelessly shambolic (his word) until the cultivated light of David Hicks burst upon him: Bold colors, balanced mixes of antique and modern furniture, all topped with a cherry by contemporary art. With rapturous tones he would finish his thoughts, lean back in his retro comfort, wet his palette, and praise Hicks, whom he called his favorite bird – his nightingale.

Tamari laughed as tossing her coat probably "shambolized" his birdy mojo.

She came into the kitchen and found Aimes around the far side of the fridge looking happily occupied with something.

"I do apologize, Miss Banks, for getting started without you."

"Started what?" Tamari asked

"Field instruction, an object lesson if you would," he said, looking over his shoulder.

"What are you up to, Aimes?" Tamari said, walking around the fridge. "Woah!" She stopped.

"You see, Tamari, this little darling is a Boska Holland De Luxe Stainless Steel Brie Soft Cheese Knife. I picked it up on Amazon just the other day for under twenty dollars, free shipping."

"Free?" Her eyebrows went up.

"I have Prime," Aimes said, smiling.

"Good thing. Looks handy," she noted.

"Indeed, Miss Banks. You see the narrow blade helps to keep the soft cheeses from sticking to it."

"I see," she replied.

"And it's dishwasher safe." Aimes added.

"Uh-huh." Tamari folded her arms and leaned back against the counter.

"But the real test of any blade is stress, Miss Banks. Various pressures always try one's tempering. Ah, and there I go slipping into analogous philosophy again - an old habit, I'm afraid." Aimes looked at her over his shoulder.

The blade, stainless and good in a hot wash as it was, quivered, partially buried into the thick wooden trim around a doorway. Tamari leaned over, wearing an amused look. There was a man pinned up against the wall. His face was sweaty, eyes bugged.

"You see, my young associate, the first part of the lesson is already over. It was a sort of practical exercise in disarmament, if you would. Mr. Hammoud here, if such is his real name, had the audacity to come into my house brandishing that Walther TPH twenty-two caliber. Say, bub," speaking to the man, "did you really think you were going to get *that* close? Such a small diameter is entirely insulting."

Tamari noticed the gun on the floor. She saw blood. The man's hands hung down. One dripped like a broken lava lamp. Red drops painted his shoes.

Aimes wiggled the blade.

"Ouchy!" the man said with a thick accent, his voice heavy with pain.

"Seriously, dude?" Tamari bunched her face.

"Oh, don't mind him, Tamari. It's a sort of *'gentlemen's agreement'* we've worked out."

She moved around behind her partner. Aimes' thick left arm was holding the blade in place. It was pierced neatly through the skin at the edge of the man's neck. His right arm crushed the smaller man into the corner of the wall and fridge like a hydraulic jack, pressing firmly, just below the sternum.

"Some agreement," she snickered.

"Well, let us call it an understanding, then." Aimes clarified. "You see, I made it clear, once I pinned him in place, that when I wiggled the blade he was to respond appropriately."

"You couldn't think of anything better?" She asked.

"Actually, no. And for all my pains I found it gratifying to make him say it." Her partner sounded wickedly amused.

"Uh-huh. I'll get back to you on that." Tamari said.

"Certainly. Presently, however, I am engaged with Mr. Hammoud on the ground rules of our little tête-à-tête. I have him in quite a predicament, you see. Notch this to the right and I sever some serious cordage and jugular. To the left and I painfully, yet cleanly cut through the tender flap of skin. He is truly boxed in, my dear." Aimes sounded matter of fact, like a clinician discussing a check-up.

"I'll say." Banks smiled.

Aimes wiggled.

"Ouchy," Mr. Hammoud through gritted teeth.

Tamari looked over Orville's shoulder.

"So, Hammy-dude, what *were* you thinkin' trying to snuff my partner?" she asked the captive.

"He is crazy!" The man's face absolutely ran with sweat.

Wiggle.

"Ouchy."

"Crazy?" Tamari reached around Aimes and shook a fine-nailed finger in the captured man's face. "That ain't none of your business, Hammy. He's my crazy to kill, not yours."

"Ouchy! Ouchy!"

"Why, Miss Banks, I am sincerely touched." Aimes, quite pleased.

"You're something, alright," she said sarcastically. "So, what do we do with Pita Bread here?"

"I think a good sitting down is in order, a real father to son chat about the facts of life and terrorism." Aimes replied.

"Then we turn him in." She stated.

"Why, yes. Then." Her partners voice became a bit more threatening as he drew his face closer to Hammoud's.

Aimes stiffly pulled the knife out and ushered the bleeding man to a chair in his small dining area. Banks went to the bathroom and got a kit, patching him up with gauze and tape. They handcuffed him. While Aimes began his talk, Tamari walked out to her car to grab her field gear. She returned, put on gloves, took pictures, and scooped the gun up with a plastic evidence bag. She left everything else as is.

Taking the man's picture, she ran it through a secure OIS app which analyzed key points of his face and began churning it through the data base for recognition. She touched the screen to a couple of his fingertips and began a print match.

She knew Aimes was seriously probing into a very dark world. But it was his world. He understood it. She was just learning, just coming to taste how pervasive and interconnected, how truly deep and deadly this game and its players were.

Aimes joined her briefly in the kitchen. He spoke low and evenly.

"He's a clown. A stooge, I guess you could say. There is little to nothing professional about him. That piece," nodding to the bag on the counter, "he handled it like a cheap, old camera – just point and click. He got one round off and I'll be blast if I didn't just have that room painted."

"You okay?" She wondered.

"Am I slipping?" Aimes looked at her. "No. But this little piggy was handled for a good while. Mr. Hammoud has been in this apartment complex for as long as I have. That's the trouble - I saw him so regularly he became background."

"Did you know him?" She asked.

"No," Aimes said nonchalantly, "just casual greetings, incidental, really. 'Hello, goodbye, nice day,' sort of things. He was a neighbor, and thus to me became no one in particular, just scenery – a lamp post, a fire hydrant-"

"Low budget assassin." Tamari stated and held up her phone, watching the display as it searched through the data.

"More of a messenger, really," her partner returned.

"That's why you let him in?" She said, looking at him over the cell.

"Well, my paper *was* missing." His brows made two perfect arches when she made a face at him. "I know, I know, I'm a fossil. But I like to read it, tactile experience and all. Not having it leaves me somewhat mentally peckish. However, to find it missing was no great concern, you know. That boy who delivers it, honestly sometimes he just draws a blank. He's been bringing my morning paper for two years. Every once in a while, he just..."

"Forgets," she finished.

Aimes nodded. "And our dear Hammy remembered and brought me his copy."

"With a nice surprise," Tamari said.

"Yes," he agreed, smiling at Banks. "He came to my back door down that little hallway just off the kitchen. Two steps past the threshold and out the weapon came. The rest is, well, let's say he lost his 'good neighbor' rating today."

"Zero him. One you. So, has he said anything?" She wondered.

"Few words, but reams of fear, though not of me. I think he is just a game piece. Someone knows I'm pressing my finger into the pie. Someone, quite simply, wants me to stop. This one," nodding towards the seated man, "is a reluctant sock puppet." He looked at Hammoud almost pityingly.

"Let's take him in." Tamari moved to speed dial the office.

"Yes. Let's," Aimes agreed. "Call the Director, if you please. We can question him in the meantime. And do make sure they bring the big black van with the tinted windows, spinning radar dish, and 'Al's Plumbing' splashed in bright yellow on the sides. We don't want to be too conspicuous."

Tamari closed her eyes and shook her head.

Chapter 14

Reverend Pearce stood at the township office.

"What was the name?" the young woman glanced up.

"Michael Pearce-"

"No, sir, I meant the park."

"Oh, uh, Erma Henderson Park." He looked at the map she had on the wall. "That one," pointing, "there."

"Yes, sir. I know where it is," a bit of snark thrown into her politeness. "And what is the permit for?"

"I want to hold an open air meeting," he said, smiling.

"Is it political?" The office worker asked.

"Political?" Pearce said quietly, wondering what on Earth it mattered. "No, religious."

The young woman looked at him, her eyes clearly speaking disdain. She knew she couldn't say anything. She knew he knew she couldn't either. Crisply stamping the form, she took his permit fee, stamped another paper and handed him the receipt. He thanked her and left for the street.

Across Detroit Michael Pearce had labored for God's kingdom. He was not ashamed of the Gospel of Christ and knew it was the power of God unto salvation. People wanted to change neighborhoods – so did he. They wanted to pull the needy out of poverty, drugs, crime, gangs. He did as well. Only, he believed, or rather knew that in order to change lives, you must change hearts and minds first. Who they were, what they believed, how and why they lived were the most powerful currents. But Michael understood his limitations. He knew he couldn't change souls – only God had that power. He also knew that the message of God's reconciliation to a lost and searching world was universal, from Wall Street to these streets; from the REN CEN to the most broken-down neighborhood. God is no respecter of persons.

Most of the time the meetings he held were in the worst parts of the city – places he was told to stay out of. They were too violent, too poor, too full of anger, hatred and bitterness. He was told at times they were too Muslim. Other times, they were too secular, worldly, carnal. It didn't matter. He couldn't let comfort, prejudice, or fear guide him. As a minister he must take the light into the darkest corners. Even if only one was reached, like Andrew, that one was worth it, and may well be the key to reaching deeper into their broken streets.

Erma Henderson park was not in what might be called a "war zone." It wasn't bad, as Detroit neighborhoods go, was on the river, had access to a marina, and was not far off Belle Isle. He had worked tirelessly with local Evangelical and non-denominational churches to organize this rally, praying for a harvest of souls and the planting of a new hope for the people. Even some of the larger, mainline churches offered support by one means or another. Yes, he had a bright outlook for this rally.

He got in the old car and closed the creaky door.

"Yes, sir," Andrew, talking on the phone, "yes, sir, I'll let Reverend Pearce know right away. Thank you, sir. Thank you. Goodbye." He ended the call.

"Well, Rev," he called him that when things were up.

"Good news?" Pearce asked, grinning at the young man's enthusiasm.

"That was Pastor Phepps," Andrew responded. "He has thirty volunteers to help get things set up."

"We're up to sixty eight now." Michael gripped the steering wheel, his smile widening.

"Thirteen churches, fifteen pastors, and yep," he checked his notebook, "sixty-eight, well sixty-nine counting me."

"I always count you," he patted him on the shoulder. "Now, we trust the Lord of the Harvest for souls."

Pulling out into traffic, Michael glanced over at Andrew.

"You haven't been to White Castle yet, have you?"

"No, sir. But you've been makin' my mouth water for days talking about their burgers."

Pearce laughed. "C'mon, kid. Let's go eat."

The car sped up, disappearing into the heavy traffic.

Chapter 15

"**A**re you family?" the young, pretty nurse asked Dane. Dane looked up at her thinking of how Jia would react. How Jia would scratch her eyes out. No, wait – first she would hack into her bank account and dump it in the trash, double her student loans, blow up her credit cards, and post her address and social security number all across the internet. *Then* she would scratch her eyes out. He sighed and smirked. How he hoped that was the old Jia, not this supposedly upgraded one.

"I've been told I'm funny," the woman looked sideways at Dane, "but I don't see the joke."

"Sorry," the crooked smile melted from his face, "I...we're best friends."

"That's the funny part?" hand on her hip.

"Naw," he shook his head, "naw, it's just me. I'm just thinkin'."

"Thinkin'," the nurse jutted out her bottom lip, rocking her head side to side. "Who isn't?" She checked Rick's IV and started for the door. Her colorful shoes squeaked a little as she walked.

"Nurse?" He caught her at the doorway.

She stopped. "Yes?" smiling.

"Uh, so, how is he?"

Her smile faded and she adopted a more professional demeanor. Folding her arms over the clipboard she took a step back into the room.

"That's really something that should be discussed with the doctor," she said evenly.

"That bad, huh?" He looked at her through glassy, dark ringed eyes.

She stared at the floor and sighed. "I'm sorry. You're not listed as kin. It's best you speak with his family."

"I will," breathing out forcefully, "I will." His hand ran through the curly hair and squeezed the back of his neck. "He's like my brother. I was there – *we* were there at the protest."

The young woman hesitated. She glanced at the clipboard. She looked at Dane, then at Rick. Moving closer to his chair she put her hand lightly on his shoulder. Without a word their eyes met. Her brows pulled together, a slight gloss of liquid rimmed her lower lids. She shook her head. No words. None needed.

A slow breath escaped the sad, young figure, half bent in his chair. Sucking in and out the machine kept Rick afloat in this world. There was no promise he wouldn't sink. There was nothing in Dane but that ache, that void. He hid his face.

"The doctor will be in again in the morning." She squeezed his shoulder once and squeaked her way out of the room.

"Why?" softly, into his palms. "*Why?*"

The survivors, the healthy, the unwounded always ask the painful questions. *Why had they gone? Why hadn't it been me? Why wasn't I here earlier? Why?*

"Dane?" a voice gently called.

He looked up at the lady, tears pooling around the swollen capillaries of his eyes.

She cried too.

"Mrs. Mata." He stood and walked towards her. Putting his arms around the little woman he burst out in anguish.

"I am sorry. I am so sorry." A thick stream poured around his cheeks.

"Dane," she patted him, ever the comforting mother, "it's a-right...is okay." They stood there embracing, rocking back and forth. Rick's sister Luisa came up, her keys jingling. Opening up the circle Dane pulled her in and they ate the fast of families – the bitter crusted bread of sorrow.

Luisa stepped back and rubbed at her face. She was a mess. They were all a mess. Moving to his bed they touched his arm, hugged, and said the agonizing, empty things that people say when reality is too hard to ignore. Mrs. Mata picked up her son's hand and kissed it.

"Such a good boy," her heavy accent even more lyrical with pain. "Ah, but such a smart mouth."

The three of them laughed, sniffled, wiped their cheeks and stood in silence.

In and out sucked the machine.

"Dr. Rames," Luisa began and choked, "said his brain is toast."

"Luisa!" Mama chided. A few more reproving words in Spanish and she leaned over, kissing Rick's forehead.

"Mama, how else am I going to say it?"

"Something that no makes it sound like bad TV," the older woman said defensively.

Luisa sighed and nodded. She put her hand on Dane's and held it. "He has extensive and irreparable brain damage. The way he is now is about as good as it gets."

Ms. Mata began to sob, pleading with God in husky, native tones and entreaties. Her very soul, as the soul of all good mothers, was laying on that bed, wounded, damaged, broken. She sorrowed not for herself, or her future, but with the artless selflessness of her sex she bled over the pain of her child, her boy.

"Mi hijo. Ah, Dios, ten piedad. Mi hijo." Her heart groaned beyond the voice of tongues. Over and over she kissed his hand. She had kissed his newborn, crinkled skin with the tiny pale fingernails. Her lips had comforted his skinned knees and bruises with soft caresses to the back of the same hand. She kissed it now, holding it alternately to her cheek, then to her forehead, bathing it with her tears. Over and over she pleaded. Out and out it poured from deep within her breast, a bleeding of her very life onto the silent man. A woman may mourn a dead lover the day, but a mother her son to the grave.

"Mi hijo. Ah, Dios...Ah, Dios," Mrs. Mata sobbed.

In the cold light of a winter morning they held one another, cried with each other, and kept the same secret from each other – the whisper of a better death than such a broken life. The thought was at once instinctive and abhorrent, surreal yet pragmatic. It was both the cessation of pain, and the abandonment of hope. It remained between them as death – unspoken.

Luisa and Mrs. Mata left for the cafeteria, leaving Dane alone. He pulled out the small, but soft recliner tucked into a corner of the room.

He sat.

The machine sucked.

It pulled.

Pushed.

Beeped.

Rick's lungs by themselves were flaccid, useless bags. Like strands of kelp they simply flowed back and forth, in and out, lost in the larger, fluid force around them.

The machine hissed. It huffed. Beeped again.

Dane had not realized how tired, how exhausted he felt. What of the body? What of it? Its eyes close in fitful slumber for a time. Waking it finds a weary, foot worn soul to cart around, a depleted psyche, a mind whirring and spinning in fitful gasps against the brain, clenching the neurons and shouting, "shut up! Shut the world down! Shut it all out!" Yet the brain sucks in. It pulls, it pushes, it whirls and clicks, autonomically maintaining the hollow, two-legged cart currently hauling around the present dung heap of a poor, beaten man.

There he was, eyes open, heart numb. He stared at the numbers and the flowing curve of graphic waves. He cursed. What did they mean? What was the point? A red and a black probe stuck into a stalk of celery proving some measure of resistance, some electric property to the piece of vegetable? Yet this was his friend, his brother. How could he ever let him go? Sadly glancing at Rick, then the medical display, he listened to the rhythmic click-hum-suck-push cycle.

Over and over.

Over again.

His head dropped. Numb. Alone.

A slight, subtle noise scraped behind him. He slowly turned toward it. Standing in the doorway was a woman: a beau - *scratch that* - a gorgeous woman. "Great," he thought with an odd, displaced humor, "Jia will really freak now." A strange, unhappy smile inched across the flesh of his face. He was in a weird funk, sort of like Rick's normal sense of the comedic. Offbeat, emotic, both sides of his heart needled with the Novocain of "who gives a rat's rear-"

"Dane?"

He stopped his mad hattery and pulled back his head. That voice. The voice.

"Dane?" The click of a heel on the cold tile. He turned and looked at her. The thick, lustrous hair glittered a band of light.

"How did they do that?" he mused. "My hair's as glossy as a brillo pad."

"Dane." Another click cut across the machine.

Her frame was slender, though accentuated with soft, feminine curves. An elegant wash of brilliant red was exquisitely draped, held close to the perfect waist by a small, thin line of gold. One shoulder was bare. The poor, grieving man was painfully captivated by its smooth, rounded shape, flowing from the sculpted upper arm to the long, beautiful fingers. The nails were painted an intoxicating black. He never forgot the nails. The figure began to bend down toward him. Like that tender spot of memories where things are warm and peaceful, a sweet, gentle scent lay its silky webs on his brow. Dane closed his eyes. The woman bent closer. Was he lost in some diversion, some escape hatch out of reality? Everything whirred and clicked, and sucked, and pushed, and he didn't, couldn't care. All was red dress and fragrance, shining hair, black, long finger nails, and-"

"Dane!"

He popped his eyes open.

There was a face an inch from his. Two ocular globes peered, watery, brown and large, framed by tortoise shell.

"Dude," the dream said, "you look rough."

He blinked.

She blinked.

He blinked again.

"Nuh-uh!" He blinked some more. It couldn't be. He rubbed his face and looked again. Miss cinnamon red hot couldn't be the admittedly cute, but chronically frowsy, pajama wearing, never-use-makeup-and-if-you-don't-like-how-I-look...

"Jia?"

"Yeah, fuzzy brain, it's me."

She did a thing she had never done, not because she hadn't wanted to, but because she never had the courage to. She reached up and lovingly, gently stroked his hair. That touch, oh, that lovely, wordless lifeline - only the truly desolate know the burning sense of human contact, the kind where someone deeply cares and asks for a seat on your soul bus, an upfront place in your heart.

That touch, that slender key opened a deep inner door in Dane, behind which was all the hurt, all the guilt, all the anger, and every haunting question. It pressed him down, the lingering weight of her black-nailed hand pushed his control out of shape, ballooning an emotional aneurism.

"Oh..." Jia didn't know what was happening. "Oh, sweetie, oh."

Dane's head fell forward and his inner world exploded. Wrenched from him in sloppy, immoderate vomits came all the tears, the groans, the sobs and sorrow of his worn, weary heart.

Jia yanked over a metal folding chair and sat, cradling the long distant love in her hands. Her hands that would now be his stay and defender, her palms that would ever embrace the broken man she loved.

"To be needed!" she thought. "To be wanted!"

Tears fell from her pretty, graceful eyes. She was changing so rapidly, so wildly. Out from the shadows of her nursed misanthropy she was unfolding long cramped wings, and they were filled with the wind of a fierce and burning love for Dane.

Off came her glasses. Down went her lips, kissing the shaking forehead, held on both sides by long, slender fingers. She loved him, oh, for the first time she began to understand a greater, giving love.

"Dane," she sobbed, "sweetie, I'm here for you."

He fell into her arms and heaved with pain. She stroked and soothed, and clung with all her might. Once she had him she would never let go. Once he had her, he would have her all.

In this sad ocean floated two tiny plankton, drifting together with the unstoppable sway of immense currents. A single green strand waved back and forth beside them, oblivious to the depths.

Whir-suck-beep-push.

Click.

Chapter 16

Yusef sat nervously in the spacious home office. He was a good poker hand in the normal course of life, but this took all his effort, every ounce of focus and mastery. He shifted. He cleared his throat.

"Is it 'yes' or 'no'?" The man seemed to tower over Yusef.

"Well," Yusef put down the teacup with affected nonchalance," that depends."

"On whether the answer is 'yes' or 'no'," the imposing figure said.

"Ah, Asan," Yusef smiled, "they said you had a sense of humor. Yet again, I have not been disappointed."

Asan stared at Yusef. His jaw worked slowly back and forth. His eyes never changed. They didn't just give him the jitters, to borrow the American vernacular. No, they did what no one else could do – squeeze his stomach cords into knots.

Yusef hated him. He despised this man. There, looming in front of him was an ever-hungry weapon, made for one purpose, wielded by unmerciful hands. Yusef, somewhat cowardly and focused on the more gratuitous adventures of this whole affair, felt nothing but disgust for him...for *it*. There were many, even plain dealing Muslims, who suffered at this one's hands. All of these blood merchants were off the rails. Why couldn't everyone just settle their problems in a day spa? He thought of Asan's hair wrapped in a white towel and almost snorted his drink.

"Ah," the seated man shook his head, "no, they will never change."

Yusef knew most of the actors in this little game of religious "vie et mort" were hardened, fanatical, and suicidally devoted. This Asan, was, well, *inhuman*. No, machine was not the word. "Let's see," Yusef pursed his lips, "if you crossed the Death Angel with a...a-"

"So, which is it?" Asan's voice rose in pitch.

"The answer, Asan, is 'yes.' 'Yes', 'yes', and again, 'yes'. The shipment will be in, on time, at the price paid, no questions."

Black eyes stared.

Yusef shifted again. His guts turned. He sipped and looked down at the carpet.

Bunching the thick muscles of his neck and shoulders Asan turned sharply and began a slow, measured pace to the window. Parting the blind, he peered into the tired grey of late afternoon. His hand habitually rested on the black item strapped to his right hip. It was a karambit, a small, wickedly curved knife shaped like a claw. Above all other tools in his arsenal, this was Asan's favorite. They had a long history together. Both seemed to relish the silent, effortless piercing of flesh. Many a life had ceased when met at the crossroads of this assassin and his steel servant. Crouching in its tension holster the precision edges and impossibly sharp blade almost screamed to its master for action and blood.

Asan was well-known, or rather well-feared within Islamist circles. There was no weapon he was not a complete master of. No one could outfight him fist to fist. Many tried. All failed. He had been gassed, stabbed, shot, and peppered with shrapnel, but he always pulled through. Thus, his natural endurance and ferocity became coupled with legend. Even his enemies began to believe some otherworldly protection hovered over his inexhaustible life.

Glancing up Yusef spotted something stamped into the dark leather of Asan's knife sheath. He saw the unmistakable tree symbol and his heart began to involuntarily beat faster. Sweat trickled by his ear. There was no need to read the Arabic. Yusef knew it all too well. But this was the first it ever surfaced with this particular group of clients.

These were the fanatics that made other fanatics shut their mouths with respect. Tons of money, political chess playing, a cultic, divine prerogative and an unquestionable, holy leader were propelling them forward. On top of that they had boatloads of tech, hardware, and advanced weaponry at their disposal. Yusef had now regrettably seen to that.

And they were obviously growing bolder. He had never seen this emblem surfacing except in the rarest and most secretive of circumstances. That could only mean that it was all coming down soon, very soon. Bad things were going to happen here. Yusef suddenly realized that this would be a good time for him to get out.

"But how?" he wondered. "What was the best way?" Wheels began spinning in his head.

It would be no easy task to remove himself from these connections, from this life. He had dozens of clients and not one of them would let him quietly slip off into oblivion. Yusef knew too much. The arms dealer had dirt on them all. Serious dirt.

But he had always had an exit plan. Only a fool in this business thinks he will see old age without a way out, and tons of insurance. Over the years Yusef had stashed both paper and digital documents in several dozen places. Banks, attorney offices, safes in the basement of mosques, and an old man he didn't know, but paid well to hide things in a sock drawer. If ever he gave the signal or failed to make his quarterly check in with three designated individuals, all sources would be given specific instructions on how to disseminate the information.

The savvy merchant also had pockets of cash, gold, silver, and jewels stashed in strategic hideouts and safe houses around the world. He had also worked out transportation lines from private jets, cargo holds in drug dealer airplanes, trains, busses, cars, and even a goat cart. It wasn't paranoia that drove him, it was the gallons of blood he watched his clients paint the world with that taught him the necessity of planning.

"So, they are setting up to make their final move," he mused in his head, "and I must make mine."

Yusef resolved then and there how to get away from this as cleanly, *and* swiftly as possible. He would quietly slip into luxurious anonymity, but not before taking a dose of long simmering revenge. The demon currently standing on his plush carpet not only made him disgusted by principle, and not a little afraid, but several of Yusef's personal associates, and their families had bled at this one's hands. No, the arm's dealer was determined to make him suffer.

He eyed Asan. Turning again at a right angle the brutal man headed toward the other wall. Once there he pivoted, moved back to the window and checked the road again.

"Don't worry," Yusef assured, "the street cleaner drives by at 12:05 AM on the dot."

Asan didn't acknowledge the comment. He certainly didn't smile. Pacing to the other side of the window he lifted the edge of the blind once more.

Yusef sat his cup on the desk, leaned forward, and steepled his fingers. Many pressing thoughts were swirling through his mind. The clockwork of his scheming began to assess his current situation and the possibilities of its conclusion.

As a conduit for arms, explosives, and other such sundries, Yusef was familiar with all the current plans for Detroit. True, no one trusted him with the finest details, but he had ways of finding things out. After all, he was the one who helped supply most of the toys for the game they were playing. They just gave him a wish list and threatened to flay him slowly if he didn't fulfill. But as he always came through, they rewarded him as avidly as they threatened. He knew the game. And he *never* failed.

But every relationship had its breaking point. It's the moment where it all plummets or pivots. So far as Yusef and this nutty "bathe-in-blood" club was concerned, it had now officially dumped straight down the outhouse hole. He enjoyed all the benefits. But he had enough with his life constantly hanging by a string, and men like Asan holding the scissors. It was coming soon. It had to come. Better to stick it to them, then to get stuck.

Yusef twisted slightly and sat back. He eyed the dangerous man cautiously. The sooner this one was gone, the sooner his stomach would sit right side up. A slender sprout of a plan to rid himself of Asan came to his mind. He smiled. "The sooner he was *gone*..."

Making money off of this latest deal was no problem. There was lots to be had. But a bonus? There was a sideways connection he had in his network – sort of a friend, of a friend, of an informant to an enemy. And the enemy was in a particular branch of government that hunted people like Yusef and Asan. However, the first one across the finish line would get the prize.

As Yusef had always used his head and not his fist to do business he carried no delusions that he could physically handle this matter. He had never wielded a knife or even fired a gun. No, he knew he was an orb weaver, not a wolf spider – a spinner of webs, not a hunter. Thus he would use his cunning and let others provide the muscle. It wouldn't be hard to leak credible evidence and set up a little trap. The thought almost made Yusef giddy. Asan was good. So was Yusef. And this time the trophy would belong to him.

He picked up the cup and sipped the dark liquid again. "Never miss an opportunity, my boy," nodding to himself, "never let it pass." He imagined a world where this Great White was stuffed and mounted on his wall. Yusef's gut relaxed a bit.

Once more Asan stared down into the street, working his jaw. The muscles of his frame flexed and shuddered like writhing coils beneath the tight, black, long sleeved shirt.

Yusef cursed under his breath. "He's like a neurotic shark, back and forth, back and forth." Yet despite his quite rational fear of Asan, and the whole tree thing, he couldn't help relieving some dread with humor. Hiding a smile in his cup he suddenly thought of how much fun Asan would be at a party. "Probably dances a mean robot." The image in his mind nearly made him bust out laughing. Such a thing would be ill-timed.

"Ah," he mockingly contemplated to himself, "I am a disrespectful man, truly blasphemous."

Smiling again he stood and motioned to the door.

"Fi Amanillah, Asan."

The dark figure swam silently into the depths of the hallway and was gone.

Clicking the lock in place Yusef bent over, hands on knees and exhaled long and slow. He stood abruptly, walked to the window, and watched the hated man get in a car and leave. In a few seconds Yusef poured concrete into the mold of his plan. Time was short and there was much to pull together.

So, they had eyes on him? He had eyes on them too. *All* their actions were known to him. He would deliver this last shipment as promised, *and* he would simultaneously deliver Asan to another buyer as well. It was time. Standing upright he moved over to his desk.

"Gone." He savored the word. His mind began to calculate. Sitting down he picked up his cup and stared into the fire.

"Gone...the answer, Asan, *is* 'yes.'"

Chapter 17

"**C**an I trust you?" Jia asked Dane.

"You want to read me in or something?"

"Dane, c'mon."

"Ok – yes, I'm good," he said, weary, but smiling.

"Promise?" her left eyebrow lifting.

"Jia!" Dane laughed.

"Ok, ok." She paused. Rubbing one arm she looked around. "Are you cold?" She tried to stand. Dane pulled her back to her seat.

"I just came in from the cold. It feels fine to me," he said.

"Alright," Jia's sigh came out long and low. "I..." she paused, looking at him, her crooked fish clock on the wall, the coffee table, then back to him.

"You?" Dane, grinning crookedly.

"Me?" She began wringing her hands. "Ok, I'm just gonna say it-"

"Eventually," he interrupted.

"Stop. Ok, yes, it's true – freakish tech chick goes out on a limb." She looked through the round lenses and blinked.

Dane tilted his head.

"Ok," clenching her eyes, "I wore make up."

"Uh," uncertain if this was a huge girl thing he was clueless about. "Wait, *this* was the big thing you had to say to me? I mean, I'd come over if you made Ritz crackers and peanut butter."

"Oh, I did! I can't screw those up." Jia patted her hands with excitement and slid a tray across the table.

"You know, my 'freakishly gorgeous Asian,'" Dane said, "you don't need make up. Buuuut..."

"But?" her forehead bunched.

"But, you looked amazing!" His voice gushed fanboy. "Jia, you have blown me away. More than that, you were there for me. I-"

"Don't," putting her hand to his face. "Don't thank me. Don't apologize. Don't say anything." She brushed aside his thick hair. "I *was* hot, wasn't I?" smiling impishly.

"Flame throw-a," Dane said, putting his fist out. She bumped it.

"Woosh!" they both said, pulling back their hands.

A silence fell between them, ponderous and awkward. They were in that swirling cloud of new love that conversed in excited, disgustingly affectionate tones.

"We *are* nauseating." Dane put his head in his hands. "If anyone ever heard this conversation they would probably hurl."

"Yep," she looked to the side, pushing up her glasses. "Cracker?"

"Thanks." Dane grabbed some of the snacks. "Do you have something to drink?"

Jia reached down and pulled two bottles of Jones from a cooler. "Green apple. I saved it from college."

"Wait, you had that six pack." Dane pointed curiously. "Is this?"

"Uh, huh." She smiled and the slightest little dimple showed on her left cheek. Dane never told her, but he always loved that.

"Girl, you *are* nuts." He leaned forward. "You kept these?"

"It was your favorite," Jia said. "Well, I mean, I liked them too, but-"

"But it was the last day we saw each other." Slumping back in his seat he looked at his

hands.

"Yeah," she breathed out and glanced toward the throw rug, wiping at one eye.

"Shhh," sitting up, Dane carefully took her hand. "Don't say anything." With great tenderness he reached out and caressed her cheek.

Jia twisted her lips together. She met his eyes and gave a teary, little laugh.

"Anyhow," pulling her close to his face, "yes, please, pass me a soda."

"Pop," she teasingly corrected.

"Not this again." He laughed and fell back into the cushion.

"Look, it says SO-DA on the label, see?"

"Ok, you're right for once, Dane Banson. But that's your monthly quota." She leaned in and their foreheads touched. Dane twisted off the cap and took a sip, then put the bottle to her lips. She giggled, yes, stupidly, happily, an in-love-like-an-idiot kind of giggle and she didn't care. Green, sugary liquid went down her chin and spilled on her knee.

"Ah!" Jia screeched. "What a slob!"

Dane threw his arms back and laughed. It felt good. She put her hand to her mouth and giggled again. They quieted down and looked at each other.

"Jia, what did you really call me here for?" he asked, leaning forward.

"Everything we just did...and more," she said, playfully her shoulders.

Dane sighed then dropped his head.

"Ok, ok, ah..." She looked at the ceiling, nervously squeezing her hands together.

"Didn't we just do this, like three minutes ago?" Dane asked.

"Ok, Mr. Pushyface," she began, "You know I'm, ah, really good with computers."

"Yes. And, uh, incidentally, Bach was good at counterpoint."

"Right," she blushed.

"Hey, you're blushing." Dane sat up. "You're-"

"I'm in love, stupid," she turned positively crimson.

The words stuck to everything in the air like cooking oil. It was again pleasantly awkward.

"You had me at computers." Dane sipped the soda and thought a minute. "Girl, you know it's bad when you start scabbing on old movie lines."

"This is like reading a digital techie bodice ripper," Jia said.

"What?" Dane's face screwed up funny. "That's not a thing."

"Is now." She did the neck thing at him.

The stared at each other.

Jia straightened her glasses and cleared her throat. "Okaaaay, here's a segue: I work for the NSA." She paused, trying to read his reaction. The last three letters seemed to hang in the air.

"Dun-dun- dun!" Dane made three musical notes. "Is that all?" casually. "I thought you were about to tell me you were a man."

Up came the pillow. Out went the pillow. Off his head bounced the pillow.

"I'm *not* apologizing this time!" she hissed.

Dane laughed hysterically.

"Dane," she whined, "this is serious."

"I'm sorry," he gasped, "alright, I'm sorry. I'll behave." He let out a breath and calmed down, though a few laughs still escaped him. "Ok, so you work for the NSA."

"Well, not really *for* the NSA," Jia explained, "but a tech group, a-"

Dane interrupted her, "a high end bunch of super smart American computer nerds who provide services that help combat the infiltration of super smart foreign computer geeks into the governmental computer infrastructure."

"Did you Google that or something?" she smirked.

"Nah, I asked Siri," he smiled weirdly, "right after where to bury a dead body, oh, and a romantic recipe for Tuscan risotto."

"Wait, are you going to 'wine, dine, and brine me?" she asked, grabbing for the Jones.

Dane laughed. "Yeah, the secret love of Bundy. Sounds like a Tim Burton Valentine's Day Special."

"I was thinking more Shyamalan," Jia said between slurps.

"Siri, how do you say 'shut up' in Mandarin?" Dane said to the cell.

The phone complied.

"Dumb phone," she smiled slyly, "how do you say 'loser' in English?"

Dane covered the phone. "Aw, you've gone and hurt her feelings?"

"Her feelings?" Jia said, handing him the bottle. "How did we go from the NSA to 'I'm a man' to this?"

"Sorry. I don't get out of the house much." He put the phone away with mock sheepishness. "OK, Chapter Two – The Deep Mystery," his voice dark and sinister."

She exhaled and sat blinking at him.

He puckered his lips and sat like a good boy.

"So, I work with this group and I love it," Jia hunched her shoulders. "I never leave the house. Yes, I have groceries delivered, do my banking online, even buy my clothes there."

"So that's why Amazon ran out of sweats and hoodies." Dane chuckled.

"Toe socks too." She held up her foot and wiggled the multi-colored digits. "Alright, I am like, the master of encryption, conjuring magic up here in my little hole-in-the-wall".

"At the end of a dark, creepy alley," he noted.

"Dirty too," she sighed, looking around.

"Yep!" popping the "p". He took a sip and set the bottle on the coffee table.

Jia began to fill in the blanks. "My little hideout is invisible to the glorious world of data. I not only have the mother-of-all firewalls and," she air quoted, " 'équipement spécial', but with all the old metal mesh and concrete in this cave of mine, I'm practically sitting in a faraday cage. And, as I am the smartest brain in the stable, my company gives me liberty to not just 'man the fort', as they say, but to, how shall I put it delicately - explore? Surveil?"

"Probe," Dane's eyebrows arched up.

"Ooooh, that sounds so 'Empire Strikes Back-ish' " Jia said then took a swig of Green Apple.

"You Spelunk." Dane said with a knowing smile.

"Hey," she brightened, "you remembered my word."

"Yes, I remember," he poked her cheek. "How did you put it, 'the best place to sneak is *under* the ground.' "

"I am a cwafty webble," her voice comical.

"So, you do clandestine probing into other systems, other networks?" Dane ventured.

"Yeah, that and a some other geekity things. Dane," she paused, "I should get to the point."

"Let me know when you do." He leaned into his hand.

She gave him a look over the fishbowls.

"Are we there yet?" his voice petulant, childish.

"Brat." She smacked his arm. "Look, I know how important Rick is to you."

At this Dane's eyes sharpened and he sat forward. "What about Rick? What do you-"

"Dane, please," her voice softened and she slipped her fingers into his hand. Jia still couldn't believe this intimacy with the man she loved, hated, loved again, cried over, shook her fist at, and finally was close enough to hold him at will. "He matters to you so he matters to me."

"Who are you and what have you done with Jia?"

"No, the question is, mon chéri, 'who are you, and what have you done *to* me?' "

They stared at each other again, deep black iris reaching into chocolate brown. Jia looked away feeling as foolish as a seventh grader, though quite glad of it.

"So, what have you found?" Urgency simmered in Dane's voice.

"Uh," she breathed in and wiped at one eye, "I was nosing around a particular group the higher-ups were targeting. Some kind of chatter, some traffic triggered red flags. Sorry to be ambiguous, but they strictly compartmentalize. I only know a piece of the puzzle, and that's my piece to study, to observe."

He motioned for her to go on.

"Ok, so, they had some decent firewalls," Jia sat back and folded her arms, "but walls were made to be breached."

"Go Genghis!" Dane said.

She raised her fist. "I was looking mainly for conversations, dialog, communications, names, emails, blah, blah, blah. I found some, but most of it was in an obscure dialect, apparently from Kazakhstan. Sort of like the Navajo Code Talkers from World War Two. If you have no real bearing on the words, the syntax, no base reference, it's really hard to make sense of it."

"Puked the Japanese," he said, picking up the drink again.

"Yeah, and these fine fellas did the same to me." She adjusted the fishbowls and went on. "I, having a fairly decent handle on Arabic, did catch a few words, however. The only name repeated was Asan."

"Sounds like a sports car made in Dubai," he laughed.

"U so funny – and cute." She pulled at a coil of his hair. "Ok, handsome, quit distracting Mama while she in da pipe."

"My bad. Proceed, smart chick."

She smiled cheesily and continued. "Asan is a fairly common name, all things considered, but I haven't completely sorted out the mystery language. I'm working on that."

"No doubt," Nodding his head.

"However," Jia furthered, "I did come across a blunder in it all. Some careless, and forlorn suitor sent a love-sick email to a girl named Destinie in Thailand."

"Dude," Dane sounding like a surfer, "never date a girl named Destinie,"

They laughed at the joke they heard at college.

"The email was in Korean, *North* Korean to be exact." She held up her index finger. Don't ask!" Dane closed his open mouth and let her continue. "Now 'Tristan', as I call him, the amorous author, was quite careless with 'Isolde'." She looked at him sideways. "He probably broke protocol, or what have you, by opening the door and lobbing his kiss-covered, digital *lettre d'amour*."

"I love when you talk techy-funk French smack literary with me," he said.

"That's a genre?" cocking her head back. "Huh, I learn new stuff every day."

Dane shrugged.

"Well, I'd prefer chick-lit at the moment," she batter her eyes in the fishbowls, "something with kissing, and big, sweeping promises."

"And muscular, shirtless men that come riding down the beach on white horses, their hair flowing in the wind," he said dryly.

"Catch me, Lord Dane, I swoon." She fell against him sideways. Sitting up she grabbed the soda and sipped. "Back to the business at hand."

"Proceed."

Jia nodded. She reached over and fired up her slim, silver tablet, it's solid state loading in seconds. "Dane, uh...they'd kill me if they found out I was showing this to you."

"I promise I won't say a thing."

She looked at him, lips pursed, weighing things out. "Bah!" a blast of breath released from her mouth, "why do you have to be so sweet looking?"

"You know," he put his hands behind his head and leaned back, "you'd be surprised how much I've been asked that question."

Jia backhanded his stomach and focused on her screen.

"Okay, here goes," she sighed forcefully. "It seems Lady Destinie's lover had much to say, and a few things of particular interest to you, thus to me."

"Thus," Dane nodded.

Jia clicked a screen. "Here is a translation of something important: 'The Bay'ah sent some of the gang members-'"

"Bay'ah?" he wondered.

" 'Bay'ah' means pledge, or oath, if you please. More specifically 'Bay'at ash-shajarah'. means Pledge of the Tree. Without going into the thorny details of Islamic history, this oath is basically a death pledge of absolute obedience to an Islamic leader and/or cause."

"I didn't know you were such an Islami-wonk," Dane said.

"Darling," lowering her glasses, "I am an *everything*-wonk, if you please." Dane laughed. Yes, the Brain knows all.

"And right now, I am particularly a Dane-wonk." She sucked her lips in like a fish and leaned towards him. He pushed her face away laughing.

"Okay, okay, Brain – read some more."

"Pooh!" she pouted and moved her cursor. Scanning down the screen she picked up her place.

" 'The Bay'ah sent some of the gang members they've been training to a protest at a bus garage or something. Several were hurt, including a police officer. One guy had a block smashed into his skull.' "

Jia looked at Dane apprehensively. She wrung her hands, blinking in thought.

"Dane." Her hand found his shoulder.

Dane shook his head. He breathed in and out slowly, deliberately. "Jia, what does this mean? Should we show this to the cops?"

"Whoa, big boy. First off, I don't exist, remember. And I *shouldn't* be sharing anything with you. One of those scary para government spooks would throw me down a hole at a supermax or something."

"Maybe they'd give you a laptop," Dane reasoned.

"Yeah, that and roach room service," she sounded a little more serious than she meant to, but not more than she felt. Neither the good guys or the bad guys in this scenario were to be toyed with.

"So..." Dane pushed the conversation forward.

"So, I don't know what. I'm not sure what all this means. I'll have to dig more and find out."

"Jia, we can't let this go. Was that a joke?"

"No. It was an idiot move by some doof guy with cranial deiectio regularis. Though what a North Korean guy is doing with this very terrorist sounding organization I can't tell yet." She noticed him staring at her. "What?"

"I forgot you spoke Latin," he said, shaking his head.

"Tu pulcher es," Jia said passionately.

"Now you're hitting on me in a dead language." Dane laughed and tipped the bottle of sugary liquid to his mouth.

She smiled, happily floating along in the vapors of requited love.

"Dane, I don't know if this will go anywhere, but I promise you I'll do everything I can to find out."

"Jia," he breathed heavily, "you have to be careful. I mean, I know you're three bags of chips, two Slim Jim's and a Rock Star, but this group, these people are probably dangerous."

"If he only knew," she said to herself. "If he knew the places they have me go..."

"I will," she squeezed his hand. "I promise."

Dane stood. "It's late and I am beyond tired. I can't thank you enough for yesterday, and this evening. We're really just getting to know each other again."

"Again? I'd say for the first time." She stood, hands in front, looking down at her wiggling toes. Her shoulders were hunched forward and she began sliding one hand up the other arm.

"Do you have to leave?" Her voice was soft.

"Yeah. Jia, I'm a mess. And this thing with Rick, and-"

"And us?" Jia lifted her eyes.

"Us." He smiled.

She smiled. "Us!" danced in her head.

"Well, no rush and all." She grinned and sighed. A strand of hair fell across her glasses. Dane gently reached over and brushed it away, tenderly tucking it back in place.

"There's an us!" the collective voices in The Brain bumped hips.

"I'll be over tomorrow, okay?" he said.

"Okay. Yeah, that's great. Bring coffee, or," she hesitated, "or lunch if it's later."

"Okay," he said.

"Okay," her voice wavering.

He reached out his arms and she had to stop herself from vaulting into them and begging him to stay. How she wanted to be caught in a rainstorm and kiss. She held off on it all and gently put her arms around him.

Chapter 18

"I hope this little bird was right." Tamari said.

"Oh, I'm fairly confident, though he *was* a starling." Aimes said enigmatically.

"What?" she wrinkled her face and looked at the bald man.

"Sturnus Vulgaris, an import, noisy, makes a general mess of things, and not especially pretty to look at or listen to. Still, he brought me *this* fat, little grub." Aimes nodded toward the dingy, rust-painted warehouse. It hugged the west bank of the river like a homeless man clutching a bottle. They gathered at the southern corner opposite the wide strand of water.

Banks tapped her com, "Team two leader, report."

"In place." The whispered voice was crisp and clear in the headset. The second four man unit waited behind barrels and old pallets at the northern end.

There was a listlessness, a disturbance in the dust of this place. Banks could feel it. Even though she had trained for days on end, replaying these types of scenarios, she still got that slick sensation on her upper lip. She sucked it in and breathed out slowly through her nose.

Large, twin boat motors surged on the far side of the building, pulling away from the loading dock.

She saw movement.

"Well, Miss Banks?" Aimes split his rumpled mouth. It sort of looked like a smile.

"Cue the DJ," she said.

"Yes," Aimes searched for the phrase, "uh, party on." His raspy voice whispered like a croak. He tugged at a strap on his vest.

"Go!" Banks triggered the mouthpiece.

The partners slid in through a bent, corrugated panel. Two men slipped in behind. Head to toe in black they were armored with vests, helmets, goggles, and balaclavas. One carried a submachine gun, an H&K MP5, the other a twelve gauge breaching shotgun he nicknamed "Mama-san." Every clip and pouch was loaded with goodies meant to bang, smoke, flash, and pummel the targets into submission.

The second team slid in through a broken door frame, silent, with complete discipline.

Banks moved her men quickly and efficiently into covered posts.

"Team two, move into position one," she ordered. "Cover the roll-up door."

"On it," the leader responded.

The old, mottled metal beams seemed to suck in the echoes, the soft scrape of boots on the dirty floor. Banks signaled. One by one they advanced north taking up new places of concealment. She held her weapon with both hands in a firm grip. The Glock 19, Gen 4 nine millimeter was satin black and seemed welded to her dark, webbed field gloves. She loved how it felt – solid, unyielding to her crushing fingers. Wiping her upper lip she pressed them forward.

"Team two at the door." The leader's voice sounded calm and confident.

"Good job, JB. You have eyes?" Tamari asked.

"Affirmative," JB responded. "I count six hostiles. Two in a speedboat. Three loading bags into it. One on his cell."

"Focus on *him*," Banks ordered, "line of site."

JB swiveled around, carefully shuffling over three feet for a more direct view of the face. His helmet cam auto-focused on the movement ahead. The man talked quietly, walked two steps and casually turned south.

Tamari looked at the live feed on her watch. "Mother, confirm."

"It's Sanders," coming in on the headsets. There was a pause. "HQ confirms priority target. Capture alive if possible." Sanders worked under the Director and ran most of the OIS field operations from their command room in Detroit. A dual feed of every man, camera, headset, and conversation was fed to the suits in D.C.

"We're a go, JB. Move in!" Agent Banks felt a surge of energy as she gave the command.

"Affirmative." He quickly signaled his team and pulled up his fat barreled POP gun, a little beauty cooked up by OIS eggheads. It was huge improvement over the XREP Taser charges – greatly increased velocity, slim, multi-stage impact, strong tissue penetration, plus it not only shocked the snot out of someone, but its multiple tips had just enough "sleepy juice" to daze a cow. It was still a risky thing as stinging too small a person could cause an overdose. But, chances being what they are, it was better than shooting them out-right.

"On me," JB whispered.

He lined up hairs on the man.

Asan stopped. He saw something: The smallest glint, the faintest motion from beyond the raised shop door. Something moved in the next room. Instinct took over.

JB squeezed.

Asan flattened heavily to the floor, the tin wall behind him ringing with a projectile.

Team two executed. Flash bangs blew by the loading dock, dark canisters rolled out and belched choking screens of gas. They flew from cover, guns up.

"Team one on me!" Tamari sprang like a panther, sleek and black, not an ounce of fat to weigh her down. She sprinted effortlessly, weapon forward, charging north in a perpendicular line to JB and his men.

Aimes and the two operatives kept up, scanning outside the expanding cloud for cover.

JB pumped another cocktail into the chamber and let fly, just missing Asan's calf. The wanted man rolled into the gas and launched himself towards the dock. Team two's leader hustled forward, spitting another round at the moving target. One of the panicking workers crossed the firing lane and took the dart just under his armpit. He flailed like a Voodoo trance, muscles convulsing and shivering with the charge.

JB swore and pushed forward. A bullet tore at the outside corner of concrete blocks, showering him. He threw himself against a wall. A second shot sailed past him, knocking one of his men to the ground.

"Smitz?!" JB called over the com.

"Good!" a figure in black began dragging the dazed man. "Stung him..." slapping his sternum, "vest."

JB nodded, pulling up his weapon.

Two armed men took off to the south, ran around a crooked stack of pallets and straight into Tamari's charge. The first whipped up his pistol. Plugging his gut, her bullet jerked him sideways. She kept running, never missing a stride. The man grabbed his belly, stumbled over his own feet and fell. Aimes veered towards him. He quickly pinned him to the ground.

Screaming some kind of oath, the second man raised his semi at her from fifteen feet away. Mama-san shook the rafters and made wet confetti out of his right bicep. He slumped backwards, rolling in viscera.

Banks headed for a door with a frosted window at the end of a tight, L-shaped wall. The heavy wood was warped and peeling from age. She grabbed the tin-stamped handle with her left hand, holding the weapon steady and straight with her right. Her breath quickened, her body tensed. Sensing movement behind her she let go and flashed her eyes right, detecting one of her own.

"McVelcro," she whispered to herself, smiling, lips throbbing with adrenaline's pulse. He was her most experienced team member, and had a Scottish name she could never remember. *And*, he always stuck by her side on tactical missions, like hook and barb, like a burr. Bobbing in a crouch on thick boxer's legs he held the sub tight to face, ready to plunge into danger at her elbow.

"C'mon, V."

He nodded.

Finding the knob again she turned it slowly. It squeaked and snapped the latch under protest. The old, rust-welded hinges gave way only enough for an inch wide crack. She reset her grip and pulled. Bursting out an assailant launched himself through a hail of dust and shattered glass, forcefully slamming Tamari into the blocks. She gasped with the impact. V drove forward and rammed him back against the grey wall. Lowering her shoulder Banks swept in , thrusting full body weight. The flat of her right forearm cracked up under his jaw, snapping back his head. She swiveled and pounded him on the side of the skull with a left, the carbon fiber knuckles of her glove crushing like peens. Wobbly legs buckled. V grabbed his hair and hurled him to the ground. He was down.

JB ran out on to the dock, watching the small, but powerful boat surge away. He pumped out two more rounds. The first skimmed just over the pilot's head, the second embedded into the upholstery of the watercraft. Asan lay in the back staring at the OIS officer. His eyes were black, emotionless, unchanging. A slight, knowing smirk played on his mouth.

From another old building Yusef watched the boat escape. He focused his binoculars on the bearded man sitting in the back. Through gritted teeth his breath hissed out disappointment and concern.

"Now what?" he said. Swearing, he pressed a hand on his midsection. Tension coiled his stomach. "Now what?"

Quietly, without being seen, he left.

Chapter 19

"I'm what you call spitting mad," the Director fumed, smacking the report on the table.

"Sir, we captured four-"

"I can not only read, Banks, but I can count too. Surprisingly, both of those happen to be requirements of this job." He muttered and let out a long breath. "The doctor says," a bit more subdued, "that I have too much stress in my life." Picking up the icy water he took a long drink. "Sit down, you two. I won't have you standing there shifting from foot to foot."

"I was dancing, sir." Aimes unhelpfully chimed in.

"Well, you're going to dance some more!" Looking at the printed pages a moment the Director breathed in and out dialing and back his anger.

"I'm just frustrated," the older man looked at his agents. "Not at you, really. You did what you were supposed to do, and none of our people got hurt. But not one shot hit the target? That man *is* slippery. And to top it off the satellite system mysteriously decided to do a full diagnostic? This sounds like a bad film script. Too many convenient things happening."

"That is the most disturbing part, sir," Aimes said.

"Yes," Marz rubbed the back of his neck. "I don't believe we are directly compromised, but our link with the DOD network may have some bugs."

"Or a mole, sir." Aimes added.

"True...true." The Director and his agents were each lost in thought for a moment. The implications were more than troubling.

"For now," Marz continued, "we must trust that they will soon have things sorted out. And, on the bright side, yes," nodding at Tamari, "we captured four. One of them isn't in the best shape, but they think he'll live."

"Yes, sir." Banks agreed.

Marz studied her curiously for a moment.

"You ever shot anyone before?" the Director asked.

"Once, sir," sitting on the edge of her chair.

"Where?" the director pulled off his glasses.

"My short stint as an MP at camp-"

"Short?" Aimes lifting his nose.

Banks gave him the look. He turned away, smiling.

"No, I mean *where*," the Director spread his hands outward.

"Oh, in the, uh," searching for the polite word, "posterior, sir."

"In his backside?" Marz leaned forward.

"It was the portent of her career," Aimes added.

"I didn't *mean* to hit him there," eyes flashing at her partner.

"No?" the Director.

"He jumped." Tamari pulled her head back, a little defensive.

They all stared.

The Director cleared his throat, wiped his nose, snickered, then rolled into an outright laugh.

Aimes sat, twisting his lips, exhaling calmly through the nose. He looked everywhere but at Tamari.

"Oh," the Director gasped, "I really needed that." Relief seemed to wash over him, to calm things down. "You can add 'gut' to 'butt' now, Banks." He snorted and let out a few short, choking sounds. This cascaded to another round of belly shaking and chair arm pounding.

Tamari grimaced and glanced at Orville. He was busy, politely inspecting the crown molding.

It took the Director a moment to catch his breath. Sipping the cold water, he sat the glass down on the exact same spot.

"Well," he continued, "we gained intel, a cellphone, and three men. But the primary target slipped away. He's good, Aimes. Hard to get anything on him, except that he's good."

"At least the information paid off, Director." Aimes said confidently, hands threaded loosely in his lap.

"Yes, yes – not a bad day for the OIS, I suppose. But things are really heating up. Everyone wants answers. There's a ton of pressure on us to come up with something. I'm sure the agencies will all help squeeze those four oranges. We'll get every drop we can."

"Yes, sir." Aimes bowed his head slightly.

Tamari and Aimes stood and made to leave.

"Oh," the Director held up a hand, stopping them. "I want you two to head up to the Tech Department and talk to the, uh, new guy. I can't remember his name. Dr. Tell will introduce you."

"Will do," Tamari nodded.

The door shut quietly behind them.

Chapter 20

"There's about two to three churches for every school. These schools are filled with boys and girls, and young men that are at risk, drifting into trouble on our streets. Minus a father, or a father figure, and stable homes they are gravitating towards gangs, drugs, vagrancy; not just a purposeless life, but a life of crime. Ladies and gentlemen, brothers and sisters, we are here to do something."

"Doctor Grayson," Diedre Grant, a bright, young woman asked, "what of the rumors regarding recruitment of these young men by militant Islamist groups?"

"I have spoken to many clerics and leaders of the Muslim community. They know and I know that, religiously speaking, we are not on the same team."

Doctor Grayson peered over his glasses at the thirty or so gathered. A small ripple of laughter worked through the rows.

"Having said that, there are many that would prefer to influence these young lives to some productive end. Every individual who turns to gang membership of any kind makes all neighborhoods that much more dangerous. Now having said *that* let me say, yes, this recruitment is happening. And it is on the increase.

It is a volatile mix of young, rebellious adolescence mingled with a purpose, a belief system, and a cause that strikes back at the government, other religions, and society at large. Not only are they feeding into the "helpless victim" narrative so commonly propagated amongst our youth, but they are giving them a cosmic reason to join their brotherhood and shed some blood. It is heinous." Doctor Grayson paused, wiping his forehead with a handkerchief.

"Adding to that all that madness, cities across America, Detroit being no exception, have seen general violence increase dramatically. While nationally such things have been trending downward, yet we are seeing unsettling spikes in the last six months. Something bad is brewing. The racial, political, and economic divide seems to be intentionally opened wider and wider.

But what is our response? What is our perspective? While it is absolutely just to protect ourselves, to stop crime and criminals, yet is there no redemption? Is there no way to prevent these young lives from become just another tragic statistic? Every one of those statistics is a soul, a person, and those souls matter to God. We must not embrace violence. We must, as the scripture in Romans twelve counsels us,

> 'Recompense to no man evil for evil. Provide things honest in the sight of all men. If it be possible, as much as lieth in you, live peaceably with all men. Dearly beloved, avenge not yourselves, but *rather* give place unto wrath: for it is written, Vengeance *is* mine; I will repay, saith the Lord. Therefore if thine enemy hunger, feed him; if he thirst, give him drink: for in so doing thou shalt heap coals of fire on his head. Be not overcome of evil, but overcome evil with good.' "

Grayson paused a moment. His nostrils flared as he adjusted his glasses. This faithful man lost a son to the roving mobs of the street. Through all the movements that sprang up in this nation, midst the agitation that boiled over in Detroit's broken blocks, the prevailing thought became "no lives matter." Samuel, his second child, ran with fools and so became one. A bullet became his end, a small hole in the head, but a crater gouging out the very pith of Grayson and his beautiful wife. This wasn't an academic exercise, or just a do-gooder community thing to ease his conscience. No, for Grayson, he had skin, flesh, and blood in this game.

"The real question is," the good doctor picked up again, "are we willing to do for the truth what they are willing to do for a lie? Many of you know Reverend Pearce," gesturing towards him.

Michael had drifted away in thought. He remembered Sydney, a handsome, young black man he met thirty years ago. Sydney was a few years older than Michael, and Pearce had looked up to him. He came from good people. Sydney's dreams lit up his eyes and they lit up Michael's imagination. Straddling his bike, young Pearce would talk while Sid sat on his small, front stoop. Sydney had gone to St. John Berchman's, now closed, it buildings vacant, decaying, a sad reflection of the state of the neighborhood.

"I'm gonna make somethin' good outta myself," he'd say, "somethin' good."

Before he hit twenty-two, he was killed going to the grocery store. One life, one small soul in this seething mass – snuffed, done, gone. There were thousands, tens of thousands of Sydney's around Detroit. Michael wanted them to do something good with *their* lives – both practically and eternally.

"Reverend Pearce?" the Doctor called to him.

Michael snapped back to the present and stood.

"Doctor Grayson," he hesitated then picked up speed. "I thank this council for inviting me."

For fifteen minutes he shared his heart, outlined his plans, spoke of the work he had done in Chicago, confirmed his rally, and appealed for their help. These were folks from various backgrounds and Christian denominations, determined to be world changers by the Grace of God. The Hold Forth Life council was fully supportive of Reverend Pearce and his efforts. They knew that only God could change hearts, that changed hearts meant changed habits, changed habits meant changed homes. Things were ugly in the streets and of paramount concern to them.

"As Miss Grant mentioned earlier," Pearce furthered, "we are facing a new and dangerous pull of gravity, particularly for young men. It has historically been religious groups and communities on one side, with drugs, gangs, and crime on the other vying for the hearts and minds of our people. I don't suppose I could put this in sweeping or elegant terms, and I do suppose that this is nothing entirely new – radical Islamists are increasingly offering a pathway for troubled youth.

In the majority they have been targeting young men, to what specific end is hard to speculate. Not simply content to exist alongside others of different faith, or creeds, they have desired the destruction and subjugation of all they encounter, and the full, regimented implementation of Sharia Law. They do not simply have some grudge against our nation, though they use such complaints as a pretext to disorder and violence. The framework they operate in is a belief system, an ideology that grants them divine license to conquer, to kill, to commit crimes against humanity without question of conscience or mercy.

With our faith in God's Grace, and in the Good News of our Lord Jesus Christ, we will leave the investigations and arrests to the appointed officers. Our work is the salvation of souls, to bring His message of forgiveness, reconciliation, of redemption. That is why I call you to join me in prayer for this work. As the Apostle Paul said, 'Pray also that I would have boldness to proclaim The Gospel as I ought.' Let us unite together at the Erma Henderson Park and begin our outreach in the neighborhood."

Reverend Pearce sat.

Dr. Grayson wrapped up the meeting with prayer and exhortation.

"What do you think?" Michael asked Andrew in the hall.

"Reverend Pearce, I have never felt the hand of God like this. The street's full of men just like me. I wasn't much, but he still came for me."

Michael put a kind hand on Andrew's shoulders. "Son, that is why we do what we do – even for the least of these."

Chapter 21

The stars are always watching, crossing and favoring as their own celestial temperaments dictate. And what of the lovers, those happy fools, loving and being loved, abandoned to the thought of only one face, one hand, one heart. All the world is cast aside for such a jewel. Kingdoms have fallen, wars long and desperate fought, treasures forsaken, and all for perchance a kiss, a look, the favorable fan of feathers in the heated pulse of our passionate ritual, the mating dance of courtship.

Below the stars were the lights of the city, transmuting the powerful, incendiary spheres of other galaxies into an overhead decoration of winking sparks. The square was open and ringed by small, white bulbs. Music gently played, mingled with the soft sounds of couples pressing into the warmth of the restaurant, back out into the cold sea of virgin Spring.

"This is it," Dane grinned.

"I can smell how good it is from here." Jia took in a long, satisfied breath through her nose. "Mmmmm..."

They were hand in gloved hand, a fatal step of intimacy. Both had it bad – really bad. Dane was coming out of a long tunnel of pain and isolation; Jia was ever ascending into a euphoric cloud of "I can't believe this is real."

Skirting the fountain, they stood below a decorative street lamp, just in front of the empty outdoor café. She faced him. Breath steamed as dragon plumes in the frost. Nothing need be said. Nothing was. Ever conscious of the twin headlamps resting on the bridge of her nose, Jia tucked them away without a word.

Dane stepped closer. "Jia...you are beyond beautiful." Her high, curving cheek bones lit up, glowing the belles étoiles of a perfect smile. Streams of breath rolled and curled around the lovers, young, uncertain, bold.

A song melted the frosty night as they drew close and began to dance – absent of care, slow, lost in each other.

"Baby, baby, baby, I was blind, oh, so blind,
Not to see you here, loving me..."

The words rolled out with the pain and hope of a blues diva, calling desperately to her estranged.

> *"All I know, all I know, all I know,*
> *Is that I need you, and I've been dyin'"*

Jia began to sing along in a low-toned whisper.

> *"So many years I have waited, for you to wander back down my*
> *street,*
> *Could it be, could it be, you are in my arms again?"*

A drop made its slow, lazy way down her cheek, pooled in that crazy dimple, and got lost somewhere along the way. Dane thought for the first time that a woman was never more beautiful than when she smiled through her tears. Jia's lips parted slightly, and she leaned in, the press of love behind her back.

"Jia," Dane hesitated, hating the slightest mar to this moment. "Jia, I...I love you."

Stars sparkled.

"And I need your help," he said, his voice tinged with desperation.

She put her hand to his face. The fuzzy, pink glove was strangely warm. He couldn't believe how in love he was falling.

"I'm having a hard time. My heart still aches, still hurts about my mom, about Micka, about Rick. I'm lost. I just...this is all so wonderful, but really fast."

With a look of tearful compassion and understanding she took his face in both hands. "I love you, Dane. You have given me my life back, or, like I've never had it before. There is no rush." She brushed aside a curl that strayed from his Red Wings hat. "I know you loved her. I won't push you. Time is one thing we have plenty of."

They embraced in the artless honesty of a loving fire, within the music, out in the cold, under the glowing strings and city lights, seen ever by the immortal spheres. With the surprising patience of older, wiser souls they simply trusted to things taking their own course, growing with what moments they had.

Out from the frost, into the warmth and comforting ambience they pushed through the door arm-in-arm.

Chapter 22

Sticky and dark it clung to her tiny fingertip. She looked at it curiously, sniffed it, and daubed another finger. Laying on the carpet the big, art paper book was open, beckoning a new creation. Her fair face glowed with cheeks, rosy and round, haloed by brown, curly locks. Large, beautiful eyes, "daddy melters" as her father called them, glanced between the figure reclining on the floor, her painting medium, and the broad page.

"Daddy," she lilted with adorable, English tones, "when will Mummy be home?"

The supine man did not respond. He lay with one arm draped over his eyes. The mid-morning sun filled the front room with a diffused, non-committal light. She looked up and squinted at the white glare.

"Mummy will be cross at the *mess* you have made," the little elf quipped. "I'll make her a picture."

She dipped her finger in again and began to sketch out a childish abstract of a man lying down.

"You're taking a nap. See?" She tapped him. He didn't move. Turning the picture to her favorite stuffed toy she was happy with its silent approval.

"And here is me." The girl dipped her finger in again and made a few concentrated strokes. "And here is Mummy. She is *very* cross."

Her mother worked for the British Government. That's all anyone knew. She commuted through the tunnel or across the Ambassador Bridge to a non-descript office on the Canadian Side. The girl's father, an American, was one of the primary officers in a high security internet firm, working mainly with the NSA and FBI. Eighteen months ago they had moved from England to outside the northern bounds of Detroit, in the upper neighborhoods of St. Clair Shores.

The lock on the condominium door clicked once, twice.

"Huhhh," the little one grasped, bringing hands to face. "You are in trouble now, Daddy." She pulled her fingers away and left two dark, red, sticky splotches on her jaw.

Turning slowly the handle gave way to the swinging door.

"Hello, dear," came the cheery greeting. Susan was away at a friend's wedding. She so looked forward to returning and being home with her husband and daughter.

"What are you two about?" setting down her luggage.

"I made a picture of you, Mummy." The girl jumped up and ran across the room.

"Oh, how lovely." Down on one knee she hugged her girl, daubing at the stains. "Red paint? Daddy knows better than that." She chided with that tone too effuse with happiness to sound like scolding.

"He made a mess, Mummy, see." She pointed to the red marks on the white paper. "Here is me," pointing a chubby, stained finger, "this is Daddy lying down, and you coming in and being cross."

"Oh, darling, it..." she caught herself rubbing the paint between thumb and finger. It was *too* sticky, growing tacky on her skin. She smelled it. "Oh, no. No!" She shot up and ran to her husband. "No! No, no, no! Jeffrey, Jeffrey!!" her voice shrieking through the house. She knelt beside him and pulled his hand away. The eyes were open, slightly opaque, staring into emptiness. She quickly checked his pulse. He was cold. A pool of thick blood had flowed out onto the floor beneath him.

Her instincts flared up shouting "*protect the cub, save the cub, spare the cub.*" Scooping up her daughter she grabbed her cellphone and ran for the door.

Chapter 23

"**D**espite the fact that it is designated a 'cafeteria' the food really isn't that bad." Aimes picked discretely at his teeth. He walked beside his partner to the bank of two elevators accessing the upper floor.

"What did you want them to call it?" Banks smiled sideways at her partner.

"Oh, I suppose 'eatery' would be a bit more aesthetic," he said.

Banks shook her head. "Why not 'grub hub'? No, wait, I got it, I got it." She alternately stabbed both her index fingers at him, mouth open in a teasing smile.

"Oh, dear," Aimes shot his eyebrows up, "here it comes."

" 'Orville's Eats.'" She threw her arms wide, her eyes bulging with mock excitement.

"Somehow, I knew, Miss Banks, you would work that in."

"Don't cha like it?" Tamari nudged him. "I bet they'd start serving popcorn."

"As long as the coffee cups are glassware-" Aimes sighed.

"And sterilized," she added.

"Of course," unperturbed

"Aw, you don't like *any* of my bright ideas," flicking his shoulder.

" 'Bright' being the qualifier," he responded sarcastically, glancing and grinning at his partner.

A short ride up the lift and the door chimed. Opening to the tech department revealed a hive of buzzing, busy cubicles to the left, and glass walled, administrative offices straight ahead. The OIS shield stood tall and black on the supervisor's door. Unlike larger U.S. agencies, the OIS had a diminutive organizational footprint. Instead of occupying several floors, it filled only two stories in a small, old office building on Lafayette, a few blocks away from FBI headquarters at McNamara Federal. Yet, it was well-funded, especially in the technical and computing quarters, and staffed with hand-picked professionals considered cream.

"Agent Banks, Aimes," a man took crisp, energetic steps towards them.

"Doctor Tell, a pleasure." Aimes extended his hand.

Tell shook his hand, then Tamari's and took them both in as guests on a cruise ship.

"Honestly," he bubbled, "I am so happy you have finally come to see our new floor. Well," he hesitated, "nothing about this structure is new, per se, but we are *finally* done remodeling. And, oh, does she hum."

"Miss Banks plays a mean kazoo. Perhaps a duet?" Aimes smiled oddly.

Tamari folded her arms and smirked amusingly at her partner.

"Duet?" the doctor looked puzzled. "Oh, humming, yes, well, our systems are on the extreme cutting edge and connected from one end to the other. This entire floor, ceiling and walls too." He leaned forward confidentially. "It's like one big, technological organism."

Aimes knew if they stood there any longer Tell would tap roots into his byte gushing creation and they would never get him to stop talking about it.

"Indeed, Doctor – a marvel, I am sure. But on to the business at hand, if you please."

"Well, yes, the reason you are here." He smiled apologetically and gestured to his left. "Do follow me." The three of them walked on the grey, commercial grade carpet toward a large, stainless steel door. "You will meet Victor Claussen, our new Lead Technical Director. He has some most interesting things to tell you about your manhunt."

"Victor?" Tamari mouthed at Aimes. She envisioned a short, pudgy Dutch man that smelled like pickles.

"Our manhunt, Doctor Tell?" Aimes queried.

"Yes," enthusiastically, "the OIS is privy to some advanced technology - way above consumer or corporate devices. We may be a small division, but we are well supplied."

"See," Banks poked Aimes, "a popcorn maker, just like the movies."

"A what?" Tell turned, smiling. "You two are rather full of code words." He pulled out a pad and wrote a few things with his stylus. They came to the door. The doctor looked up.

"Here we are." He put his hand on a platen waiting for the green light, then centered his eye on a retinal scanner. As a last tumbler Tell spoke his full name and the door unlocked with a loud, hollow click. He motioned them in. "Unfortunately, I will not be able to join you. There are other duties I must attend to."

He bowed his head and Aimes nodded courteously.

Tamari walked down a long corridor and entered a tight, rectangular room that would have made any CSI movie set drool. She could see several spacious labs and stations through the glass walls to the left and right. This first area was comparatively tight but packed with perfect order. Lights winked and flickered like a busy city. She imagined the data traffic flowing and hustling, moving at incredible speed through thin, conductive highways. What secrets were they divulging? What criminals had their end forged here, the forming of the first links in the chain of justice? What-

"Hi." A warm, deep voice broke into Tamari's thoughts.

She turned. She froze, mouth slightly open, eyebrows up.

"I'm..." she stuttered, "I'm here."

"Yes, you are. Tamari?" the figure pointed an index finger at her.

"That's my name too. I mean, we have the same name, uh, you are?" The bottom of her stupid dropped away and she hung in the air like a dope.

The man laughed. He was over six feet, a perfect V of muscle, dark, long hair, with a square chin, shadowed by light stubble.

"*I'm* Victor." He held out his hand.

"Mr. Pickles?" her head voice wondered.

She put her hand forward.

"I'm Tamari," she stated.

"Not Victor?" he smiled, taking a step toward her.

"Um, no." Tamari said with a small voice, looking shyly to the ground. A part of her hated being caught off guard like this. She didn't know why it happened. With her job she could face any number of dangers straight up. But when a good-looking boy came into her circle, sometimes she just turned into a pile of mush.

"How about I just get it over with and nickname you 'Victoria'?" the young man laughed with an easy, teasing sound.

"Um..." Tamari didn't know what to say. She took Victor's hand in her's and enjoyed its warmth and strength.

"But what am I saying? A nickname would be very forward and unprofessional. So, I guess I'll stick with Tamari."

"You could call her Miss Banks," her partner broke in. He walked up beside them, eyeing Tamari. "Oh, my," he said, smiling sagely.

Tamari's hand shot out of Victor's. Her face burned and she watched her boots scuffing the ground.

"It's nice to meet you, Mr. Claussen," she said.

"Please," Victor said, turning toward Aimes, "my friends call me Vic. Mr. Claussen makes me sound like some fat, little Dutch guy selling pickles."

"I thought the same-" Tamari burst out.

Aimes cut her off with a disapproving look.

"Never mind," she said in a tiny voice.

Vic stopped and looked back at her curiously.

"Vic, is it?" Aimes stepped up and offered his hand. Victor readily accepted it, gripping with confidence.

"It's a pleasure to finally meet you, sir. I've heard so much about you," Victor said.

"Thank you, young man," Aimes replied warmly. "I look forward to working together."

Tamari could tell her partner liked this man. He appreciated intelligence coupled with a dash of humbleness.

With a swift movement Vic snatched up a pad linked to several larger displays. Turning back to the partners he continued to manipulate the device. "In case Dr. Tell didn't mention it, I'm the lead tech here."

"You, uh, don't look it," Tamari noted.

Aimes shutter his eyes and shook his head. His chest rose and fell.

Victor smiled a GQ set at her. "I know, you expected a lab coat and titanium pocket protector. Yeah, yeah, every team needs the introverted geek, socially awkward, always talking tech speak. I watch cop shows too."

"You don't look...like...a geek." Each word out of Tamari's voice got quieter as she spoke. She took a few, subtle steps behind her partner, unsuccessfully trying to hide her tall frame.

"Ok," Victor walked toward the monitors, "let's spin things up." His hand rapidly tapped the pad, firing images to three screens. "Your last action on the dock yielded some good results, as I'm sure most of the other departments have filled you in."

"Yes," Banks nodded. "Some good intel."

"Yeah. So, here's the technical component." The younger man pulled up a few last windows.

There was a sound at the doorway.

"Hey, JB," Victor called, "c'mon in – perfect timing."

JB nodded at each in turn and entered the room. He wasn't a large man, but wiry and quick in his movements. He wore a black, one-piece outfit, his last name threaded with dark strands over one pocket.

"Okay," Victor continued, "on this end we have a few things left to explore." He brought up the schematic of POP gun ammo. It looked like an elongated electron microscope picture of a virus. "The POP gun JB so graciously field tested for us, has some additional features you may not be aware of. I am sure you know that its primary function is to disable a target by shock and drugs."

"Goose and juice," JB chimed in, grinning.

"Right," Victor smiled. "It's quite an advancement over previous iterations. But there is one last trick up its sleeve. In addition to the aforementioned features, the injecting tips also deliver a healthy dose of nano trackers into anything they pierce."

"But I missed, Vic." JB said.

"I mean anything, dude," Victor said, getting into his toys, "manflesh, orcflesh, and...dramatic pause...upholstery. The little critters are way out on the front of current technology. You missed the target, but not the boat.

"So, we shocked the boat into submission," Aimes, with a bit of sarcasm. "Once located we can fit it into the basement. I'm sure the mean boys will work it over."

JB chuckled.

Tamari started up, a bit defensive, "I'm sure Victor has something more to say about the nanotech."

Aimes slowly turned his head and knowingly raised his eyebrows at her.

She snorted air and raised her chin.

"Yeah, a bit more on the nano. The OIS, in conjunction with MIT, and a half dozen other abbreviations, have worked on a tracking system. Each of the little buggers has a charge that lasts about thirty-eight hours on a good day. It sends a trackable radio pulse coordinated with GPS. Every tracker's code is specific to the POP gun round it was loaded into. As long as they are in proximity to each other their signals are synchronized, creating a chorus of voices, if you would. Together they send out a continuous loop of the same

ID. And, at the risk of an unnecessary effusion of geek speak, I will leave it at that."

"And that makes them traceable?" Aimes.

"Yes," Victor turned towards him. "With satellite, cell tower, and high-powered portable receivers we should be able to pick up on something."

"What's the range?" JB asked.

Vic referred back to one of the screens. "In truth, only about one hundred to one hundred fifty yards. We're workin' on that. It would be harder if they were just general beeps being thrown out into the radio field. But these give their own ID code on very singular radio tunings. So, in the morning, the suits want us to loose the drones and comb the river."

"Cool," JB.

Tamari chipped in, "so, we send out the birds with radio receivers and attempt to triangulate the little buggers."

"Yep," Vic nodded. "We had it on cell for a while, but it faded. At least we can pick it up from there."

"Faded?" she asked.

"Yeah, probably stashed in a metal boat shed, or hauled up into a building. Remember, the range is pretty short, all things considered, yet very specific. At least if we find the right haystack, we can say we are looking for the glowing needle."

"That helps," Aimes pursed his lips and nodded. He pulled out a padded stool and sat down.

"Oh, yeah, and since I'm on a roll I'll show you this." Vic moved over to a lab cart and hauled up a POP gun. "This little beauty is the very one JB used." He flipped open a small panel. "In here is a USB port, and settings for Bluetooth and wireless. In effect, I can download in real time all the activity relative to this unit – where it's at, where it's been, the ID of each cartridge loaded and fired, when it was discharged, even who held it."

JB flicked up his thumb and pointed at the print with the other hand. "I had to login before it would click off safety."

"Cool," Tamari. "Do they make it in pistol size."

"Well, I hear it will be in this year's summer wear catalog." Vic smiled. He caught Tamari's golden eyes. Her toes tingled.

Aimes smiled wickedly and whispered to his partner, "If you throw another one of your tantrums, I'd advise shooting me twice."

"Make it three...in the head," she whispered back at him. "How does the dentist put it, 'you'll feel a pinch'?"

Aimes snickered. He stood. "Well, gentlemen, what time and place tomorrow morning?"

"Seven's good. We'll meet at the Coast Guard Sector and work towards the Ambassador Bridge."

"Sounds wonderful. It was a pleasure meeting you, Victor. We will see you tomorrow, bright and early." Walking over to JB, Aimes traded a few words with him.

Tamari approached Victor. He set the gun back in place.

"It was nice to meet you," a smile trying to take over her entire face.

"You as well. But 'meet' is not the same as 'get to know.' Maybe we could remedy that." Victor smiled and raised a set of thick brows.

"Maybe," Tamari said, trying not to gush.

They shook hands and Tamari left.

Out in the hall Aimes was waiting for her.

"So?" he asked.

"What?" sounding guilty.

"Did you get his number?" Aimes said, looking at her sideways.

She huffed at him.

"Miss Banks, as I hold you in the highest regard, I have a great respect for the value of your genes. Thus, I would only encourage you to find a good mate, marry, and add to the wealth of the general pool."

"Oh, that sounds so romantic, especially coming from you, Orville."

"Romantic? Oh, indeed, Miss Banks. And no wonder you think so little of my amorous history – I have never told you about Margaret." Aimes spun on his heel and marched away, grinning.

"Margaret?!" Tamari shouted at her partner's retreating form. "Hey, wait...wait up. Hey, old, bald, white dude - you have to tell me about Margaret. Who's Margaret?" She chased after him down the corridor.

Chapter 24

He looked out over the cold, murky water, across the western tip of Belle Isle to the hazy Canadian shore. The last of the winter ice had melted away, leaving a brooding, steel colored strait splitting twenty four nautical miles between two countries. The sun was pushing its way over the Windsor skyline.

At five AM Victor helped pack the OIS field truck. By six he pulled onto Mt. Elliot Street, curved through the roundabout at Wright and lumbered the vehicle down a narrow lane leading to the Coast Guard parking lot. Hands buried deep in coat pockets he waited, lost in thought. The breeze was stiff and uncomfortably chilly. He shivered.

This was nice, getting out of the "box", as he called his work room. The cold he didn't care for, but the application of all his testing, all the tech, all the time made it worthwhile. He had thought of going into forensics with its fingerprints, crime scenes, lab tests, and long, often irregular hours. But he found he liked things that whirred, clicked, flew, and shot. Gadgets, yeah, he was a gadget guy. Not in a consumer jones kind of way, but a build it, test it, break it, rebuild it type.

He hoped this really worked. This nano pulse tracking system, NPT for short, may prove to be quite useful. Then again, it could be one flipping pizza dough that landed on his head. Time will tell. Time will *really* tell.

Two cars pulled up at six forty-five. Tamari, Aimes, and JB got out of one, four techs, and another grunt in black emerged from the other. They had coordinated with the U.S. Coast Guard, who in turn worked out details with their Canadian counterpart. In the full course of their sweep they would cross the international boundary line which invisibly split the waterway. It was best to have all parties on board.

"Hello, Victor," Aimes gave a happy greeting. "I do love the early morning wind. It is quite bracing."

"Ignore him," Banks motioned a steaming coffee at her partner. "He was shivering by his fireplace when I came to pick him up."

"Now, Tamari, aren't we supposed to cover for each other? For instance, you were extraordinarily giddy on the ride home last night. Why, I thought you were channeling a school girl crush. It is my observation-"

"Alright, alright," she cut him off, quickly walking toward the watercraft, "brace the morning wind, seize the frigid day, just tempus fidget your twitchy self on to that boat." Pointing over to the Coast Guard vessel she said a quick "hi" to Vic and hustled past. She hated being that vulnerable, *and* that obvious. Yes, she was lonely, yes, very few people would understand her life, yes, the last guy she dated was El Creepo, but – she looked back at Vic – he *was* easy on the eyes. Smiling, she laughed at herself and lightened up.

Aimes watched her scurry away.

"Well, young Victor, it seems I hit a nerve." He smiled slyly and followed in her steps.

In half an hour two smaller ships pulled out of the dock, four drones were launched, and a sweep of the river began. Two of the drones were set in a slow, zig-zag pattern in the middle of the water, flying about twelve feet above the surface. The other two followed the western coast, winging back and forth like large, slow dragonflies.

Victor hunched down behind the windshield of one boat, keeping a close eye on the tablet. Its screen showed clear and brilliant in the growing light of morning. Gripping the rugged case with his left hand he played his fingers over the touch surface with swiftness and dexterity. He was excellent at his job. His eyes were deftly attuned to the feedback he was receiving. Nothing would escape his notice – *nothing*.

The humming drones searched and probed, listening with acuity, bristling with an array of antennae and small communication discs. They were hunting one signal, one scent, like bloodhounds, ignoring every other smell, pursing their prey to the end.

No trace, no blip, no sign of that boat showed up anywhere. Victor was trying to be patient. He believed in his work. He believed in the technology. At the moment, as he was anxious, and a bit tired, he also believed in strong coffee. Picking up the Styrofoam cup he sipped. It was hot and felt *so* good. Ducking down again he made a few adjustments. The screen had four windows open, each giving a critical readout of the drones. Altitude, telemetry, speed, wind, temperature, battery life, all critical things, and all working well.

But they did little to soothe his jumpy nerves. He just wanted was a sign. Something. Anything.

And, Vic found himself wondering what Tamari thought. Shaking his head, he picked up the coffee and took another sip. He must focus.

For three hours they slowly, painstakingly worked up the bank towards the Ambassador Bridge. They stopped to charge the drones on one of the boats, grab a bite to eat, and make plans, for the next leg of the search. The breeze had died down and the weather was turning mild.

"We've got a greenlight from the Canadian side," an officer from the U.S. Coast Guard informed them on their radios. "They know the basic pattern the drones will be taking, so no problem there. If we spot anything, *anything* it's important that we notify them right away. One of their lighter vessels will accompany us."

There was nothing more to be said. The search resumed.

Combing their way up the Windsor coast the same approach was used. Back and forth the drones searched, listening, sensing, probing. Behind them a small group of vessels trolled slowly in the water, waiting for the telltale sound, the digital baying of a pack on the hunt.

Vic exhaled. Glancing at the time he sucked in his lower lip and rubbed the back of his neck. He sipped his coffee and tapped the screen, fussing with settings that were already set.

"Any hope?" the man piloting the watercraft asked.

"Nope." Vic inhaled and looked up at the clear sky. "I was thinking-"

A signal came in. Drone three chirped, hovering over a spot almost midway in the river.

"Hey," Vic keyed the radio, "hey, I think I've got something."

"Which unit?" JB's voice came back.

"Three, buddy." Everyone could hear Vic's tablet singing over the radio as he talked. "I'm focusing all units on the area." Like flies on barbeque all four drones converged together over a thousand square foot area. They confirmed a reading. The box tightened to three hundred square feet. It was a weak, but persistent pattern, repeating with precision.

"We've got it!" Vic was pumped. "It's locked in."

"Where is it?" the Coast Guard officer's voice.

Vic gave him the coordinates.

"Great," the officer said, "at the bottom of the river. I'll let our neighbors know."

The general feeling of elation deflated. One didn't find living suspects at the bottom of a river. And, water erased a lot of evidence in a very short amount of time. But that they found the craft was a victory, however small.

A call went out for a heavier vessel and divers. They would find the boat and pull it up out of the muddy silt. Sure, the craft would bring up clues, and hopefully leads, but no warm body would be there. No names, or contacts, or manifests, or destinations awaited their discovery. The leader, the weapons buyer, the potential terrorist wouldn't be there – no eyes, dead and animal-like. There would be no hardened soldier defying the world, no ardent zealot despising the infidel.

"Well," Vic muttered to himself, "at least it worked."

Chapter 25

S he knocked frantically.

"C'mon, Dane!"

She looked up and down the street.

Knocking harder she made the old door jump in its frame. A hissing sound came from her mouth. She tapped her feet and wove her hands together.

"Dane, hurry up!"

The door clicked. The handle turned. Dane looked like an old, rumpled shirt hiding in a fuzzy blanket. Jia shoved past him.

"Quick! Shut the door!" She pointed frantically. "Shut the door! Lock it!"

"Okay, okay. Chill." His voice was thick and drowsy.

She began pacing, blowing into her hands. Her glasses fogged.

"You need wipers?" sarcasm mingled with amusement.

"Dane," she shook her hands, pacing, turning, pacing. "Not now, hon, not now."

"Jia, what's-"

"I'm in trouble. Oh, this is bad. Bad! Dane," she stopped for a second, "it's bad." Back in motion she clenched her fists.

Dane had seen her get worked up a good hundred times or so. He had a view to wait it out and talk her down.

"Girl, nothing could be that bad."

"Then it's way worse than you think." She marched, pivoted, marched. "Way worse!"

"You want something to drink? Coffee, tea?" he offered.

"Nothing," she paced.

"Wanna sit?" His head tilted toward the couch.

"Can't," shaking her hands.

Dane pulled the blanket tighter. His t-shirt and pajama bottoms were comfortable enough but made him feel not quite dressed for the occasion.

"I'm gonna go change," he said and began to turn away.

"Please stay here." She stopped and pleaded. Her lenses were clearing. There was no mistaking this was something urgent, something beyond her normal level of spastication. "Please, Dane." Two cold-blushed circles were drawn on her face making her look childlike, vulnerable. She resumed her indoor sprint.

"Alright. Alright." He walked over to her, stepped into her lane and took her by the shoulders. She was rigid. "Jia, what's going on?"

"I...I," she shook her hands again. "The Bay'ah – you remember?"

"That, uh, cryptic thing from the email dude, right?" Dane responded.

"Yeah." She paused and swallowed. Her foot drummed. "It means Oath of Allegiance."

"Okay," he shrugged. "You mentioned that."

"It's a death pledge." She said, eyes swirling around the lenses.

"Yeah, I remember." His hand slipped to the base of her neck, comforting, caressing.

She took off again, pacing away, then back.

"I studied the mystery language," she spoke in a breathless flurry, "tracked the roots, the syntax – you know, my company has a lot of linguistic resources." Jia nodded her head rapidly and pushed up her glasses.

"They have you for starters," Dane smiled.

She sniffed in heavily as her nose thawed. Her speech began to thaw too, rapidly increasing speed to keep up with The Brain.

"I figured once I deciphered the language I would break into all communications." She stopped and poked Dane's chest. "And let me tell you, chocolate bar, whoever set this up was good – better than good." She turned and marched.

"Like, your level?" he ventured.

Jia stopped and looked at him. "Something like that."

"And I'm thinking you found the red pill and went in." Throwing the blanket over his head Dane leaned against the wall.

"Some make you larger, and the one I found made me small." She stopped moving and shaped a gesture with her thumb and index finger. "Like, *really* small. I got in everywhere. Everything was coded to the dialect and so become the basis for decoding on the other end. Once decoded, though, it didn't explain the symbolic references they used."

"You mean, 'Elvis rode the UFO', or somethin'?" Dane asked.

"Right." Jia bobbed her head up and down.

"Mary cooked the little lamb?" He laughed a little.

"Yeah. You can decode the name Elvis, but you have no idea *who* it stands for and what exactly *is* the UFO." Jia shot this out in a flurry and began pacing.

"I see." Dane paused. "Did they really say Elvis?"

"Dane!" She stopped. Hiding her lower lip, she began to cry. Her hands shot straight down to her sides, fists balled.

"Hey, hey," tenderly, "you really *are* scared." He stepped forward and hugged her. Jia grabbed him tight, trembling and tapping her foot.

"Dane," her voice tremulous, "they're going to do something, something bad. I could only grab pieces, but Iran is involved, somebody mentioned Putin, and hinted at North Korea."

"And the doof?" Dane asked.

"No," she shook her hands. "I didn't find anything more about him. They mighta spanked him for opening his mouth. It was all so sketchy. Something about a little island, captives, and lots of 'Victory for Allah', 'Conquer for Allah', and all the usual 'kill everyone who isn't us' stuff."

"When?" he pulled the blanket off, throwing it on the couch.

"Soon. Very soon. Things are heating up, apparently." Jia shifted from foot to foot.

"Okay," Dane nodded sensibly, "so, we pick up and move out of the city."

"Dane, that's not the worst part." Her eyes begged him to understand. "I'm...I'm." She gripped him so tightly he winced.

"Jia, were you caught?" Did they trace you? Did-"

"Not from them. Not from outside." She stepped closer to him, her mouth in a tight grimace.

"What do you mean?" He leaned closer, caressing the left side of her face.

"Listen," her voice low, confidential, "our company has its own 'Elvis' and 'UFO' shtick. I've never met anyone except my direct boss. He recruited me, handled me, arranged my pay."

"And?" Dane looked through the fishbowls at a very scared woman.

"I saw the news, the reports, my boss Jeffrey is dead. He's dead, killed in his apartment. His wife and daughter are missing. He's the only one who knew who I was."

"Jia, that's terrible! But how would they know you were poking around?"

"They got it out of Jeffrey, I guess...the hard way." She swallowed and sniffed. Her lips pressed together, a fresh stream of tears falling. "And...and I got an arrow from Baby Doll?"

"Who? What?" Dane ran both hands up into his messy hair." This would be kind of comical if it wasn't so serious."

"Baby Doll is another worker for the company," Jia said, shaking Dane a little. "I'm Dragon Lady, remember?"

"And the Jeff guy?" he wondered.

"Mordred," she returned.

"Do you guys do comic cons?" shaking his head. "I bet they're avatarpaloozas."

She threw out her shaking hands and let out a little series of frustrated stutters. "Dane!"

"Okay, sorry," he held his hands open.

"I've never met any of the others." Jia fired rapidly. "I only know a few by their handles. Baby Doll sent me little notes in the past. Not even notes, really, but one or two words that have pre-arranged meanings. Some of them silly, most are serious. They're like little papers tied to an arrow – one offs, nothing deep or long. We were given specific codes warning us or instructing us in case of a breach, a mole, danger, or the need to wipe everything and so on."

"Jia, what do these people really do?" he leaned down to her face.

"Play in deep doo-doo. Read bad people's mail. Well, that's part of it. They surveil. Infiltrate." She exhaled and leaned on the wall throwing her arms around herself. "I got the news about Jeffrey and then the warning from Baby Doll."

"And?" he cocked his face.

"Pitch," she said matter-of-factly.

"What?" Dane looked around.

"That's the message." Jia paused her nervous motion, searching him for understanding.

"Pitch?" he scrunched his face.

"Yes!" She tightly threaded her fingers together. "And in our circles, it's a freakin' nuke. It means 'we've been found out, destroy everything, run for your life.'"

"Pitch?" Dane said with disbelief.

"Well, what did you want it to be?" stamping her foot.

"Okay, okay...so, *pitch*." He looked around at the apartment. "You can hang out here."

A car door closed softly, but noticeably outside. Jia went to the window and peeked out through the blind. She swore. "This is like a dumb cop movie. Dane, throw on your jeans."

"Why?" he asked.

"Because there's creepy guys with tattoos and goatees who aren't part of a rockabilly band. And, they just got out of a white van. Why is it always a *stupid* van?!"

"More room to work?" He felt mildly insensitive. "Sorry." Still thinking she was a bit paranoid he went to the window himself. Yep, two guys, a van, and now a second one pulled up.

"Why *is* it always a stupid van?" He cursed. Several times. Creatively.

"I'm sorry, hon. I really am. I'm scared. I didn't know where else to go." Her voice was high pitched. She shook her hands.

"I'm glad you're here," he said quietly, walking over to her. "You *should* be with me."

"I've thought that for a long time," she said, smiling weakly at him.

He smiled back and wished he had kissed her already. With a sudden burst of motion, he ran past her and grabbed a pair of jeans off the couch. Ducking into the tiny kitchen, he pulled off his sweats and threw them on. Hopping back out, trying to put on a shoe.

"Jia," Dane leaned against a wall, pulling on his other shoe. "We should really call the cops now."

"If they got to Jeffrey," she said firmly, "they can get to us. Who knows who's been bought off and at what level. Once we're in custody we'll be in the system. They'll know our friends, our family, everybody. I'd rather make it hard for them to fish me in open waters than to shoot me in a barrel."

"I hadn't thought of all that," he said.

"But I have to! They apparently know where I live, but I wiped everything – all of my work. The whole life I presented to the world online, *and* in real time, was a forgery. This," motioning to the window, "is the very reason I did all of it from the beginning. Even Jeffery didn't know my real name and connections. I don't exist."

"How did you get paid, and stuff?" Dane asked while pulling on a hoodie.

"Figure it out, Sherlock. I'm a hacker," she said, harsher than she meant to. "As far as the world knows I'm Yu Yan from Hong Kong, clutching to her green card and working at a local deli. I left a fake paper trail at my place to mislead them. All of my picture ID with immigration, the FBI, and Homeland have been altered just enough to fool facial recognition. Jia isn't in the system anywhere – I've seen to that. I even designed my own fingerprints on file. No one official has a clue who I really am."

"But they were watching your place. They followed you." Dane filled in the blanks.

Jia nodded.

"Jeffrey must have surrendered my location. I got out just in time, but I think someone spotted me walking down to the Uber. Otherwise, they don't have a clue who I really am."

"You rock, tech chick," Dane said, turning his head at a noise outside, "but we gotta go."

"On your heels, hunky," she said, taking in a deep breath. "Oh, you should destroy your phone. It could be used to track us. Throw it in the toilet tank."

"Really? Is that from a spy manual?" Dane said, shutting the cell down.

"No. Someone tweeted it." Jia said. She kept looking from the front door to the window.

"Okay, I will in a sec," Dane replied, shoving the device into his back pocket.

Jia heard a voice from the sidewalk. "Dane," she hissed.

"C'mon, girl!" Grabbing her by the hand he ran toward the tiny, back bedroom.

"What are we going to do now, hide in a closet?" she said sharply.

"No, Jia, I've got it worked out."

"You better!" her nerves speaking with irritation, " 'cause we're some bad history."

"Not if I can help it." Dane pushed her in and glanced behind him.

"I'm so freaked! So freaked." She shifted from foot to foot, clenching and re-clenching her hands. They stood by a small, cluttered closet. Jia's chest rose and fell spasmodically. Cold, trembling fingertips pressed against her mouth.

"Dane!" she hissed.

"Just a sec," he said, pulling out a box and setting it down.

Someone tried the front door. They stopped and looked at each other briefly. Dane launched into motion, explaining as he moved.

"I'm renting this apartment from old friends of mine," he said, burying his head in the small space. "This used to be Marco's room. I would spend the night and we would sneak out."

"How?" she shook her hands.

"Through this." Under the hanging clothes Dane fumbled with an access panel on the back wall of the closet. "He never said why this was here, but I know this building used to be an industrial laundry. This is a big vent or something, or at least it was. All the sheet metal was long gone by the time Marco and I used to climb up it. There's a really cool hang out." He snapped the panel out and stood up. "Got it. Yeah, there's also an access down a fire escape."

"Hurry!" Jia danced.

They heard the sound of glass breaking.

"Hurry!" she whispered.

Gripping Jia's elbow he pulled her toward the opening. "Reach straight back and grab the iron bars. Start climbing."

Dane watched her pretty, little figure go through the hole, latch on to the metal and begin to ascend. Slipping in behind her he turned around just like Marco showed him. He pulled the panel by the handle on the back, snapping it up and in place. Unless you knew where to look this little access was hard to find. If nothing else, it could buy them some time.

He hadn't realized how fast his heart had been pounding. The climb was fifteen feet, but adrenaline made it seem like three. Jia was at the top waiting for him. There was an old, dirty window throwing milky light down the dark shaft. Taking her arm, he led her through a dusty hallway.

"This place is creepy and cold," Jia shivered.

"It's just old and unused." Dane said. He came to the door where the hiding place was. It was screwed shut. "Great!" He quietly fumed. "We can't stay in here forever. C'mon. If we go down the ladder we can get out and run."

Run. In all the excitement Dane had grasped at something new. He was tired of all the chains, the heaviness, losing people. *It was a good life*, he consoled himself, *but only half a life*. He really was in love with this nutty chick, and the thoughts of leaving it all for a bit, running away with her, forgetting everything for a while was enticing and romantic. Dane wasn't just living; he was now on the cusp of thriving. Now he had someone to be passionate about, someone to protect. There was an old camp he knew. It was farther north. With a wood stove and a hand pump in the sink they could make it. If he emptied his account, they'd have more than enough to live on for a while. He had an idealized plan – just the two of them against it all, and that was enough to sink one's teeth into. No more drifting, no more hollowed-out, empty, listless soul. Grabbing her by the shoulders he hugged her.

"What're you doing?" her voice croaked out. "You're crushing me." Her face was smooshed against his chest, mouth puckered, glasses askew.

"Sorry," releasing her. Stepping back, he leaned in and kissed her forehead.

Jia pulled back stunned, pleased. "That...that was so tender." They looked at each other honestly. "But, curly locks, your timing *reeks*."

"Timing," he sighed and rolled his head in a figure eight.

"Not that I mind, sweetie," Jia said, straightening her glasses, "but maybe when we're dancing, or something."

"How 'bout going down a ladder?" Dane asked, unlocking the window.

"You sure know how to make a girl feel special." Jia patted him on the back.

Dane fought with the old double hung and managed to force the sash up. Peering out he spotted no one in the alley. He turned and faced Jia.

"Out you go," he pointed.

"Great," she grabbed his chin, "hug her, kiss her tender-like, then kick her out - typical man."

"Hug her then save her. We've got to move. There's a hole in the fence we can slip through and get to that other building." Her eyes drew to the old, grey hulk across the alley.

"That looks inviting," she smirked.

"It looks safe," he stated, "safer than here, anyhow."

Jia swung her legs out of the window and onto an old iron platform. It shuddered at the touch of her feet, probably the first contact in ten years. Easing her body down she pivoted and glanced several times at Dane.

"Go on," he motioned. "It's only one story. Hurry!"

Without hesitating Jia grabbed at the top rung, hooked in her foot and began the descent. Dane slipped out and waited. She made it to the ground and looked up. He motioned her to step to one side. This thing was shaky, and he always had a fear of it pulling out of the wall. She moved. Dane began to come down. He was almost to the end when the bolts bent slightly under his weight, breaking loose an old, corroded bracket. The piece fell, bounced off a metal dumpster with a loud bang, and clattered to the street with a series of sharp, echoing tumbles. They might as well have rung a bell.

Dane swore.

Jia shook her hands.

"Hurry!" he urged her, "I think the whole neighborhood heard that. C'mon, this way!"

They slipped through a hole in the beat-up fencing just as a van pulled down the alley. Running with young legs they made a quick retreat to the old apartment building. All the doors along the back cul de sac were locked. Dane tried each one he came to. He pounded a door and cursed. At the second to last one he grabbed the handle and smiled. A small rock was stuck in the bottom propping it open just enough to keep it from latching.

"Smoke break," he called it and pulled the door. Once they were in, he nudged the rock out with his toe and shut it. It locked and they breathed. They stood in the bottom of a stairwell.

"Let's go up," Dane said in a rush.

They took the four flights to the top floor. There were no apartments here. It was all storage, dust, and the super's living area.

"At least it's a little warmer in here." She shuddered.

"Yeah," he took her hand. She tingled strangely from the excitement and his touch. It seemed they both had strange timing.

"Maybe we can find an empty room to hide out in." He pulled her forward.

"Okay," she said, exhaling rapidly.

The hadn't gone ten steps when the superintendent rounded the corner, jangling his keys. Dane panicked. He froze. There were no open doors. The stairwell was too far away.

Should they ask him for help? Should they hide? His thoughts swirled in the panic.

Jia, the brain, the quick thinker, the young woman in love took a scene from a movie and made it fit. She grabbed Dane and swung him around, slamming him into the wall. Her glasses were already off. She threw herself at him, but time seemed to forget its nature and all the world slowed down.

He saw. He knew.

She had waited and waited.

Through all their loneliness, in all their blossoming love and passion, less than a second became more than a lifetime. In the crush and cascade, in the pain and pleasure their lips met in one sparking flash, intensely filled with the dream they had both desired. Jia clutched him, held him with long expected hope and desperation. Dane felt the world and its weight give way beneath him, all its burdens lost in this one, incomprehensible moment.

The super stopped in his tracks. He tilted his head sideways and shook it.

"If you kids want to make out, find some other-"

He never finished.

Down at the far end of the long corridor a sound like a muted bang and the quick hiss of an opening pop bottle rang. It was followed by the clink of a hollow metal tube bouncing off the cement floor. The old man fell like a truck had blown up out of the pavement and hit him square, planting his face dead on. His hand still clutched the keys. Dane saw the goatee, grabbed Jia and ran for the steps.

Exploding next to his head the wall showered fragments and dust. Down they ran heading for the bottom. They spotted a figure coming up from the floors below.

"Quick," Dane yelled, "in here." He dragged Jia through a wide, metal door with a large number three on it. It opened to a long hallway with a row of doors on both sides. Midway down the corridor an alcove recessed into the wall, adorned with a smudged window and an old, tartan love seat. They ducked in and hid.

Jia stood up near the corner and kept stealing glances back down the way they had just come. Her eyes were focused on the main door.

Dane crouched down behind her. He remembered that he had his cellphone. Being shot at drove out all other concerns from his mind. Pulling it out he pressed the power button. A luminescent gray logo appeared on the screen.

"C'mon," Dane seethed at the device. "Hurry up!"

There was a noise from down the hall.

Jia quickly looked and pulled her head back in.

"Dane..." Jia turned to him in panic. "Someone's coming."

The phone booted up and Dane unlocked it. He dialed 9-1-1.

"I live at 944 Swanson, Oak Park," he shouted. "I'm in the One Bridge Apartment building to the west of where I live, third floor. The emergency?" he listened. "I'm being shot at!" he yelled. "Yes...yes, my name-" A bullet slammed into the wall by Jia, showering her with dust. Dane ducked involuntarily and dropped the phone, kicking it under the small couch behind her. He fell to his knees and began searching.

"There's no shots that way," Jia pointed down the other leg of the hallway. "Maybe we can run." She snaked her head out to look for the shooter.

"Where is it?!" Dane fumbled around on the ground.

A spray like fine mist covered his right ear and cheek. Jia leaned against the wall still facing around the corner to the left.

"Are they shooting paint balls at us?" He said, rising on one knee. Wiping his face, he looked at his hand. Panic blew through him. "Jia!" He grabbed her and spun the mannequin body around. The delicate, high boned features were limp. Her eyes were closed, glasses gone. She looked almost peaceful. A hole the size of a dime sat neatly in her forehead. Blood and fluid began to ooze out. The legs, the torso, the arms, the shoulders drooped, her head pitched forward and she folded like Jack back in the box.

"Jia! Jia, no! Jia!" Dane cried out.

Fog enveloped him. Time abandoned him. Reason, hope, heart fled him in this hour of need. He sunk with the body and cradled her.

"Jia!" he screamed, sobbing.

Out of the dark the monsters came, hissing and laughing, the kind you fear as a child, the kind you dread as a man. They stretched out their claws to tear him away. Her head fell forward and he could see the back of the skull was missing.

Poor little rag doll, sad little thing, lifeless and breathless she slumped to one side. It was the last he saw of her, the last he traced the delicate line of her face.

Black night came down as a hood. A blow from the creatures ended what was only the beginning of a waking nightmare.

Chapter 26

Cold. Dane shivered uncontrollably. The bliss, the unconscious bliss, the little cave he longed to crawl back in to. His feet – what was wrong with them? Wet, clay, mud, cold. A tongue, thick and pasty, wormed across paper-dry lips. His body shook. One foot scraped another; bare, no shoes, no socks. Muddy. Wet. Freezing.

"You know what I love about your country's leaders?" The voice floated, in the dark, through the dark, from the dark.

Tick-tock, tick-tock – the sound was constant.

Wet feet, the deep, thick voice, the clock, they were all there, together, surreal, and cold. He shuffled his feet. They were bound. He couldn't pull them up.

Breath came rapidly. Trying to rise he fell back. Throbbing, beating, his skull pulsed.

Tick-tock.

"They are so unwilling to deal with the reality of Islamism that they have made up a version of their own." The voice floated in from somewhere to the front of Dane, a little to the right.

He began to panic. His hands were tied, his head hooded, and his feet – what did they do to his feet? They were in a hole filled with water. It was the early weeks of Spring. Some days were nice and warm this time of year. The nights were cold. Too cold to lay on the ground with your feet strapped into a hole. The frigid liquid seeped and ached up his legs, into the bones, to his pelvis, in his gut, up his spine. It settled, kicking merrily in his head.

"Why am I here? Who are you?" Dane shouted.

"Ah, the dead speaks." The voice said calmly. "And the appropriate litany..."

"Where is this?" Dane's anger and stress rose together. "You need to let me go!"

"If I had a coin for each time..." the captor mused.

"Let me go!" Dane sat up. Exploding stabs and brilliant spikes shot through his head. He tried to stand but his feet were two wooden blocks, numb, yet burning. Sitting heavily, he tried to pull at the fabric on his face.

"It's a pity," the refined, eloquent voice took on a sympathetic tone, "that your girlfriend died. She *was* beautiful. Some spoils are, well...spoiled. Ha! How witty." The sound died into subdued laughter.

"Jia," Dane slumped, "why did you kill Jia?"

"An excellent question. Half a moment." Changing directions, the voice began to speak in a language Dane didn't understand. A question was posed to a guard who shrugged his shoulders, nervously avoiding the eyes. "Ah," turning back to Dane, "yes, an unanswered pity. I, for various reasons, would have liked to know her better. I am sure she had something of value to tell me. And," as though reasoning out his like of a favorite dish, "she would have warmed a bed nicely, though a bit too old for my tastes."

"Freak!" Dane shot at him, "what's wrong with you? Some kind of," he struggled with his wrists, "religious nut?"

"Ah, the dead questions." A chair creaked back. "I am so going to enjoy our repartee. So, what shall we discuss at the outset, your Christian faith?"

"Mine?" He tried to sit up. An almond sliver of hope dropped onto his dirty, empty plate. "I don't really think there's a God. See, I'm not one of your religious enemies. I...I'm a nobody. A friendless-"

"*Girl*friendless, at any rate," the voice said dryly.

Dane grunted in anger. He managed to slump forward and stay upright. A knot on his head throbbed and pulsed. His stomach heaved.

The voice chuckled. "You so remind me of that Russian lad taken into custody."

"Are you a cop or something?" Dane said, straining at the ropes.

"Tsk, tsk," the mouth clicked, "perhaps a bit too euphemistic. Let us say 'captured' shall we?"

Dane groaned.

"He was a smart one," the voice continued, "and, like all good Russians, loved to argue. Ah, the talks we had. It was a pity he had to be dismantled – such spirit! But one cannot help oneself."

"Dis-what?!" The slight bile of panic splashed into his mouth. "Are you freakin' Hannibal?!"

"What a pleasant comparison," slapping a knee. "A great general. What a tact-"

"No, dude, the serial killer," Dane corrected. "He ate his victims."

"Oh, Allah forbid! That is most distasteful. What a dreadful comparison." The voice sounded mildly offended. "True, there is a physical component to each project, but it is really a game of breaking the psyche, of dismembering, not so much the body, as of the person. Soon, little pet, you will forget your life, your occupation, and ah, even your name."

"Oh, God," Dane moaned. "Let me go!" He cursed the thing in the dark, accusing it in the vilest terms. He thrashed his feet. He yanked at the bindings on his wrists. He pulled, fruitlessly, helplessly at the strap cinching the hood to his neck.

"There, there, young man," a cooing, consoling tone. "One is called many things by many people. Some of them," the sound paused thoughtfully, almost whimsically, "not so nice. By some, those who know my work, I am called the Pet Maker. What do you think? Quite an appellation for a disembodied voice in the gloom, no? And what shall I call you? Hmmm...what was that older American movie? Ah, a Man called Dog."

"Horse," Dane said.

"What?" the voice questioned.

"Horse!" Dane shouted.

"Horse? Horse – yes, yes, that's it. And what was his name?"

"Richard Harris." Dane wondered what on Earth he was doing playing a casual game of trivial darts with the Devil. How freakishly absurd it all was. He remembered that particular movie and that particular actor from a Film As Social Commentary class at University. Why? Why, of all the stupid, stupid things to remember? And why had he so willingly shared it with Sinbad (the name he secretly called him). Why?

Ingratiation.

The bound, helpless man despised his weakness, his urge to appease, to please.

"Yes," the dark, cold voice spoke up, "Al Kalb. It looks like it sounds like 'corn cob', but really," a long exhale filled the room, "it is dreadful at times to make the sweet Arabic work with English." Distaste spilled from the tone. "But I shall carefully sound it out for you – al-KA-leb. Is that better?"

No answer.

Slow, paced footsteps walked to Dane's side. "But there you have it. When you remember nothing else, perhaps you will remember that: The man called Dog. Hmmm?"

More measured steps and a chuckle lilted out, set against the unfamiliar, ambient sounds that hummed just beyond conscious thought. The cold figure on the floor moaned piteously. He lost his love, he lost his freedom, and he was in the hands of not just a religious fanatic, but a twisted sadist – one determined to break him down piece by piece.

Things were not looking up.

As it slowly rose to his ears a persistent hissing became a part of the background noise. It was louder now, bubbling with a tinny echo. The sound had to come from a large pot, a tub of something hot and violently boiling. It all ate at him – the cold, the sucking sound of his muddy, tingling feet, the tick-tock of the large, cabinet timepiece, the eloquent, maniacal voice, and the rolling thrum of liquid dancing to the flames.

The clock chimed.

"Ah," said the voice, "the hour has come for bed. Yes, punctuality and discipline, I do like a brisk schedule. Makes one feel that one has, how do you say it, 'get a jump on things.' "

Stress laughed like an idiot Dane's his head. How stupid. How insane. It was like discussing hemoglobin with a vampire. Repartee? "It" was strapped to the ground. "It" had its feet in a hole. "It" was not going to get "It" in any deeper than "It" could help. Such was the vanity of hope, the fain scrabbling for the purchase, the traction of dignity down the slippery shaft.

The man stopped abruptly. "Oh, how thoughtless – to be a host, yet so remiss in duties. You are my guest and I have offered you nothing. What a breach of etiquette." At some signal two moved from the corners of the room. They seemed to lift something heavy, shuffling toward Dane under the load.

"You are no doubt cold," the voice shivered. "It *is* getting quite frigid." Something was spoken sharply in another language. "Let me offer you something hot before we part."

The two carrying the load moved closer. Liquid began to pour into the muddy hole. For a moment delicious and brief his feet warmed up. A thrill of comfort and rest effused through the stressed, weary man now on the floor. But the boiling water kept coming, burning, scalding, stinging beyond any pain Dane had ever experienced. He screamed and lurched forward. His hands reached out instinctively. These too were doused in the liquid fire, channeling some on his chest and into his lap. He lunged backwards, throbbing and convulsing on the floor in acute agony. Dane twisted in his bonds and blacked out.

"Good night, Al Kalb. Until the morning."

The voice departed. The guards took their places. The clock ticked on toward the dawn.

Chapter 27

Quietly threading his fingers together and pulling them apart, Pearce sat staring into his cup of coffee. He looked up at the clock – Seven AM – and back down, tumbling around some thoughts.

Anything ecumenical, particularly with someone of an altogether different faith often made him a little nervous. Over the years He had met with many diverse people in a wide range of communities across several countries. Somehow, he never quite grew comfortable with it. Ironically, the needs of a community, like politics, often made strange alliances.

True, the people who lived in any given neighborhood generally wanted to live in peace, in places that were safe, on city streets where they didn't have to fear for their children's lives. That was true of Christians, Muslims, Jews, Buddhists, atheists – any decent person. But he could only join their efforts so far before what he felt was an untenable compromise. It was one thing to work on his approach, another to violate his principles. He would do all he could to be "all things to all men so that some might believe." What he would *not* do is water down the message of Christ regardless of pressure, public opinion, or political correctness.

"Political correctness," he muttered out loud, laughing a little. Picking up the creamer he poured some absently into the black, steaming liquid. He mused the utter stupidity of using politicians, political mores, or the ever shifting, self-serving winds of political approval as a basis for what was right and wrong. When did we become the toadies for elected officials or their orbiting bureaucracies? When did a nation lease their mind out to a group of ever offended social justice warriors safely nested at universities and fringe think tanks? The idea of making politics, a profession more known for its vice and sleaze than anything else as a-

The bell on the door softly chimed.

Michael looked up.

A man stepped in – heavy, full length overcoat, full, greying beard, dark sunglasses and a broad-brimmed, black hat.

Michael pursed his lips and put the knuckle of his index finger against them. He knew Nasri and thought his get-up mildly amusing. He had never seen incognito so "cognito" in his life. The figure walked over to his table, looked out the window, leaned to the side and searched the back where the bathrooms were. Pearce raised his brows and waited.

"Go ahead and laugh," the enigmatically clad man said. "I certainly did when I looked in the mirror."

The Reverend started to snicker, then began a somewhat polite series of heaves into his mug. Finally, he snorted, put down the cup and stared out the window.

"How are you, Nasri?"

"Michael," he greeted, "I am well."

"Please sit," Pearce motioned to the opposite bench. The man took the seat in one fluid motion. "Do you think you were seen," leaning in toward Nasri, a stifled grin on his face.

"By everyone...and no one," the heavily cloaked man remained straight as a rod on the bench. Michael shook his head and leaned out, getting the attention of the waitress. She nodded, knowing the order.

"Rye toast, no butter, black coffee?" Pearce offered.

"That is fine, Michael." The figure looked out the window, scanning up and down the street.

Pearce looked out on the empty road, then back to the man. "I know some people gave you static for working with me on the food bank-"

"This is a more urgent matter," Nasri said, glancing to the back, "far more dangerous."

"Nasri, what's wrong?" Pearce suddenly sobered. This wasn't like Nasri. The normally cheerful cleric was unusually somber.

"There is not much time," he answered Michael, hissing between his teeth.

"Okay," Michael leaned back, crossing his arms, "lay it on me."

"I cannot give you specifics. No names. I am a peaceful man." Nasri continued to scan the area.

"Of course," Pearce, nodding his head.

"But there are those, you know, who interpret things differently, the words," the bearded man breathed in quickly then let out a long breath. "The words of The Prophet, peace be upon him."

"Yeah. I mean, you and I don't fundamentally agree on theology," Michael sipped his coffee, "but we do try and work together at times."

"Peaceably," Nasri added.

"Yeah." A grin hooked Michael's mouth. "Well, I'm good on my end."

"As am I. But not all are," the brim of the black hat tipped toward Michael.

"Can't please 'em all-" Pearce added.

"Michael, I-"

"Okay," Pearce held up a hand. "Spill it, Nasri. We've never lied to each other."

"No," the man wove his fingers together, bending them up and down. "We have not."

The waitress came and set down two plates of toast, one fresh coffee, topping off the other. The covered man shifted, keeping his rigid posture. His eyes never settled, roaming from the street, the back of the restaurant, back to his hands.

"Something..." his voice became low. "Something is going to happen, Michael."

"Something?" Pearce set down the cup, growing serious.

"I am not sure." Nasri sucked in air almost painfully. "We are a simple gathering. Our mosque is not overly wealthy, but our people are honest and hard working. Many of us left places on fire with war. We only want to live peaceful lives."

"Okay, okay," Pearce nodded again, turning his cup slowly. "I hear a 'but' coming."

"Yes. Well..." Nasri put a hand on the table. It rattled the spoon near his steaming coffee. "We work with men, young men, teaching them our beliefs, our pillars, pointing them to a life without drunkenness or thievery, a life of faith. Many come for help, food, you know."

"Yeah, I do," Michael agreed.

"Many come for their needs, but few will listen," the older man said.

Michael motioned him to go on.

"There are other voices that rise up." Nasri almost whispered.

"Others?" Michael cocked his head.

"Please," Nasri looked to the cold, treeless street again. "The less I say-"

"Alright, alright." Pearce took a swallow of his coffee. He had never seen Nasri so disturbed. "Take your time."

"Yes. Yes." The man paused, pulling his sunglasses down an inch. Pearce could see the worry etching his face. "There are others who offer them a very violent version of Islam, a chance to spill blood for what they say is a higher cause. It especially appeals to those in gangs, the unstable, the desperate, the lonely and fatherless."

"They're recruiting." Pearce's fingers tightened on the porcelain cup handle. This grieved his heart. Setting the cup down on the table he shifted in his seat. Michael brought a message of forgiveness, redemption, healing, of belonging. Arms, however humble on this earthly plain, were opened to the lowest, the least of people. It brought him great pain to think of young men and women, young souls like Andrew being pulled into a radical belief system that promised other worldly rewards for violent and deadly actions. In practical terms did it matter if it were vicious gangs, skinheads, or neo-Nazis? Preaching the message of malice and destruction could only lead to one end. Had he not seen it in Africa and India, Mexico, as well as America? Drug cartels, brutal warlords, religious extremists – they all became vortexes that sucked young lives down into death, war, and the hatred of one's fellow man.

"All they that take the sword," Michael muttered, "shall perish with the sword."

"Yes," Nasri said sadly. "The recent violence at a few of the protests – the bus depot, the carpenter's unions, those thugs were stirred up and sent as part of a larger game plan."

"Game plan?" Reverend Pearce sat back in the booth. His chest rose and then slowly deflated. He reached down and picked up his coffee.

Nasri held up his palm, head slightly bowed. "Something big is coming. I heard rumors of killing Christian leaders, especially in public. I fear I only know a small, small piece." The cloaked man turned brown, tired eyes out into the emptiness. He bunched a hand under his nose. A silent car passed by like a shadow over the asphalt.

"Now, I know you're not just trying to shut me up," motioning his cup at Nasri, "as much as you might like to."

The unsettled man turned his face back to Michael. It broke into a feeble smile.

"Michael, this is more than just religious conflict – more than militant Islamism."

"Strange," Michael leaned forward, replying a bit too sarcastically, "but I feel neither surprised nor relieved at this news."

"My friend..." Nasri paused as one about to take a serious plunge. Even through the dark shades obscured part of his face, Pearce could see in his kindly eyes how weighed down he was.

"Sorry," Michael sat back. He slid a finger across his lips, cupping his chin in his hand. "I'm sorry, Nasri." Michael said quietly. "Please continue."

"Yes." The greying man paused. "Yes." He flexed his fingers and took a deep breath. "The followers and those in power behind what is coming believe a great leader has revealed himself, one who has long been hidden. This leader is to usher in the complete, worldwide rule and justice of Islam. And, depending on which branch of belief, which scholar and/or spiritual group one follows this dominance will be achieved by different means."

"Means?" Pearce asked, tapping his finger on the rim of his cup.

"Look, Michael, I could get very nuanced and technical with all of this. Without much thought I could begin throwing around Arabic and Persian words, names, and titles. This is something I have studied for a long time. But I am stripping all of it down to, uh..." Nasri searched for the right phrase.

"Where the rubber meets the road?" Michael offered.

"Yes." Nasri nodded. "That. I do so not because you are not capable of grasping it-"

"Thanks," Michael interjected, motioning his coffee at the man.

"No, Michael, I do so because I fear taking too much time, and, would it really matter? My warning would not change. Your danger would not be less, I fear."

"And, Nasri, the less you throw around buzz words that may cause nosey ears to pick up on, the better."

"Yes," the cleric replied, shifting his glasses. "You understand me."

"So?" Pearce wondered.

"So, this particular group believes that it follows this prophetic leader directly," Nasri furthered, "and that he has finally been revealed to the world. This leader and his followers undeniably affirm that great destruction and bloodshed must be brought upon this Earth until it is completely surrendered to their rule."

"Ah, Sha-" Michael corrected himself and began to whisper. "Sharia."

"Yes. And more." Nasri leaned closer to his companion. "They want total control, complete subjugation. They believe that by the sword, bomb, chaos, rapine, deception, or any means necessary they will utterly stand on the back of the world's collective neck."

"And let me guess," Michael smirked up the side of his mouth, "this leader will be God's chosen one, fit to bathe in blood and enjoy the wealth and power of his office."

"Yes." Nasri looked out the window and sighed. "Yes."

"Gott mit uns," Pearce dropped his head and said quietly. "Gott mit uns."

"But the world is too obtuse a target, Michael."

"Ah, America." Pearce shook his head. "I assume they see it at the satanic hydra to be dutifully slain."

"Yes. It is the biggest of many targets at which to focus their hatred. A particularly virulent strain of this belief has grown out of the religious incubator of the Middle East. 'Death to America' must be on a lot of t-shirts by now." Nasri smiled faintly. "Sorry," he said sheepishly, "bad attempt at humor."

Pearce chuckled. "Doesn't hurt to laugh a little."

"Michael, you must understand, though, that Muslims in the west, those who are happy to be here do not generally hold this view. All we want to do is to be free to worship our God without persecution, to raise our families in peace. We do, however," Nasri shrugged his shoulders, "disagree with many aspects of the moral bent this society has taken."

"I disagree with much of it as well. I too believe in conversion, but not at the point of a sword." Michael's voice became harder. "I stand for freedom of conscience, individual rights, and certainly don't see the moral high ground in slitting people's throats and rape."

Nasri spread his hands. "Michael, please don't shoot the messenger. I meant no harm."

Pearce huffed and stared out at the passing cars. "I'm sorry again, Nasri. I know you are trying to help, and certainly putting yourself at risk. Will none of them see reason? Can't any of your good people talk to them?"

"No. These radicals are too far gone. They have taken a death pledge," the black-hatted man said softly.

"A what now?" Pearce's eyebrows went up.

"They have pledged to Allah, to the Prophet, and to the leader to fight this battle to the end or die in the effort."

"I see," Michael muttered. "I see."

"Some I know have tried to talk to relatives, to friends. But you must understand, Michael. We are not one monolithic group – no, far from it. Most are very afraid to mention a word of this. Some have lost their lives. Islamist elements in Iran and Syria in particular have carved out the most vicious and determined group of radicals I have ever seen. They have campaigned to rope in every man, woman, and child around the world they can to their glorious cause. Those who will not submit they will destroy.

And it would be easy to dismiss them as a cult were it not for the power, money, weaponry, and support of these nations and others. They will kill anyone who stands in their way, Muslim or not. Add to that an unshakable 'end of days' belief in one man, and all the 'God ordained' license to fulfill bloodlust and bodily passions. Even nations that aren't predominantly Muslim have back-channeled funds to help thrust a spear in the side of America. Bad things are going to happen not only here in Detroit, but across this nation."

Michael thought a moment then spoke. "If all of this is going to happen soon the whole Greater Detroit Area must be crawling with this guy's followers."

"Yes, Michael. And I do not now know friend from foe."

Pearce was himself becoming a little paranoid. He watched the cars flow by. Did that one slow down just a little too much? He rapidly shook his head, clearing it from fear while shooting up a silent prayer for courage. His life, Andrew's life, and the soul of every volunteer was in God's hands, not his. Michael was held by the deep conviction that he must unashamedly move forward.

"But you know," Pearce sipped the black liquid, "that I cannot hide, or back down. I must hold these rallies. I must reach out to everyone that I can."

"I know...I know," Nasri looked at his fine-boned fingers, eyes rimmed with dark concern. "I just felt that I should be honest with you, to give you a 'heads up.'"

Michael didn't speak. He studied the man in the black outfit across from him. They were oil and water; they would never really mix. Each of these men sincerely held faiths that, at their core were not compatible with one another. To the unlearned or novice, to the surface skimmers these differences seemed a matter of semantics. But Michael knew it came down to one person: Jesus Christ.

To the Muslim, Jesus was just a good man, a teacher, an inspired prophet of lesser station than Muhammad, a human created to be part of Allah's plan. To the Christian, Jesus was God incarnate, in whom all the fullness of the godhead dwelt bodily, through whom all things in the cosmos were made. He wasn't just a moral instructor who knew the way, but as Jesus himself said, "I am the way, the truth, and the life. No one comes to the Father except through me."

Discussions of the Koranic Jesus were as scholars pinpointing the exact time of a given sunrise and sunset, and how that day affected humanity. For Biblical Christianity it was the presence or absence of the very sun itself, and the entire existence of humankind.

But that gave no reason to hate. In fact, that same Jesus that Michael was dedicated to had given his followers the injunction to love – even their enemies. It was a hard thing for a human to do. Michael knew his weaknesses. He trusted not to himself, but to God's unmerited love and favor to give him the strength to follow this command.

Besides all that, Michael actually *liked* Nasri. He was a good man. True they were canyons apart on faith, but this man was made in the image of God, and one for whom Christ died on the cross. Moreover, he was gracious, not to mention good company – at least not when he dressed like a folksy goth and was scared out of his wits.

Some called these notions of loving your neighbor idealistic or naïve. Others sharply criticized him for even cooperating with Nasri on a community outreach last year. He couldn't live his life based on other's opinions of him. As King had said, "a genuine leader is not a searcher for consensus, but a molder of consensus."

"Nasri," Pearce spoke softly, "I thank you for warning me. Have you considered going to the authorities?"

"Michael," he leaned forward. His voice, though quiet, became ragged, colored with desperation. "I have put my life, my family in danger just doing *this*." He motioned to the table. "And there are many unfriendly eyes and ears in places of authority. Many have been bought and paid for." Nasri leaned back, crossing his arms. "No, Michael, I cannot."

"I understand," slowly nodding his head, "maybe we both have to consider our courage." Pearce sipped again. "You have been more than kind, my friend. Thank you."

The cleric nodded his head slightly towards Michael. Staring at the man across the table he moved his mouth as though there was something more to be said.

"Be careful, my friend," Nasri said. "May mercy be upon you." He stood, turned, and left, never touching breakfast.

Chapter 28

The gentle hum was entrancing. Quiet. Solitude. Scraped concrete hung in the sky, irregular, heavy, and strangely translucent, pathetically pushing a dull light into the room. Floors were cleaned, shelves arranged, sheets changed, and the machine with empty, hanging bags was checked, clicked, generally fussed over and disconnected. Men and women in blue scrubs and green scrubs and soft shoes whispered in the dim, grey-lit space.

A doctor came in pushing a cart. He checked boxes on the screen. His signature went on a pad. Two others logged in and signed, confirming the time, date, event, and causation. The PICC line was removed from the patient, the humidifying mask already off.

Reaching over, the physician threw off several switches.

The sucking stopped.

Watery eyes peered through the doorway – a mother, a daughter. They cried. They agonized silent words.

"Where was Dane?" they wondered. "Why wasn't he here?"

The clicking ended.

Grief unyielding blurred beautiful faces.

The beeping ceased.

Rick was gone.

Chapter 29

"Good morning, sleepy one. It is time to get on with the day's adventures. Ah, I see they have moved you...splendid!"

To Dane, the disembodied voice from the night before sounded cheerful in a "hi, I'm your Inquisition Cruise director, and have *we* got a full schedule of events to fill all your masochistic needs," sort of way. All of Dane's emotional and physical gyroscopes were spinning in an end-over-end tumble. His body felt like he had run a marathon. Dry sand seemed to roll around his mouth. Deprived of fight or flight he was backing down into the hermit shell of complete panic, thoroughly mixed with a perverse sense of humor.

"You add an agreeable sense of the macabre to any delirium[i]," kept running through his mind. He began a high-pitched, panicked hiss that elevated into a squeal.

"What?" came the voice. "You are upset? Ah, I see the problem." The man moved over to the table Dane was strapped to. His arms and legs were pinned, the hood was on, and his feet hung out beyond the table, naked and vulnerable.

"How are they today?" He flicked the tender, blistering skin of Dane's instep causing him to jerk his head forward, screaming between clenched teeth. "That good, eh? Well, the day is young, you know."

"Do you really get your kicks out of this?" Dane fired at the voice.

"Uh," the voice hesitated as in thought. "Yes. Immensely so!"

"You're a freakin' Cardassian," Dane fired.

"Kardashian," the man protested. He turned back and forth looking at himself. "Now that is impossible!" He hit Dane's arm. "Nothing on me is big enough." Sitting down he let out a huff. "You sure know how to insult a man."

"Nuts," Dane grumbled to himself, "he's totally nuts."

"We have much to discuss, Al Kalb. But first I must put something in order – you know, one of those 'matters of business' things that must be dealt with." Standing up he moved the chair out of the way and went to a cabinet. It was opened, then closed. Dane, disoriented, frightened out of his mind had no real context in which to place this chattering madman. He was a bug caught in a hopeless trap with some hideous thing come to suck him dry. And the thing was brimming with serial sadism.

"Have you heard of the Shahada?" the voice asked.

The question hung empty in the air.

Dane finally answered. "I don't suppose that's a restaurant," he said flatly.

"What?" the voice nearly laughed. "If my guards could speak English, they would insist that I peel off your skin in strips for saying that. Well, okay, it *was* humorous. And come to think of it I bet you *are* hungry. Yesterday you fed on fear and adrenaline. Today you would like some food and water, yes?"

"Yes," Dane responded, weakly.

"Ah, good. But first, let us conduct our, oh, how do you say it?" The voice hummed. "Housekeeping. Yes, let us conduct that. I have much to ask you. Yes, there is much to discuss."

The figure moved over by Dane's feet and stood. He spoke something in what Dane assumed was Arabic.

"Have you ever heard that, Al Kalb?"

"No."

"You poor soul." The man clicked his tongue. "Well, today is your lucky day."

"I doubt it," Dane said in a small voice.

"I doubt it too, but then again it is a matter of perspective. You see, the words mean, 'There is no god but Allah, and Muhammed is his Prophet.'"

"You are Muslim?" Dane asked.

"Very good, very good, Al Kalb. There is nothing slipping past you, is there?" The voice spoke in unknown words. A few of the guards laughed. "You see, to be fair and all, I am going to give you three warnings, three lessons to teach you your need to make that very same confession."

"But I'm not Muslim."

"No, not yet," the voice said. "But it is important that I give you the opportunity to convert."

"Then you'll let me go?"

"Ah, do not hope, Al Kalb. Whether or not your soul is Allah's is not up to me. I am only a humble messenger. But your body," clicking his tongue, "perhaps even your mind – they are in *my* hands for the time being."

Dane groaned. How could he make sense of this?

Without warning a whistling sounded through the air. A heavy, thick rubber baton smacked the bottom of Dane's foot. It felt like he had stepped onto shards of glass. Violent sounds erupted from his mouth. The impact and pain shuddered through his whole body, lifting up the small of his back. His bladder, already full and strained released involuntarily.

"Ah, what a pity...so soon," the voice, sounding disappointed.

The hooded figure's body fell back to the table. He convulsed and arched again. Rags of breath sucked in and out.

"Now," the man patiently instructed, "you will repeat the confession."

Dane swore – loudly. "I am not a Muslim! I don't even believe in-"

A powerful crack hit the sole on his other foot. The tender, scalded flesh split like ripe fruit, sending little knives scratching up his skin and into his gut. Everything ached. His mouth, dry and pasty, sent out a torrent of screams and curses.

"It is important that we start off on the right foot. Oh, forgive me," a sub-dued chuckle, "what an insensitive pun." Steps walked to his side. "Al Kalb, can you not be reasonable?" The voice pleaded as though discussing the sale of an automobile with an unruly customer.

Dane hissed, his neck a web of taut, red cords.

"Very well, back to business." The profession was repeated steadily, wait-ing for Dane to respond.

He did not. He moaned with anger and frustration through his teeth. The hood was suffocating him, the straps chafing him.

It whipped. The sound was like throwing a large fish at a wall. The supine man's body shook and slammed on the table in agony.

This went on.

And on.

The voice spoke, confident and soft. The beating continued. At last, with acute and clenching pain turning his vision white, Dane surrendered. His will to resist fell to his instinct to survive, to stop hurting.

One brick fell from the solid wall of his psyche.

He confessed.

The breaking had begun.

Chapter 30

Dane's breathing had calmed down. He ached all over, terribly, persistently. What was this game? Which would give first, the sailor or the storm? What would bend or break, the nail or the hammer? Clearly, he was overmatched, put in such a weak, vulnerable place. He was both relieved at the cessation of the beating and ashamed at complying.

A chair pulled up next to Dane. The sitting motion made it creak.

"Now that the rubric is attended to, we shall move on." The voice reached across to Dane's head, unlocking a strap cinching the throat. Roughly the hood came off, and not a few strands of hair besides. Dane gasped from the shock of fresh air and bright light. His head swam. He was exhausted, hungry, thirsty.

"There you are, Al Kalb."

Danes eyes could not focus at first. He stared at the dirty, industrial ceiling, then around the room. It was an old shop of some sort. Several rust-flaked, metal frame windows lined the wall to his left. Silent men stood at different points in the shadows.

"Over here, Al Kalb. We must be introduced."

Dane didn't want to look. He didn't want to see this freak, this maniac.

"Come, come, don't be rude," the voice chided. "It is improper."

Dane forced his head over. He hated this man. Hated him. Hated all of them. Wanting to pretend this didn't exist was his first fall back. Yet, he wanted to see, to confront this...thing, this inhuman beast.

"Yes, I am over here, Al Kalb." Dane was looking at a Middle Eastern man, wiry build, wearing a green army jacket with a red and white patterned scarf around his neck. He had a handsome, boyish face wearing a perpetual, devilish grin. The eyes seemed to vibrate with intelligence and viciousness. Smiling, he spread his lips showing white, even teeth.

"You may call me Sidi," bowing his head slightly, hand on chest.

" 'Seedy,' Dane mused, "great name for this jerk."

"Do you not have a name?" Sidi asked, his eyebrows lifted high with anticipation.

"Dane."

"Excellent. You see what good talks we are to have. There is so much to discuss," patting Dane's shoulder.

"Like what, uh, Seedy?"

"No, no, 'See-DEE'. I prefer more stress on the second syllable."

Dane stared at him.

He stared at Dane.

"Water?" Dane asked quietly.

"Oh, yes, of course. My manners have slackened as of late. I have been so busy." He reached for a crank at the side of the bed and spun it inclining Dane's head. Pulling over a tray he unstrapped his right hand.

"Here you are, Al Kalb." He handed Dane an open bottle of water. The parched man lunged at the container taking it in one draft.

"Easy now, Al Kalb. You must moderate your appetites."

Dane glared at him but remained silent. The man handed him a chunk of bread. Dane ate cautiously. A wave of pain and nausea rolled over. He hunched forward, hand over mouth retching acid. Breathing heavily through his fingers he forced it back down.

"So," the interrogator settled back in his chair, "I must ask you about Dragon Lady, and, Mordred. What kind of lives do they have? Do they live in their computers? What fanciful names."

"I'm sure you're already know the Dragon Lady was my friend Jia." Dane looked at him with smoldering eyes.

"You Americans kiss your friends like that? Perhaps," Sidi wagged his head side to side, "but I think she was more than a friend."

"Yes, she was. And now she's dead." Dane's voice was angry, but low and constrained.

"Yes, yes, regrettable - I said something to that effect yesterday." Sidi crossed his legs and sighed heavily. "So, your girlfriend, how much did she know?"

"About what?" Dane's face couldn't hide his irritation.

"About us, our plans." Sidi looked at him, unblinking.

"Everything was coded. She couldn't figure it out. Even though she translated the words nothing made sense." Dane felt that since he really knew nothing there was nothing to hide. Also, he was dealing with a psycho so he may as well give him something, anything to mollify him.

"There were no words, no phrases that made any sense?" Sidi lifted his eyebrows.

Dane swallowed heavily and answered. "She had struggled with some phrases, stopped at my place, then your goons came, and we ran. That was it." Dane let his head fall back. His feet ached with a deep bone pain. They oozed a slow steady mixture of broken blister and blood. Throbbing, his head and body pulsed together.

"Think, Al Kalb, think..." Sidi's voice became quiet, menacing. Standing up the man moved to the end of the table. He reached down to one of Dane's feet and began to squeeze.

"Hey! Hey! Okay! I'm thinking," Dane said in a rush.

"Think faster, Al Kalb. I *hate* losing my patience."

"Something about an island... And some captives." Dane covered his mouth again and swallowed. "The rest was all nonsense."

The captor studied the figure on the table to discern the truth in his words. "So, that was all you heard?" he asked.

"Yes." Dane had a few more bits but thought it best to hold them back.

The tormentor casually stepped back to the chair and sat.

"So, Al Kalb, who else heard of this 'island'?" Sidi asked.

"No one. Like I said, she came to my apartment. Ten minutes later we were on the run. I swear to you, dude-"

"Ah-ah," Dane's captor held up a finger, warning him.

"Uh, Sidi. That's all. Then you killed her."

"What a repetitive theme with you." Sidi gently slapped the bound man's thigh. "You must let these things go. It is bad for the mind."

Dane sighed.

Sidi turned to one of his guards and spoke some orders. Dane thought he heard a few names that referred to their discussion.

"Well, we shall set that aside for now." Turning back to Dane, Sidi re-crossed his legs and calmly folded his hands together. "So, you have questions?"

"Can I go home?" Dane asked weakly.

"Ah," the man smiled grandly, "you never fail to hit it on the head. Unfortunately, no, you are at present a permanent guest."

"Oh, joy." Dane's head dropped.

"Yes, joy. Unlike fish you will only smell better to me in three days." He sat expectantly, looking at Dane. "Was that not funny?"

"Yes?" hesitantly.

"Okay. I am no comedian," Sidi absently looked up at one of the lights, "though I do have a rather robust sense of humor."

Dane smiled weakly and chewed another lump of bread.

"So, you are wondering about me. 'What is this man's deal? What kind of disturbed person has me like a rat in a cage?' All of these are fair questions, yes?" He touched Dane's arm and confidentially leaned in. "You see, Al Kalb, I do not have to worry about the media, or even my men for they do not understand a word I say to you," he poked him, "or you, to me."

Standing up the man shoved the chair out of the way and moved across the room. He began to push a bigger chair toward Dane.

"Al Kalb, I have a few personal indulgences, whims, I suppose you could say, that I take advantage of. My work is hard, there is a lot of traveling involved. I mean, the mileage points are great, but I do need some comfort along the way. And so," he wheeled the chair next to the table and stopped, "some things I insist on taking with me. This chair, for example, is one of them. I cannot quite manage without it. I meditate in it, sleep in it, read, eat, and above all else converse in it - such as we are about to do."

"Uh, cool," Dane, not knowing what else to say.

"Yes, cool." Sitting comfortably, he propped his feet up, the head of the chair reclining back. Its faded, black leather looked rather inviting, especially to a man bound to a tilted, metal table. Sidi pulled a white, plastic bag of candy from his coat pocket. He shook out a small, orange cube into his palm. Popping it in his mouth he closed his eyes and blissfully chewed.

"Don't you have to let me go?" Dane ventured.

Sidi's eyes popped open. "Let you? What?"

"I said the thing you wanted." Dane persisted.

"Somehow, I doubt your sincerity," Sidi said around a mouthful.

"My sincerity?" Dane threw his head back. "Why do you keep me here? I've told you all I know."

"Stop!" The man held up his hand.

Dane complied.

"You are here, Al Kalb, because it *pleases* me. You are alive because it *pleases* me that you are. I will do with you as it *pleases* me to do so. I command my men, I drink my tea, I sit in my chair," stroking the worn arm, "and I play with my catch."

Dane let out a hopeless rush of air. He wished the nut would just kill him. Now he was stuck in this painted clown's fun house.

"Perhaps a bit of perspective is apropos," Sidi said, stroking his beard. "But first, some more refreshment."

"Great," thought Dane, "Uncle Seedy's happy hour begins." He had to find humor, some relief somewhere, and as often as he could find it. This whole thing was too much.

The interrogator gave some commands to one of his men and soon a tray of hot tea and cups were brought in. The man poured out and served one to Dane, who held it unsteadily, though gratefully. One never knew when such a thing would come again.

"Ah," Sidi pushed back into his chair with great satisfaction. "It is the simple things that bring life true pleasure. Now we can continue our discourse with civility." The boyish face looked down into his cup, brow furrowing. "What was I launching into, Al Kalb?"

"Perspective," Dane said wearily.

"Yes! Wonderful! How helpful. Perspective." Sidi sniffed and snuggled down into the cushioned leather. He paused a moment, gathering his thoughts. "When I was a young man I was in Asia once, it doesn't matter where, and having risen at dawn I walked out onto the porch of the house we were staying at. It was in the wilds, in the jungle. To my great delight I had a clear view down the hill the house sat upon to a marvelous scene. A magnificent male tiger was crouched in the woods. I quietly stole back in the house, found my binoculars and went out again to watch him. He lay there patiently - ah, such a noble beast. Wouldn't you know it, a little deer of some kind came grazing out of the woods, ignorant of the tiger, ignorant of its fate. There was a most delicious sense of anticipation. My heart was beating in my chest. The tiger didn't move. He was perfectly hidden. Every hair on him was tense, ready to spring.

The deer ate some grass, looked around, flicked its tail and took another step closer. The tiger didn't move. Munching and munching, moving towards his death, the little thing was so ignorant so, well, oblivious, I suppose one could say. Suddenly, with a leap like coiled steel the cat fell upon the deer. It was over just as it began. But there was something that happened, Al Kalb. The tiger, instead of simply biting through the neck to kill it, instead of eating it out right, simply bit it once then held it down with an immense paw. The deer would cry out in struggle from time to time, but it was useless. The Tiger held it there and began to lick it. Again, and again its tongue stroked one of the bite marks as it savored its meal. A few moments later it picked up the deer effortlessly by the neck and went off into the foliage."

"So, you will ask me, 'Sidi, what does this have to do with me, or with you?' That is a great question. In truth, Al Kalb most of my prey I dispatch quickly unless I have some other purpose in keeping them alive. Some, you, for instance, I like them to linger, to pull them apart slowly, to savor."

"Are you out of your mind!?" Dane cursed, spilling tea all over himself. "Why don't you just put a bullet in my head?"

"Now, now, how absurd. There is no point getting so upset. You, Al Kalb, are in very capable hands. I assure you."

"Let me go!" straining against the bonds. "What do you want me for? I have nothing. Everything I told you was all I know. What do you want!?" Dane breathed heavily. The man just stared at him sipping his tea, passive as a house plant.

"Would you like more tea?" Sidi leaned his face forward, wiggling his cup.

Dane turned his head away.

"Very well. So, you ask me why. Why, why, why? It is always foremost in their minds. The more pragmatic ones truly wonder 'what' I am going to do with them. But," he sipped, "to each his own. Settle in, my man named Dog, and I will tell you more than you probably care to know."

Chapter 31

Sidi shifted sideways, resting his right elbow on the chair arm.

"You have mentioned I was Muslim. And what, I am curious, does that word conjure up for you? I do wonder."

Dane didn't answer but stared up at the ceiling.

Sidi continued. "I was raised in a small village on the edge of the desert near a salty, marshy inlet of the sea. It is no concern where, really. What was important was that I had a peaceful life - poor, but peaceful. I mean, to tell you the truth, we were all poor in our village, so I didn't really know I was poor. I had food, some clothes, a small house, more of a hut, really, and loving parents. Yes, loving, kind parents. The faith I knew I learned through them and my cleric. We had many Muslim traditions, but I did not really study the Koran. We were never explicitly taught that jihad was central to the advancement of Islam. No, rather we were taught observances, morals, hard work and love of family. Life was simple, happy, and obedience to the tenets of the faith was a matter of course.

Through a series of events some wealthy hunters, also Muslims, came through our village and I became their guide. They took a liking to me and, very long story short, they made steps to accelerate my education. Books, tutoring, trips to larger cities, ah, Al Kalb, I excelled. They continued to come and hunt. Doors were ever thrown open before me. This eventually led to my acceptance at Oxford. Yes, oh, yes...surprising to you?"

Dane looked at him carefully, adding 'erudite' to psycho.

"Here I was given access to the Koran, hadith, and sira, along with all the other faiths, politics, and philosophies of the world. You may find it curious that my first degree was in comparative world religions, my second in psychology. I won't bore you with any more details. So now, I will ask you, what do you think of Islam?"

Dane despised this man and would rather talk dating tips with a rapist. He turned his head away.

"Al Kalb," the voice lower, "any answer you give will not upset me in the least. However, not answering me will force me to become, oh, how shall I say it, 'persuasive.' And you know how insistent I can be."

Dane got the point. The mistrusting mouse decided to play with the convincing cat.

"So," the captor asked in businesslike tones, "what do you think of Islam?"

Dane knew little about any faith, or *any* organized philosophy of life for that matter. What he did know he had been fed by television, by pop culture, blogs, social media, and by school - kindergarten through senior year, and finally, definitively, at college.

"Um, it's a religion of peace."

"I had thought you would say that," Sidi answered.

"Well, isn't it...with a few exceptions?" Dane asked.

"Ha! I suppose I am one of your exceptions?" the man in the recliner said.

"Yes," Dane said cautiously.

"I am," the man slowly leaned forward, "and I am *not*."

"That clears it all up." Dane bobbed his head.

"Ah, I shall be happy to elucidate." Sidi sat up a little, brandishing his teacup at the captive man. "It is really not hard to understand. What will be harder, my young, American Millennial is for you to come to terms with a few realities. And I shall be as a real, and as honest as I can be. You see, Al Kalb, as I inferred before I do not have to worry about the media, or politicians, social opinions, or the like. I do not have to concern myself with your government, or even my own leaders. Here, it is just you and me, having a conversation, a healthy exchange of ideas."

"This doesn't seem healthy to me. It's a bit one-sided. I mean, I'm fairly open-minded. I could've met you for coffee if you wanted to talk." Dane said.

"You see!" The interrogator genuinely smiled, "now this *is* a real conversation." He flicked Dane's leg and settled again in the chair, nursing his drink. "We," he motioned with the tea, "are on a little island of encounter, at the intersection of a cultural clash."

"I have no problem with Muslims." Dane looked directly at Sidi. "I can get along."

"No doubt, no doubt, but you are ever plucking at the leaves. You do not yet see the roots." He thought for a moment. "Why are some Muslims making terror attacks?"

Dane responded immediately. "America has done them wrong. We have given them reasons to hate us. If we would just get out of all their areas, the Middle East, and places like that they wouldn't be angry. They are fighting for their freedom. What they need are jobs, new opportunities."

"Bravo," slowly clapping his hands, "bravo. You have been so well indoctrinated that I could not have done it better myself. Long has your mind been rented by other masters."

"I can think for myself," Dane said.

"As long as your social sphere approves," Sidi nodded with clinical observation. "As long as the college dogmas are canted."

Disgust filled Dane's face.

"Hmm," the captor stroked his beard, "right about now you probably feel the need for a 'safe space' to nourish your wounded ego and emotions. Have I triggered something? What is wrong with you? If anyone objects or counters your generation, you either pout and cry or call them foul names."

Dane was silent.

Sidi continued.

"I love your culture, your news media, your schools. They make my job so much easier. I'll tell you what, we shall look at some foundations, the roots I mentioned earlier, okay?"

No answer.

"Very well, Al Kalb. I will assume that if I asked you of Christianity you would spout words like 'bigot,' 'homophobe,' 'ignorant,' and perhaps even 'backwoods.' Why, I even heard one of those bloated women on one of your talk shows say that fundamental Christians were as dangerous as a Islamic terrorists. I tell you," shaking his head, "if ignorance were capital even your president couldn't spend it all." He laughed at his own joke.

"Yes, yes," catching his breath, "other than these fictitious notions your only frame of reference is probably some random school assignment in older literature containing a general mention of Providence, or a Twitter post. Nothing like understanding the world through a pinhole of study, or a handful of pixels. Now, let me put some pieces of knowledge side-by-side. I will keep things simple, Al Kalb. Yes, yes, there are so many technicalities and different perspectives, but for the sake of our little discussion I will make it quite plain.

You have the direct teachings of Jesus - his example, his life, and the letters of his closest followers. On the other hand, you have the teachings of Mohammed, *his* life, example, and a collection of letters that further described his words and habits. For the Christian this is the Bible, specifically the New Testament. For the Muslim it is the Koran, and hadith. To each group these are canonical - do you understand that term, Al Kalb?"

"Not really," Dane searched. "Well, sort of."

"It means, in short, that they are the accepted authority. Authority is that which has the right to demand obedience. But over time those direct examples, teachings, doctrines can become, well, short-circuited by various traditions. Buried under layers of culture, opinion, and a lack of source material and/or the ability or desire to read they transmute into something radically different from the fundamentals."

Sidi took a sip and pressed on.

"When I began to read the Koran and hadith myself, I saw Islam for what it was. I saw Mohammed in the unvarnished light of truth. And you know something, Al Kalb, I was overjoyed. Here was a man who *knew* what he was about!" Sidi snapped his fingers and sat forward. "He was a warlord who fought battles in the name of his God, murdered those who insulted him, encouraged his men to rape enslaved women, why he even killed unarmed captives – eight hundred Jewish men and boys after just one battle. Now THAT was a man I could follow!

Yet, for all this glorious history, Al Kalb, those who claim that there are peaceful Muslims would be correct." He pressed himself back into the leather-covered cushion. "There are those who take the original faith and its founder moderated through a filter, through layers and layers of mediating commentary. Otherwise they would either get down to the business of actually following Islam for what it is or become apostates and abandon the faith.

If the Christian practices the fundamentals, the essentials of their faith, they will not follow all the various traditions, but will follow the life, the teachings of Jesus himself and the Apostles. They will seek to live consecrated lives, peacefully share their faith, stand up for what, according to the Bible, is right. To seriously follow the person they consider the founder of their faith they will forgive their enemies, turn the other cheek, walk in compassion and mercy. For me, I think this nothing but weakness. A man in my position could simply fine these 'people of the book', but I prefer to behead them if they do not convert to Islam.

On the other hand, if someone truly follows the fundamentals of Muhammed, they will follow in his footsteps, proclaim the Shahada, and pursue Jihad against all who will not surrender.

But, oh, Al Kalb, the debates and disagreements between the Muslim communities. There are those that reject such as hold my view as too radical, too dependent on extreme or erroneous texts, and/or their misinterpretation. Obviously, I don't agree with them. And you should hear me make a case for my side. What fun!

So, yes, Al Kalb, there are peaceful Muslims. But Islam – it is not a religion of peace, but of conquest, of war. Muhammed did not come to make peace with the world, but to subjugate it to the will of Allah."

"But what will you do to the Muslims who *are* peaceful," Dane asked earnestly, "those who won't go along with your 'crush the world for Allah' program?"

Sidi bent his mouth down and shrugged. "They will fall in line or I will behead them as well."

Dane stopped a beat and pulled tentatively at the restraint on his left hand. He looked at Sidi with disbelief. "Why do you have to force everyone to your way? Must everyone be Muslim?"

"It is not a question of whether everyone *must* follow Islam. It is that everyone *will* follow - or die." Sidi spoke with such a simple, matter-of-fact assurance that Dane thought for a moment he was just being a smart mouth. Yet, he sipped his tea, nodding at his captive with the most congenial smile imaginable.

"You are..." Dane weighed his words.

"Go ahead, Al Kalb. I promise I will not be offended."

"You are sadistic, psychotic, even."

"Yes, in a sense you are right." The man smiled again, set down his cup and crossed his arms. "And I am truthful. I do not sugar coat anything. Sadistic? Gleefully true. However, I am not insane, no part out of control. I am rational, logical, and pridefully brutal in my efficiency."

"But, don't you ever think you are wrong?" Dane asked.

"Wrong?" Sidi cocked his head. "You mean immoral?"

"Uh...well, yes, I guess. At least I mean to say unethical."

"Oh, such a word for pundits and pedants. In a word - no. I am not wrong. I am an Islamist. I do not shy away from saying it loud and clear. But *you*, Al Kalb, you do not know who you really are. You have nothing to live for to the point of dying for it. I know precisely what I am living for and will give all I have to further its cause."

"I want to live." Dane looked at his stinging feet.

"So did the deer. So did the Tiger." Sidi picked up his tea and sipped. "Who won?"

Chapter 32

Being unseasonably bright and warm the weather smiled on the volunteers setting up for the rally. Erma Henderson Park had not seen so much activity this early in the Spring for a long, long time. In one sense it'd been a gamble, holding it outdoors this time of year. True, Pearce had contingency plans, but as he prayed and believed, he believed and lived. There would be free hot chocolate and donuts. They erected a large tent with plenty of propane heaters. Even games were prepared for children, with frost or without it. Michael wanted to be out in the public, open, accessible, unashamed. How could he reach out to the brokenness around him if he hid away in comfort?

Andrew approached him. "Rev. Pearce, this is Mrs. Angelis."

"It's nice to meet you," the older woman shook Michael's hand. "My husband was a minister in this neighborhood for thirty years. I brought the pulpit we had in the downstairs fellowship hall."

"Thank you so much." Pearce smiled, lightly pinching the end of his nose. "I heard someone say that a pulpit was coming."

"And here it is." She pointed to a solid, oaken structure that must have been forty or more years old. It was exquisite and skillfully made, but that didn't mean half as much as the spirit of cooperation from believers coming together for God's kingdom in their community. His eyes shined with happiness as he exchanged a few pleasantries with the beautiful, older woman.

"Thank you so much, sister Angelis. God bless you!"

All through the morning people came to help, drawn by compassion, by duty, by the Holy Spirit. Things had changed so rapidly for the bad, even in the last two years. People were tired, afraid, yet together they could be helpful. They must try, and in trying felt that something was being accomplished.

The message of Christ was one of turning to His salvation, the forgiveness he won for humankind when He died on the cross. It was a message of reconciliation to God, and people to each other. Pearce was in no way ashamed of the Gospel. He knew it was the power of God unto salvation. Politicians weren't hoped for, government help would not change men's hearts, even walking through the ritual of going to church or getting clean from addictions wouldn't ultimately capture the prize. They must know the one true God, and Jesus Whom He has sent - for this is eternal life.

"Andrew," Pearce put his arm around the young man, "it's gonna be a good day."

Chapter 33

They had let Dane off the table and moved him toward a small room in the corner. The floor was grimy, with dirt ground into every crack and pore. He had to painfully crawl each inch to the door. His feet were swollen and seeping, his bones ached up into his abdomen with a deep, dull throb.

It was a tiny washroom, the kind you find in a mechanics garage or auto parts store. The kind with the curling, yellow calendar picturing a model on a car, advertising hand cleaner. There was a pair of old sweats and a rumpled T-shirt hung up on a hook. With the most painful, awkward motions Dane managed to wash himself, use the cruddy toilet, and exchange his dirty clothes for those set out for him. It was what he needed to do. It was what Sidi *told* him to do.

He slowly dragged back to the table, hauled himself up, and sat. It was also what he was told to do. The guards remain silent, motionless. They were all well trained.

He felt like a kid waiting for the doctor; like a dog that had been severely beaten, licking the hand that had done it and then fed him. No, he wasn't dreaming. This was too prosaic, too campy and un-Hollywood to be a dream, a movie, or a bad night of Taco Tuesday. He was caught by a creepy, little child who'd had him pinned to a corkboard and was slowly pulling off his wings.

Sidi came to the door and shouted something to the guards. They moved swiftly, with precision, without a word. Lifting Dane, they twisted a hood on him, hustling him outside. He remembered the cold, being thrown into a vehicle, pulled out, set in a small boat, landing, then being scraped along the dirty ground to a cold, concrete room and thrown in. It smelled like an animal cage at the zoo before they hosed it out. Sudden panic waved over him with the thought of being fed to something.

The hood wouldn't come off. There was nothing in the room. Despite always knowing thirst and hunger he still had to relieve himself in the corner. He was cold, barefoot, tired and once again alone.

Chapter 34

The tent was set up. Heaters glowed around the inside and it was surprisingly comfortable. Overnight it had dropped to a chilly fifty-two, yet there was no wind, rain, or snow. The sun had streamed down brightly, though with little heat.

"Thank you all for coming. I'd like to thank the choir of Grosse Pointe First Baptist for opening things up for us." The crowd applauded. Pearce was in his element.

Everything had been working smoothly. There were the normal logistical and personnel issues he had to sort out through the day, but nothing major. Kids had fun, local, contemporary bands played, plenty of donuts, cider, hot cocoa, and coffee were passed out. All around were volunteers interacting with the crowd milling through, handing out simple materials about faith in Christ, food banks, rehabs and community help. Now it was the time for the crown jewel - the message of Christ and him crucified. Michael had prayed and cried out to God for the souls of the city, men and women, children of every background, color, rich, poor or anywhere in between. He knew that if God captured souls, He would capture neighborhoods.

"Let us bow our heads." Michael prayed earnestly for God's hand, His presence to be with them. He prayed that he might get out of the way and let the Lord work in people's lives. Many verbally agreed with him and he opened his Bible to begin.

"Paul, the Apostle wrote in the book of Romans, chapter three, verse twenty-three, 'for all have sinned and fallen short of the glory of God.' In Romans six, twenty-three he also wrote, 'for the wages of sin is death, but the gift of God is eternal life in Christ Jesus, the Lord.' These two verses together-"

Ringing out a shot exploded through the heavy corner of the pulpit, bending up on its trajectory and striking the man standing behind Pearce to his right. Several masked men entered the tent. A young deacon in the front row shoved his wife to the ground, shielding her. Slamming into his head a bullet dropped him twitching beside her. She screamed, desperately grabbing his hand. People and panic flew everywhere. The report of controlled, disciplined bursts of gunfire punctuated the erratic, terrified screams of the escaping rush. The moans of the dying floated in between.

Rev. Pearce had fallen, showered by splinters. He crawled over to the man. Andrew, sweet, young Andrew. A dark, angry stain spread out from his chest. Michael saw him as a brother, as a son.

"No, no, my boy, my Andrew," cradling his head.

Andrew stared straight forward, frozen in shock. His breathing was wet, sick, and ragged. He didn't speak. He didn't look. Pearce wept, holding his head. He heard a noise behind him. Keeping his eyes on Andrew he ignored the movement.

The gunstock was raised, then thrust downward. Michael fell forward across Andrew like a bag of moist sand.

Chapter 35

A silent guard entered the room and unshackled the hood. Dane gasped the cold air. He heard the faintest sounds of popping and distant screams. They carried only small doses of news across the river.

The armed man brought him in a bottle of water and a chunk of bread. Closing and bolting the door he left Dane in the dirty room. There was a small window, a thin slit of ventilation, really, near the upper blocks of the wall. His feet throbbed, his head ached, but his curiosity won the argument. He had to see what was going on.

Jutting out from the wall below the window was an old pipe, broken off at the end. He crawled over to it and reached as high as he could. Too short. The pipe was about three feet above him . He slid one knee up and carefully set his foot on the ground. It felt like a balloon on the other end of his foot, filled with tiny spikes and all of them trapped against the skin. A little weight on it and sparks shot through his eyes and into his brain. The hurt, the ache, was like nothing he had never felt before. But he had to try. Hanging his head, he groaned with frustration, biting his knuckles, silently raging.

The human will fights for life as does the body. Desperation breeds in it a reckless determination. Pushing up he gasped at the violence of his nerve endings. His hand slipped around the pipe. It was too big for him to grasp, but the grit and dust on the cold iron gave him the needed grip. In one sweating effort he grunted, stood, pulled himself up and slung over it onto his belly.

Hanging in the air he fumbled like a turtle on a post. Nothing worked right. Everything hurt. His body was weary and craving food, nutrients, rest. Somehow, he managed to plant his upper shin and pull himself into a kneeling position. Carefully, he straightened. Peering out the slit he saw several dark, rubber watercraft pulling to the shore. There were glimpses of guards hauling bound, hooded figures from the boats.

"What is going on?" Dane wondered quietly.

He rested his forehead against the metal frame of the window, rocking back and forth in dismay. How could this be? In America? In Detroit? Why?

Some of the shots drew closer.

Footsteps approached the building. Dane slid to the floor in a heap. The door unlocked. Two men came in. One grabbed his hood. Picking him up between them they threw him to the back of a loaded pickup bed.

"Where did they get all this stuff from?" he whispered quietly to himself. "Will they ever let me go?"

Dane's hope was alive, but asthmatic, wheezing with the pain of reality. And with it he kept his mind occupied by what he knew were impossible thoughts. *Maybe Seedy would find another playmate to torment. Maybe there would be a rescue. Maybe, with all the extra people he could slip away and escape.*

He laughed bitterly. Sidi really didn't have to kennel the dog, he just had to break his feet. Sure, sure, he would crawl away one night, swim in the river and –

The truck jolted.

Every ache, every sore, every bruise saluted Dane, obligingly reacquainting him with pain. Vehicles and a train of desperate souls hooded and tied together headed towards the center of Belle Isle, into the thickest part of the woods.

Last summer a multinational group approached the city of Detroit through the state Department of Natural Resources, seeking permission and permits to establish a small camp on the island. They were organized, professional, educated, ostensibly representing several universities and green movements, and most convincing of all, they came with a great deal of money. What didn't they wish to study? There was the weather, the temperature, atmospheric carbon, the river, the flora and fauna. The mayor liked that he could tack a green leaf to his lapel and feel quite modern, elite, and rather self-satisfied. Plus, gold in the coffers stood on his steps and screamed incentive. The bureaucrats at the DNR felt much the same and looked forward to the reading of statistics and findings gathered not only without expense, but with several hefty boosts to their budget. These people were pedigreed, they had political connections, they had deep pockets.

Thus, a camp was established - nothing destructive, nor permanent, but fully stocked, prepared for all weather and manned by zealots of the green variety. A collective sigh ran through the city council. Even school visits and presentations were planned for late Spring.

Throughout the colder months these "assumed researchers," came and went. Studies were made, calculations tabulated, everything uploaded to a protected site accessible to the privileged few of the various government entities involved. Ever and anon a stream of supply boxes, equipment crates and storage racks made their way to the fast-growing, if transient eco-hamlet. Most of these were set aside, not opened.

Then suddenly, with little outside notice, the researchers, the assistants, the technicians were all sent to a conference in the Netherlands. Over the course of a week each of these were replaced by temps, and guards and other technicians who would "hold the fort" until their return. This return never happened. The abundant, yet mysterious boxes, crates, and racks were opened, yielding up their stash of weapons and ammunition, explosives, inflatable, motorized rafts, rolls of razor wire, communications gear, and, oddly enough, one worn, but comfortable recliner.

Sidi arrived and began to form up the camp. Wire was stretched around boundaries, empty crates were set up at tactical points around the perimeter, and boats prepared. The two or three slender threads of travel to the island were rigged with C-4. All buildings around the fringes were set to be raided, then burned or imploded. Cables, pipes and wires connecting to the mainland were to be severed. By careful planning the camp had sufficient provisions for the duration of the mission.

Their leader was precise, efficient, and swift in his efforts. In forty-eight hours they would launch a strike at a park across the river during a religious rally. He had known about it weeks in advance. With foresight, and not a little flexibility he molded the final details. Loyal soldiers would be threaded into the crowd, the police were to be neutralized. A requisite number of boots and boats were planned to obtain the sufficient number of captives. So many dead, so many escaped, so many caught, so many wounded - his men thought it too precise but held their tongues to prevent them from being ripped out of their faces. Sidi was known to apply a certain medieval flair to his inquiries. He was also known as a mastermind. This particular mission seemed relatively simple. With a long and bloody history of planning and executing successful strikes, leaders ceased to question and let him do his thing.

Dane was driven into the camp. Guards stood at a metal gate. They were let through. Following behind them came a train of bound prisoners, some weeping, all hooded. Two more vehicles slowly lumbered in and the camp was shut.

The sound of several large, distant explosions rolled through the camp. Every island edifice, road, bridge, and utility link to the main shore was now swiftly destroyed. Each of the men carried out assigned duties until all the boxes in their leader's head were checked.

Within an hour an awed hush fell over the camp. Dane had been thrown into a small, concrete hut with one window and one door. There was no toilet or sink. There was a bucket, and one recliner. He sat below the window and touched the glass. How silly, how stupid, that three sixteenths of pane stood between him and the outer world. But he knew it didn't matter. They may as well have gone ahead and hamstrung him. He was Batise. He was hobbled. They had planned that part well. There would be no running for The Dog.

"Sidi," Dane hissed, "you son-"

The door burst open.

"Ah, Al Kalb, are you not impressed?! We are like well-oiled machinery, no?"

Sidi stood expectantly.

Dane thought it best to play along.

"Uh, yep," nodding his head, "well-oiled."

"Oh, I am disappointed, my pet. I had thought you would have been overwhelmed by the sheer efficiency. In two," he checked his watch, "in two hours and forty-two minutes we have launched an invasion, killed many, captured twenty-eight, brought them here, and completely isolated this island, and all without losing a single man. Not bad, eh?"

"A record, I imagine," Dane acquiesced.

"Yes. A record, I think." The captor smiled broadly.

Sidi turned to the door and firmly commanded something. In came several men bringing a sleeping bag for Dane, a tray of hot tea and food, with a little table to set it on. The arrangement was placed next to the recliner. Just as swiftly the men left. With an impish smile Sidi launched himself into the leather chair, landing with a flop.

"Ohhhh, Al Kalb, I can't begin to tell you how good that feels.

"I'm sure you will try," Dane mumbled.

Sidi looked at him and laughed, too high on success to take offense.

"Yes, my pet, it has been a long, exciting day. I am ready for some refreshment? You?" He looked at Dane and motioned to the tray.

"Really, I'm trying to watch my girlish figure," numb with sarcasm.

Sidi's eyebrows shot up. He threw himself back in the cushions and laughed the wind out of his lungs. Howling, he held his ribs and shook with heavy, happy spasms. Two tears worked their way down his reddened face.

"Oh..." He gasped, "oh, Al Kalb - that was the funniest thing you could've said. Oh, my sides!"

Dane hung his head. His feet throbbed. His heart was like an old candy bar left on the dashboard. He'd been tortured by this clown - and Sidi played the part well, dressed in his suit, daubed on the face. This "repartee", this whole act, he knew, was the foreplay of terrible events. Cringing, he dragged his feet up only to slide them back down for the discomfort. Why must the villain monologue? Even worse, why this friendly conversation? It only sickened the poor man. He was caught by the Joker and the Bat was across the river, onshore...maybe out to dinner.

Sidi wheezed a labored breath. "So, my friend, some hot tea? Cake? Some cream? Yes?"

Game or not, Dane was hungry. He knew instinctively that starvation was a favored tool in the box of the seriously warped. Shuffling on his rear he edged away from the wall towards the tray. Survival dictated that he get all he could when he could. For now, he could, and so he did.

There are those well fed who leave half a plate and call the choicest cuts common. But to a starving man even the bitterest of scraps was sweet. How satisfying then to have hot tea with cream, and several cups of it. The cake was moist, though not overly sugary. He felt his stomach absorbing it, his body revived by the needed calories. It was the first meal he had ever eaten with the sharp edge of starvation pressed to his tender throat. Never had he dined with desperation seated at table beside him. Never had anything tasted so good.

"Oh," said Sidi, "look at you go! How happy I am to see it. You, Al Kalb will need every drop of it. As for your waistline, fear not. I will be your..." The man drew his brows together in concentration, "what is that term? Beef? Best friend?"

"BFF," flatly.

"Ah, BFF! Yes, I will be your very own BFF. Do not worry, my project, I will help you manage your health. I will not let you become portly. Gluttony is," sipping his tea, "a sin after all."

"Perish the thought," Dane exhaled sadly.

"Yes, yes, perish *many* things." The seated man reached down and tousled his hair. Dane stiffened, but did not raise a hand. "Perish the thought, Al Kalb, perish."

Sidi leaned towards his captive, dark eyes sparkling, grinning like a wicked Brownie. "So, here we are, full as fatted calves, and sitting down to a fine discussion. Please, please," he motioned to the sleeping bag, "make yourself comfortable."

Dane slid back, balancing a cup of tea in one hand. He sat on the blue nylon fabric looking into the bittersweet liquid.

"So, you might ask me, 'Sidi'," he gestured to Dane.

"Uh, Sidi," Dane repeated.

"Very good," smiling. " 'Sidi, what is this marvelous thing you have done?' "

He gestured.

Dane parroted.

"Al Kalb, I am so glad you asked." Sipping the steaming cup he settled himself more comfortably into the leather.

"I, Al Kalb, have lit a fuse."

Chapter 36

Falling like the first in a line of dominoes, the raid at Erma Henderson Park was only one of a dozen major events that flared around the city: shootings, explosions from homemade IEDs, a synagogue looted, churches burned, stores raided, their patrons savagely beaten. The locations were strategically selected to pull the first responders apart like taffy, to spread them thin, to flame havoc and misdirection.

Some of the rioters were highly trained Muslims, devoted to radical factions, willing to die for their cause. Other groups were gangs of restless, angry, young men and women, generously paid and willing to live for destruction, violence, drugs, and sticking it to the government.

It had all been well planned.

Sidi composed, then stood at the podium tapping his baton. When he swung and set the tempo each played according to the score.

Interspersed with the physical violence were masterful strokes against communications, data, and infrastructure. Hundreds of calls from hundreds of untraceable burner phones flooded the 9-1-1 system, giving dozens of ghost emergencies, spreading resources away from the actual events. For every real fire the stations had to cover dozens of urgent calls in every direction. As the systems were at the peak of being overwhelmed, hackers, who had months before burrowed into government and community servers, began creating an utter chaos of miss information and malfunction.

The personal emails of city officials were raided. Anything embarrassing or incriminating was forwarded to different news sites and outlets. Bank accounts were electronically pilfered. Social Security numbers, birth dates, and addresses of public figures were posted on a multitude of social media sites. The FBI, NSA, and Homeland Security offices were sent a flood of emails and information - most of it false reports of suspect activity, all in the wrong places.

Every electronic system that could be altered and manipulated for five miles along the shore of the Detroit River was. Traffic lights, construction zones, public works - what should be off was on, and on was off; what should be closed, opened, and opened, closed. Real and serious accidents began to pile up.

Washing into townships outlying the city proper, a second wave of violence erupted in the early hours of the morning. First responders, already exhausted and depleted were stretched beyond the breaking point. More storefronts were looted, homes set on fire, gas mains were ruptured tearing entire blocks apart. Roving bands destroyed schools, knocked over fire hydrants, put large, impassable holes in roads, and generally terrorized the people. Hospitals, police stations, and fire houses overflowed with the wounded, the panicked, and the homeless.

It was an absolute hailstorm, a blitzkrieg.

Sidi outlined in great detail all of these happenings to Dane. "Is that not impressive, Al Kalb?" He said. Smiling warmly, charmingly even, Sidi faced Dane, his eyebrows up, happily awaiting a response.

"Massive, Sidi," Dane nodded and sipped, "way massive."

"Yes, I like that – 'massive.'" The man shifted to one side and put his tea down on the table. He sank into one comfortably padded leather arm and leaned his head into his hand.

"Do you not want to know?" the captor asked.

"Know?" the captive responded.

"The big question," Sidi said, lifting his head.

"Permission to be sarcastic, Sir?" Dane's lip curled up.

"You already are, and yes, I am in a rather elated mood," the tormentor responded.

Dane looked straight at him. "Why should I care?"

"Care?" Sidi pondered. "I suppose you could roll the iron pea of hope around in your mouth. 'Who knows,' you tell yourself, 'perhaps he will let me go, or I will be rescued.'"

Dane dropped his gaze. These words skewered the truth to his chest.

"'Perhaps,'" Sidi continued, "'he is satiated and will forget I am here.' Such thoughts are not surprising, Al Kalb. After all," he gestured lazily, "one in your situation is generally more concerned with what will happen to your person, your body. It is a central part of self-preservation, yes?"

"Yes," Dane said, staring blankly into the dark, brown liquid.

"Yet, it amazes me, my project, how disconnected you and your peers are from your country. You have no clue how others suffer in this world, yet so many of you young people do nothing but complain. Here, you lose a fingernail and God, government, and Grandma are incomprehensible wretches. And this system of government, even with all its corruption, has produced the greatest earthly boon that mankind has ever seen."

Dane cursed softly. "Oh, so you hurt all these people, *killed* all these people because you have Americrush?"

"Crush?" Sidi sniffed and shook his head. "No, you are The Great Satan. I hope you burn in Hell."

Dane nearly snorted his tea. He looked around almost bewildered. Where was the camera? Was this one sick, black comedy show?

"I don't believe in any country, or God, or The Devil for that matter, and certainly not Hell." Dane said forcefully.

"Soon, my dear Al Kalb, you will not even believe in life itself. This I promise you."

What was he to say? He was a buzzing fly. There sat some psychotropic web weaver discussing blood sucking techniques he found on Pinterest. It was the oddest, bad burrito kind of nightmare. Dane laughed, loudly. It welled up at the stupidity, the absurdity, the madness of it all. His voice practically screamed with the sound of it.

"What?" Sidi sat up, a look of concern. "Your mind can't be broken yet. It cannot be. Uh!" he threw himself back into the seat. "That's my favorite part," he whined, "the cream-filled center."

Dane stopped abruptly, smacking his skull back against the wall. "I'm not crazy, Sidi. I haven't lost my mind. What I've lost is the punch line. What's the joke? I don't care about your religion, or anyone's for that matter. I don't care about your plans or your holy war. All I care about – cared about," grabbing his hair, "was my simple, broken, little life. Why, of all people, did you pick on me? I mean, who am I?" Dane cursed and wacked his head back again.

"No one," Sidi's eyes were unfocused, pointed at the ceiling. "You were simply available."

The head of the poor, weary man fell towards his lap. He hid his face in his hands. Slow, painful drops pulled from his eyes, wetting the tired fingers.

His feet throbbed. Misery sat next to him, wrapping its cold, disconsolate arms across the sagging shoulders. It was the comfort of dead souls, those yet haunting the fracted body, a bandage over the sulfurous, morbid wound.

"You do not wonder why?" Sidi's voice was flat, torpid, the twilight of consciousness mumbled through heavy lips. "Across your nation, bad things are happening all at once. New York, Los Angeles, Dallas, Miami – oh, the list goes on. Yet, Al Kalb, this is the hand the magician wants you to follow. This is the distraction to the greater play. Who will keep their eyes on the hidden trick? And this city is my particular theatre, my puppet show. For me, I do this for the reason an artist paints – I must, because I am. It is a happy place when one's pursuits align in a perfect mesh, a harmony of gears and mechanisms. I am but a pocket watch, and, tick-tick-tick, now is *my* time."

"Haven't you ever questioned what you are doing, whether it is good or evil?" Dane fired at Sidi, somewhat surprised at himself for using such absolute terms.

"This again?" Sidi muttered, slowly twirling his finger in the air. "Oh, well, yes, I suppose I have. Often I have pondered if I was truly being my authentic self."

"You're authentic alright," the captive man sighed.

"Ah, Al Kalb," Sidi picked his head up, "I see the problem. You have never truly understood who you are. What a negative vibe you have. With a little effort you could make this your 'best life ever.' " He made quotes in the air and dropped his tired arms.

"Sure, sure," Dane said, rolling his eyes, "I'll make every day a Friday."

"That's the spirit, AlKalb!" The tormentor sat forward and began a slow clap.

Dane cursed sharply at him.

The clapping stopped.

"Fine, Mr. Monday-pants," Sidi said with a mocking tone. He folded his arms and fell back into the cushion.

Hanging in the silence were all the words and emotions between them.

"So, Alkalb," Sidi continued gently, reflectively, "you asked me a question. No, I have never doubted my faith, but I have doubted myself. I mean, who am I to walk in such lofty shoes. Think of all who have gone before me. Suddenly, imposter's syndrome hits me, and I think to give it all up. Perhaps

I should live as some bespectacled cleric, gently tending people in my native land. I have truly questioned whether I was to be the one to carry this work forward."

Dane sighed with disgust. "And."

"Well, then I watched one of those cartoon movies. It was something about a princess, I think. It said to 'follow your heart', and so I did." He turned away from Dane with shining eyes and brushed his nose.

"You're freakin' kidding me?" Dane swore and laughed at the stupidity of it all.

"No, I am quite serious," Sidi insisted. "I draw inspiration from the strangest of places."

"Really?" The captive breathed in and squeezed his eyes shut.

"Yes..yes," Sidi nodded with all sobriety. "But just look at me now! My compatriots and I are dancing with laughter on your culture's grave. Your country's political sensibilities, it's 'correctness' is its own undoing. We are feeding the dragon its own democratic tail. This nation, like the Roman Empire in its day, has the strongest military, the farthest reach in all the world. And yet, like them, you have lost yourselves, your identity. You are losing all national integrity. There is no *unum*, to your *pluribus*. And what did your Christ say-"

"Not mine," Dane interrupted.

"Do not cut in like that, Al Kalb, at least not while I am in the middle of a brilliant exposition."

"So sorry," Dane lisped.

"Now, where was I," Sidi picked up his thoughts. "Ah, yes, 'A house divided against itself will not stand.' "

"Dude!" Dane shot out. "Couldn't you wait 'til morning to torture me some more?"

"Torture?" Sidi pondered. He made a slight chuckling sound. "Al Kalb, you are very funny...very funny indeed. But I assure you that you will soon long for my ravings over what you will endure."

Dane grunted with a long, exasperated sound. His head bounced off the blocks.

"You might as well get it all out of your system," he said to Sidi. "Then maybe I can at least get some sleep." The captive began to drum fingertips on the side of his head.

Sidi opened one eye and looked at the pathetic figure sitting on the floor.

"As you wish, Al Kalb, as you wish. Our goal is to, well," he shifted, "to give Lady Liberty a black eye. Soon, I will violate her – but that is for a future mission. For now, these outbreaks are intended to humiliate. And we do them because we can."

Suddenly Sidi sat up, rubbing his eyes. "I mean, look at you – a man shouts 'Allahu Akbar', obviously claiming what he does is for Allah, then kills dozens of people, and the cowards, sycophants, and toadies in Washington, in...in your news media, can't even bring themselves to say 'terrorism', or 'Islamism', let alone in the same sentence. You are too weak, too divided, and, praise Allah that makes it easier for us. And more-"

"Why?" Dane asked, wearily holding his head.

"I told you-"

"No, Sidi, why do you *always* monologue? I thought I could take more, but..."

"What? Didn't we just discuss this?" The man's brows contracted. He looked left, then right, mouth partially open. "I," putting a finger to his lower lip, "I do *not* monologue."

"You were on the rant rails. It's the ones you like to ride."

"I - the what?" sitting up straighter. "Oh, I suppose I was. Yes," smiling, "I guess this is the part of the movie where the bad man airs his grievances with the cosmos and the victim secretly cuts their bonds and escapes. You," he wagged a finger at Dane, "caught me with my mouth open. But that was your chance, Al Kalb."

"I can't walk." Dane stated.

"Ah, now don't you wish you had worked harder in gym class. You could do something acrobatic on your hands, like that, uh," snapping his fingers, "that raunchy hero you kids like, uh, Deadpuddle or something."

Dane stared at him. His legs ached, his head was thumping, his rear was numb, and he could really use a Portajohn.

"So, Sidi," clearing his throat, "don't you think this will end soon, and badly?"

"Badly, yes. Soon...not so much," the man in the chair nodded his head slightly.

"This is a small island," Dane said.

"Yes – with big news coverage." Sidi held up his index finger.

"You're part of some terrorist group, I guess," Dane said. "What do you think you'll accomplish?"

"Big picture?" Sidi looked at Dane. "To be a painful, embarrassing thorn in the lion's paw."

"Dragon, I recall," Dane returned.

"Both metaphors work, Al Kalb. Do not be such a bore."

"Sorry," the captive responded.

Sidi nodded acquiescence. "Small picture – I like to pursue my hobbies."

Dane let out an audible groan. He thought of Bundy, Gacy, Pichushkin, and other little debutantes of death. Even Vlad the Impaler haunted his thoughts. Running through his mind were racks, wheels, iron maidens, and the ever-inspiring Judas Cradle. How had it come to this? He threw his face again into his hands.

"Oh, joy. I'm part of your recreation," the figure on the floor said through his fingers.

"Too true, Al Kalb." Sidi clicked his tongue. "However unwilling."

"Why can't you just grab me and kill me, get it over with?" Dane burst out with rage. "Kill me – kill us all, all those people you dragged in."

"Now, where would be the fun in that? What would there be to savor?" Sidi said half yawning.

Dane remembered the tiger. He breathed in through his teeth and began thumping a knuckle between his closed eyes.

"Al Kalb," the tormentor calmly explained, "we *must* do our dance on the knife point. The tedious cycle of threats, questions, and negotiation with your authorities must commence. We are to hold the attention of the world for a time. Fear, anger, irritation and prejudice – it will all come out. I will act out my part dutifully and completely, and all on the stage of your simpering media. 'Oh', they will grieve, 'how have we offended this poor, beleaguered people? What can we do to make peace with them?' Short answer: Convert or die."

"You are so dogmatic."

"And you have utterly lost all principles. You stand for nothing but your gut and your zipper. You do not even grasp the basic, foundational principles of your country. What of the Declaration and Constitution? The Bill of Right? Let me guess...you have no clue. For shame, for shame – one tweet and you are all ready to riot in the streets. And do you even know the cause of your angst? What do you really believe?"

"Raving again," Dane said with irritation.

"Ah, yes, I truly am." Sidi's face darkened. "But I am tired and it is my prerogative to ramble on."

"Captive audience here," the wounded man stated.

"Quite." The captor replied.

Dane's head fell forward into his chest. The world and all its pain, lost hopes, and stupid play-doh dreams seemed crushing into his bones, pressing his soul out like guts from a bug.

"You hope you can do this alone? You think you can take over an entire country like this?"

"Oh, Al Kalb, if you only knew how many hands pitched coin in the box to help fund this. If I were indiscreet," he stretched his arms behind his head, "I might mention interested parties such as Iran, Russia, China, and North Korea. If I were a blabbermouth, I would mention these and more."

"I know them now," Dane offered weakly.

Sidi snorted dismissively. "Fortunately, you, my dear Al Kalb, will tell no one."

"I suppose you'll cut my tongue out," Dane said softly.

"Goodness, my pet project," Sidi lifted his head with surprise, "that sounds so uncouth. Your tongue is the very last thing in a long list of things I would cut out."

"That's comforting?" Dane cursed and threw his head back.

"I daresay, Al Kalb. But it is not your tongue that will fail you. You will have your own bowl of mush between those ears when I am done. Soon, you will not even *know* the words to say."

Knuckles pounding between the eyes, Dane threw his head back again, and again, sharply thudding against the blocks.

"But no, my friend, we are not aiming to take over the country via these current cataclysms. No, Al Kalb, these are just the opening acts, but the beginning of birth pains."

Chapter 37

"**B**anks, Aimes, please sit down." Director Marz motioned to the two agents as they entered the OIS conference room. He was unusually composed. For those who knew him from the old days this was the time when he did his best work. In the relative calm at the center of a cyclone he was surrounded by a terroristic eyewall, a towering ring of thunderstorms and violent winds threatening to destroy the streets of Detroit, and the nation.

"At the risk of sounding melodramatic, we are at war," the director peered over the top of his glasses at Banks, Aimes, Victor, Dr. Tell, and three other agents. Clicking a remote Marz brought to life several large, flat panel monitors mounted on the wall to his left. One displayed a map of the U.S., another a satellite image of the city, the third a montage of video clips showing destruction, riots, and flames.

"You will note, on the national scale," referring to a monitor, "the red colored areas." At the Director's words all eyes scanned the map of the lower forty-eight states. Seven major cities were highlighted. The west coast had two, the east coast had one, with Florida, Texas, Illinois, and Michigan rounding out the count. "Each of these have been struck by terrorism. It was a coordinated attack, going off like clockwork. This was not the work of weekend jihadists, or college punk activists. No, it has obviously been planned for months, if not years."

"Sir," a young, female agent asked, "how badly has Detroit been hit?"

"Badly." Characteristically blunt, the Director's voice had a tired sound to it. He paused the rolling video stock on a helicopter shot of buildings engulfed in smoke and fire. Pulling a laser pointer out of his shirt pocket he put a red dot on the screen. "This particular footage is from the Rivertown Warehouse District, almost directly across from the western tip of Belle Isle. Just about every building along the coast from Adair Street down to the Ren Cen was damaged or destroyed. And, speaking of Belle Isle, yes, it has been confirmed, a group of people were captured from a community park in the area and taken there. And no," cutting off the gesture of another person at the table, "we don't have any more information yet."

Taking a long drink of water, he cleared his throat and continued.

"And that's just the start. Key systems and utilities across the city have been disrupted. The central train depot was bombed, the people mover facility destroyed, multiple casinos had either gas fires or explosions, and twelve city buildings – police stations, fire departments, courts, and even a few libraries and museums have been attacked and vandalized. Rape, murder, and theft are rampant.

Gang members even tried to break into Children's Hospital. Fortunately, there were two off-duty police officers in the emergency room at the time. Three perpetrators were put down, two more taken into custody. So far, none of them have anything useful to say."

"Just sticking it to the man, I suppose?" Aimes asked with a low, gentle tone. He leaned forward, placing his elbows on the tabletop.

"That's probably what *they* think they're doing," the Director responded.

Orville rested his chin into his hand and nodded. "How many of them actually know the game that's being played?"

"I would bet not many," Marz said, rubbing at his neck. "Mostly useful idiots and pawns."

"Indeed," Aimes said thoughtfully.

A sort of dull silence settled on the room. Everyone seemed to stare at all the information glowing at them from the wall. It looked like something that happened in the Middle East, some battle zone in some far-off place, with destruction exploding on distant, unknown streets.

Not here. Not now. Not us. The unspoken thoughts lingered in the room.

"Director," Tamari spoke up, breaking the pensive mood, "what about Homeland, FBI and the other agencies?"

"Can't say yet about the others, but Homeland and FBI are currently operating under their respective protocols. Like us they are powered by their own generators, armed to the teeth, and are communicating wirelessly. Just glad we have our own water." Something like a forced smile came across Director Marz's face as he took a sip from the tall, clear glass.

"In addition," Marz continued, "every cop, full-time, part-time, even suspended or retired has been called up to help. It's the same with hospital staff and firefighters. Multiple State Police barracks have sent troopers to our area, and the Michigan National Guard from regions one, two, and three have sent air, ground, and medical units to keep order and assist."

At this the Director sat back and pushed away from the table. He swore softly and took off his frames.

"So, folks, what are we looking at?" He scanned the faces around the room. These were his agents, his people. Excellent, well-trained and disciplined, each person in the room was an expert at their job. With this city reeling from the jab-cross-uppercut-knee below the belt combo it had been dealt they *had* to pull it together.

"What I have shown you thus far," Marz motioned toward the wall, "what I detailed is only a tiny grain of all that has happened. Like I said earlier, we are at war. This is a 9-11 type event – and not happening in just one place, as terrible and unforgivable as that was – but in seven cities, SEVEN, people! So far, the confirmed death toll in Detroit alone is over nine hundred. And that doesn't account for those reported as missing."

Taking up the remote the Director scrolled through a couple dozen images, most from personal cellphones. Dead bodies, burned houses, men and women in masks, and one pic that caught Tamari's eye. It was on a headband worn by a young man throwing something at a window. In the center of his forehead was the figure of a tree with a word in Arabic superimposed upon it. Though it was only on the monitor for a moment a flash of recognition shot through her mind.

Motioning to Aimes she pointed at the symbol. "Bay'ah," she whispered. "Pledge." Tamari made a mental note to dig further into it.

"Later," Aimes mouthed to her, and then, "good catch."

The last six pictures Director Marz scrolled through looked like something from a city-wide purge. Though brutal enough on its own, yet more than one person in the room was strangely disturbed by how well-timed and orchestrated it had all been. And all this right in their own backyard.

"Clandestine, organized terror cells have been operating within these local neighborhoods." Marz motioned again to the monitors and sat forward. "Worse than that, elements within the very government of this city have helped this happen. And what is our response? What's the plan?"

The Director drew his chair back to the table and slid over a device. "By now each of you has the latest information packet on your tablets. This is everything the OIS has, every report and piece of data collected from every relative department and agency in the Metro Detroit Area, Langley, D.C., the other six cities, and even some from foreign bureaus. I expect each of you to research, put pieces of the puzzle together, and meet every two hours to collaborate. It's going to be a long day, and progress must be made. We need to move quickly. We need answers."

The Director picked up the remote again and shut off the screens. "Remember, our job isn't to patrol the streets, or figure out what thug did to whom in the city at large. Our job is to find the head of the snake. But before we can hunt down our prey, we must know its location and habits."

Marz stood and the room followed suit. "Agents, let's have at it."

Chapter 38

Sleep. The lie. However much a lie he wanted it, more of it, some or any of it. He wanted to be lied to, and for a long time. He wanted told he could rest, be at peace, hold Jia, be a hero, see his mom – anything but this. This reality. This terror. This horror.

Dane tried to sleep.

Long hours passed with him staring into the thick, musty darkness. Shivering, he turned to his side. Dane pulled up his knees, tucked in his chin, covering his head with his hands. The swollen, blistered feet felt like heavy, sucking fish, throbbing steadily to his pulse. Working into his hipbones the ache gnawed at his nerves, chewed at his mind. He cursed. A numb spot grew between his eyes, the place where he vented his frustration. Rolling over, his fingers began tapping at a new patch on the side of his head.

It was an ugly dawn. Cold, weak, a tattle tale light sat on the small windowsill mocking him.

"Today," it hissed with frigid disdain, "today things happen. Bad things. Painful things."

"No," he said. "No, no, no!" wretched out in spiteful sobs. Hot tears, angry tears flowed, fool's missives begging the world for mercy. He turned onto his back, lips pressed tight, eyes rolling with thick, salty desperation.

He noticed something and stopped. That sort of something at the edge of hearing, at the very corner of the ear. It was a small, faint clinking sound. The dull, stupid, little morn fairy covered her mouth to listen.

Clink...clink...clink, a bit more distinct. It nibbled at his ear, his thoughts, his curiosity.

Clink...clink.

An eerie, singsong shoved the fairy off the sill and into the room.

"Al-ka-leeeeb..."

The camp was deathly still. All of those people and not even a groan.

Clink...clink.

"Al Kalb, come out and pla-ay." Sidi's happily wicked voice pealed in the morning calm, timed with the ringing sound.

Clink...clink...clink.

"Al Kalb, come out and pla-ay."

The door burst open. Sidi stood, small bottles on three fingers, a crooked grin on his boy- like face. Without knowing why, Dane was strangely relieved. For some perverse reason he expected him to be wearing a clown mask. It was just Sidi, only Sidi. They were going to have another stupidly protracted discussion about blood pudding - his blood, no doubt, but just about pudding; nothing more, just talk.

"Gooooood morning, Al Kalb. Did you like my entrance? I got it from a movie. What a way to build suspense, no?"

Dane nodded at Sidi. He hadn't bothered to sit up. Despite the cold he still lay on the sleeping bag and never got in it.

"Well, campers, this is a day of new beginnings. I assure you that today's agenda will be unlike any other you have experienced. It promises a time to be remembered." With his arms spread wide he bowed and began to back away.

He moved from the doorframe as two guards came forward. Their weapons were shouldered, their faces blank and heavily bearded. Grabbing both ankles they slid him off the bag and out the door. Dane shuddered and squirmed with the pain, but their hands gripped like iron shackles. At the threshold his head bounce. Crying out he grabbed the back of his skull. They pulled him up a small dirt path, around the corner, and out into a large, graveled intersection of four hastily erected pole buildings, forming a sort of square.

The corrugated roofs were fairly new, the doors freshly painted. To his left was a building with metal siding and a grey door. A sort of carport ran out at a right angle from the far end of the structure. Under this was some kind of crate, or box made entirely out of wooden pallets. It was empty and the hinged door was open. To his right the door on its building was tan with a green ecology sticker of some kind.

On the building across from this the door was painted red. To the left of this the structure had a door colored black.

They dragged Dane out into the center.

"Al Kalb," Sidi swung wide his arms, a ringmaster at full cry. "Welcome to my world. You must be proud to know that you are the first one to see it all ready. And I have taken such pains to prepare a place for you."

The rollicking man gestured toward the pallet box. "That, my young, American friend will be your home. You will not only taste in the harsh delights of my play yard, but you will have a front and center seat to everything that goes on in the square."

He twirled around, gesturing at the structures.

"And which one is yours? Behind door number one" pointing at the black door. "Why, yes, Al Kalb, you have guessed correctly."

Dane was sitting up, hanging his head. He looked at Sidi enough to let the freak know he heard him, though he showed little else in the way of emotion.

"Al Kalb, really! I thought for sure you would have displayed some enthusiasm after all I have done with you in mind."

"Uh," Dane, shrugging his shoulders, "way cool."

"Massive, yes?" Sidi's face held a wide, open smile.

"Sure...massive," Dane answered.

A silent pause hung between them. Sidi bunched his lips and nodded his head in a wagging fashion.

"Okay, okay, Al Kalb, massive it is. You may not know it now, but you will come to appreciate that beautiful, black door. It holds a certain anticipation, a mysterious tension, filled with a delicious, mounting anxiety. 'What is in there?' You ask yourself. 'What will be done to me?' Is not the foreboding scrumptiously disturbing?"

Sidi came over and knelt next to him. Dane's chin was in his chest. He was folded within himself, full of sorrow, fear, and very, very much alone. To be so helpless, so useless - it tore at his very fabric. He knew this tormentor, this demon was calculating all his moves, lengthening it out, savoring, slowly licking blood from the tooth wound. If he didn't manage to psychologically get under Dane's skin, he would certainly flay his weakening body and achieve it through several pounds of flesh.

The guards came again. Sidi stood up and moved over by the black door, Hell's Concierge, showing him to his room. Once more the iron grips crushed his ankles, hauling him away to the door. In one motion they stood him up and he gasped, sucking in breath, grunting long and hard with the pain. His plump, red feet were on fire. The raw, bubbled soles popped and leaked, pierced his calves with pain at every bump and piece of gravel.

"Look, Al Kalb, look," Sidi motioned. It was hard to see. The long, dark room was awash with the gloomy purple of a black light. "Oh, wait," Sidi reached around him and fumbled at a light switch. "Just a second," Sidi strained as he searched the wall, "oh, this is embarrassing. Terrible optics," he muttered.

"If only I had a knife, or rock, or a baseball bat," thought Dane. He wanted to plunge something, to pummel this man, to kill him. His life wasn't worth a penny now. So, what did it matter? He'd rather crush this cockroach and have them shoot him. Better than to let him eat through his belly button and chew on his guts. But he didn't have anything, let alone the strength to wield it.

A light switch flicked.

"Ah, success!" Sidi triumphed.

The room glowed an evil, blood red, a bright, arterial shade. Dane retched. Nothing would puke up. He couldn't even spit. It looked like medieval-torture-meets-fun-house-meets- LSD. His stomach heaved again. A steel bed with manacles, a rack, some kind of barrel thing with chains on both sides, cuffs hanging from the ceiling, and rows of implements, sharp, pointed, blunt, serrated.

"No," Dane backed up. "No. Kill me! Just kill me!" A stream of swearing and vicious names lashed out of his desperate mouth. "You can't! You can't!!"

"Oh, but I can, Al Kalb. And I will." He motioned to the men. They thrust him inside. The black door clicked as the camp awoke.

Chapter 39

It was an hour. A lifetime. The passage of time seeped slowly by in dark, viscid waves.

They had beaten him.

They stripped off his shirt, hung him from the ceiling by his hands and beaten him. In a perverse way he was glad. He immediately envisioned thin ribbons of flesh being torn from him, or hot pieces of metal scorching his skin. But they hung him and beat him around the back and ribs. Nowhere else, and with nothing but rubber hoses.

He laughed bitterly at himself. "What an idiot! Only a fool would be thankful for a beating." Unless *that* fool was in *that* blood-lit room.

The pain had been unbearable. They hit him at inconsistent intervals. There were two of them, one at each side. Sometimes the volleys came in a rhythm, two seconds apart – *hit*, two three, *smack*, two, three – a perverse waltz in a bearded demon's ballroom. At others they fell thirty, sixty, fifteen seconds apart, interspersed with "Meat" and "Head" (his name for them), stopping to take drinks of water. He was sure that hitting a helpless man must be thirsty work.

The dithering jolts knifed through his gut and up into his lungs, until breathing was terrible. He couldn't push enough air out. His skin shivered terribly, then began to swell. The welts began to weep. Pink and slick the hoses began to paint over every new stroke they laid. At least one rib broke. Dane felt the sharp jolt, the sound like someone pressing a cracker against his side. It was a quick, crisp sound. He flailed and spasmed on the chains, uselessly shuffling his feet.

His bulbous toes were barely touching the floor. It was a desperate game – supporting his weight, taking the bite off his wrists. In doing so he merely transferred pain back to his feet. After a time, his hands went numb so he gave up trying to help them. The smacking, the whipping sound, the fine spray of sweat and red droplets overwhelmed other discomforts.

The worst, however, was not hanging there. No, the wounds the two were doling out was only a backdrop for it.

Sidi sat in a chair, devil-may-care, legs crossed, tea in one hand, book in another. Beside him sat a stack of novels, loose notes, periodicals – a well of the most contextually, acutely, intentionally irritating sources from which to draw his "mind water".

"Al Kalb, I have a fine collection of things to read to you."

One hit came, then another.

"Mother Goose – I am sure you will like it."

A whip from the hose. Meat gulped a dink, stepped back in place and hurled a blistering strike. Dane arched his back, screaming through clenched teeth.

On and on Sidi read. Fairy tales, nursery rhymes, fables. It was like watching a public execution with carnival music playing in the background.

The captor turned on a pair of slow, pulsing strobes.

The beating continued.

Women's magazines, a southern cookbook, mechanical manuals, even random haiku all spouted from Sidi's lips. Happily, with genuine nuance and inflection the tormentor read on and on. Dane began to hate him, to really hate him. Fear escaped him for the moment. He truly wanted to kill this *thing*. He dreamed of crushing his skull in with a rock. With each whip he mentally swung the rock down, and down, and down - pulping and crushing, splintering the cheek bone, eye socket, jaw and nose. A raging, angry fire blazed up in Dane, agony pouring like fuel on the flame.

He shook and cursed.

Sidi happily droned.

How could he just sit there and read about the chemical composition of panty hose, removing lawn grubs, and excerpts of Anna Kar-what's-her-face?

"Shut up!" he yelled. "What's wrong with you?!" He threw a few crude names at him.

Sidi looked up and motioned the men to stop.

"Why, Al Kalb, how rude of you! What manner of guest are you?" His tones were sincere and injured. "It is no wonder your mother up and died, what, with a son like you. I am utterly aghast."

Dane screeched. He thrashed against the bindings. Every verbal bomb he had he threw at the calm, smirking man.

Sidi quietly, patiently reached into his jacket and pulled out a large, white piece of cardstock. On it was written "ANGER" in big, black letters. He showed it to Dane, smiled, then put it away.

The hanging man seethed, he kicked, he tired. His head hung, face wet with tears and perspiration. He knew he'd been played.

Sidi motioned.

The beating continued.

Everything went dark.

Chapter 40

Tamari sat in her cubicle reading through a classified document from the FBI on her flat panel display.

"Jeffrey Bright, U.S. Citizen, former CIA Technical Operations Officer, stationed in England," she quietly echoed to herself some of the words on screen. "Subcontracted in the States for a joint operation by FBI and NSA for cyber reconnaissance and analytics." Agent banks pursed her lips and continued skimming over the paragraphs.

"Codename: Modred. Hmmm." An eyebrow shot up, "welcome to Camelot." She clicked on a link offering a spreadsheet indexing real identities and covert pseudonyms. A new window opened which she dragged to the second monitor on her desktop. "I'll dig into you in a second."

Spinning the mouse ball, she settled on a small, but highlighted section —

Current Status: Deceased; Cause of Death: hostile execution.

"Ouch!" Tamari whistled long and low.

Theories and conjecture for the identity and motives of the assassin were briefly stated. Picking up her smartphone she took a pic of each screen for quick reference, set it down and continued gleaning through the information.

"Wife, Helen Bright, née Earnshaw, employed by the British Government, GCHQ, Government Communications Headquarters. Formerly stationed at the Doughnut, Cheltenham, England." At the mention of food her stomach made a sound. How long since she had last eaten? She looked at the clock. Almost time for her "every two hours" briefing. Scrolling down she kept at it.

"Helen Bright was transferred in 2018 to a back office in Windsor, Ontario, Canada while residing with her husband and daughter in the Detroit Metro Area. Current Status: Missing." Banks paused and picked up her coffee. She sipped and recoiled with disgust. "Cold!" she said, setting the mug back down.

"Daughter, daughter, daughter," Tamari whispered absently, searching for more information. It was half a page down. Her name was Molly. She was six.

Also missing. Sitting back the young agent smoothed both hands over her mouth, following her jawline. One set of fingers wrapped around her neck and began to massage the tension out of the aching muscles.

"You look like you could use a warmup," the smooth, encultured voice of Orville Aimes sounded behind her. She swiveled her chair. He was standing at the mouth of the cubicle with a fresh and very hot pot of coffee.

"My man," she said. Swiftly dumping the last few drops of her frigid mug on top of the papers in her waste basket she held it out to Aimes who gingerly began filling it. "I needed a cup and you brought the whole bucket."

"My dear," Aimes cheerfully replied, "you will probably need this entire thing before the day is over."

"True dat," she said smiling, knowing it only took a few pieces of hood slang to get under his "oh-so-proper-diction" skin. He smiled with a knowing sneer and finished dispensing the brown, steaming liquid.

"Ah," Tam inhaled the smell, "nothing like cheap coffee to make your day."

"And paint your intestines," Aimes added with a crooked smile. He turned and handed the pot off to another agent that Tam didn't see behind him. The agent in turn placed a teacup and saucer in Orville's hands.

"Now that we're all in a happy place," Aimes said, "let's go over our notes."

"Oh, indeed," Tam mocked with aristocratic tones.

Pushing a chair over to the desk, Aimes took a seat beside her. Tamari filled him in on the Bright family, and their current state of affairs.

"Have you identified any of the team members Mr. Bright supervised?" he asked her.

"Not yet," she answered, "but I did pull up this spreadsheet." Dragging it back to the main monitor she began to go over it. "This gives us an index of their real identities, code names, working locations, contact info, and other employment related stuff. All are accounted for, one is dead."

"Oh, dear," Aimes shot up his eyebrows and took a sip from the cup.

"Yeah," Tamari continued, "her name was Yu Yan, from Hong Kong, Green Card, permanent resident. Interestingly, I saw a note about some discrepancies in her ID – something about fingerprints and a reference to genetics, among other things. At any rate she was discovered in an apartment building with a bullet in her head. It's not sure what she knew, or exactly why it happened, but she was the star hacker of the Jeffrey Bright menagerie."

"Any witnesses?" Aimes leaned forward.

"No, but the building supervisor was also found." Tamari sat back. "I'd like to say detectives are looking into the details, but with everything going on it's not a priority just yet."

"Then perhaps, Miss Banks, it is best to set that aside for now. Though do mention it at our meeting, which," Aimes checked his watch, "happens in just over five minutes."

"Yeah," Agent banks let out a tired breath. "I'll throw it into the pot."

"Have you gathered anything on the symbol you spotted earlier?" Aimes asked.

"Yes, quite a bit." Tam stretched out her long arm and touched near the bottom of the screen. A picture file popped up, a little fuzzy despite the high-resolution treatment the tech department gave it. "I'll have a full report on it soon. Suffice to say, I think it's way bigger and far more troubling than some jerk smashing storefronts."

"I get that sense as well," her partner agreed. "Let's pull on these lines and see what unravels. Well, Miss Banks, time to go collaborate."

Aimes and Tamari both stood, cups in hand.

Chapter 41

Dane dreamed.

Out of the mist, and out of the grey, out of the smoke on a warming morn he followed her. She did not run, but sort of skipped, turned, caught his eye and danced. He pursued her down the foaming shoreline. The little waves kissed their feet and flew away, back to home, to hiding, and the frolicking sea; cherubic children happily at play.

Trying to speak, he had no voice. Yearning to call her name, he could make no sound. She was fair, she was lovely. He must have her.

Flitting around a black, storm-battered boulder she slipped from his view.

Calling, he could not be heard. Looking, she could not be seen. He stepped about in the warm sand, blushed gold by the rising sun. Screaming her name, he spread his arms wide in unheard despair. She never answered. The little nymphs raced toward him, nibbled, then hissing, ran out again.

He was alone.

Chapter 42

He had blacked out. Everything throbbed. Movement was impossible. Dane felt like a fat, overcooked hot dog, fleshy and round, ready to burst the skin.

They had pulled him through the black door and dumped him into the yard. It was cold, around fifty-five. The sun of a young season teased vernal promises, raising the temperature to a relative high. Still, it was cold. Dane had on a filthy, sticky t-shirt, and stained sweats, with a sheen of bloody fluids covering him.

Lifting his head, he found a collar around his neck. Wincing, he moved his fingers, following a thin chain. He looked down his body, past his feet, and saw the tether stretch thirty yards to the box Sidi said was home. Dane lay facing the red and black doors. He knew the grey and the green were behind him. As he dare not move he could only view where his eyes wandered.

To his right, down the path between the red and green door buildings came a distant wailing. It was the first he heard anything from the captives since they were brought in. It was a woman screaming, high pitched, in short bursts. There was a struggle. She came into view, a guard at each wrist. Fighting, wrenching her thin arms, the young, black lady showed a lot of spirit. She resisted but didn't have the strength to break free.

Dane watched her, helpless. He was not apathetic, just useless. All he could do was breath, slowly, so slowly, and watch. As they rounded the corner toward the red door, she looked at him, saw him, and, he believed, pitied him. Soon, he guessed, she would never remember him at all. They were both alone.

Three guards came with a man. His wrists were bound in back, his feet bare. Around his neck was a rope, the ends slid into a pipe, the way used to control an animal. They made him stand in the path between the black and red.

He faced the woman.

She looked at him, utter shame and dismay running down her face, leaving claw trails of mascara.

"Leave my wife alone!" The bound man growled. "Let her go!"

Sidi sauntered over, casually flicking a thin, wooden switch back and forth like a cat's tail. "Deny your Christ, confess Allah, and all will be well." He spoke as though he were encouraging an intimate friend.

"No," the man throttled against the rope. "I will not," gasping, "Jesus is Lord."

"Very well," Sidi sighed. He struck a blow across the abdomen that threw him forward, face into the gravel. "You obviously have nothing with which to pay the tax," walking around the fallen figure, "so, I will extract a payment in pleasure."

The insidious man's face played a jaunty grin as he lightly stepped toward the woman with springy, little steps. He motioned to a guard. The tether on the husband was yanked, pulling him to his knees. Sidi circled the wife like a shark, bumping her, nudging her, smelling her. He pulled sharply at a blouse sleeve and tore it off, exposing the smooth shoulder to cold air.

"Charles," choking with sobs, "I'm sorry Charles. Baby, be strong for me, for the Lord."

Sidi grabbed a handful of the long, dark hair and violently pulled her through the door. The camp was darkly quiet. Irregular, wailing sounds punctuated the silence. Two distinct slaps and the sound fell to muffled cries and whimpers. Small, broken sounds of begging, of pleading, of prayer broke through tin and window.

Her husband went mad. With a tremendous surge he stood and threw himself back, plunging against the rope, the pole, and the guard. They all crashed to the ground, the man rolling over his captor, then being kicked by another. Several blows stunned him into silence. He lay writhing, his inner man torn out through the chest.

Dane watched. Numb.

It was not the bliss of an overwhelming calm he floated in. As the ear goes temporarily deaf at extreme percussion, so his mind, his person was overloaded by all the pain and humiliation suffered. He could hear the poor people, pity them logically. With abstraction he *knew* he should have great sympathy as a human and fellow sufferer. But he was flat, stepped on. Peering out from under the one-dimensional plane of self-preservation he could barely fit his fingers around its heavy plate to wiggle a pathetic finger at their sorrow.

He crouched inside this bruised, beaten shell, oblivious to the torment-
ing list of needs it petitioned him for. Comfort, food, rest, and water – these
were its supplications. But nothing could be supplied save emptiness. He lay
aloof, like some strange, little man living in the head of this unlucky fool.

Sidi came out, straightening his shirt. His men dragged the woman back
into the yard. A ragged cut bled down into one swelling eye. They hauled the
man up to his knees.

"Charles, Charles, you must give a proper confession." The tormentor
swished his stick back and forth like the twitch of a tiger's tail. "Or poor An-
drea will have such a rough morning."

Dane suddenly wanted to see Charles head butt Sidi right in the groin. It
would be poetic. Everything was at the right height. But Charles didn't. He
began to pray.

"Though I walk through the valley of the shadow of death, I-" A thin
spray of blood misted out as the man recited.

"Oh, not that one," Sidi threw up his arms. "I cannot tell you how many
languages I have heard that in. Nothing original! How predictable!" The
switch struck the supplicating man across the mouth. Blood spurted out,
down his chin, onto his pants. He fell sideways to the ground.

Sidi said something and four men grabbed the heaving, helpless woman.

"No, no," she moaned. Her fight, her tenacity had been leeched. They
dragged her by the dark strands back beyond the red door. This time it wasn't
closed.

The odd, little man sat passively in Dane and watched. He was tired. Too
tired to move, too cold to care.

They violated her for an hour. At some point along the way she fell silent.
The men did not.

Sidi, having been satiated earlier had a folding chair placed near Dane's
head. Arriving with his perennial cup of tea he sat, reserved as a high-born
Englishman at a countryside cricket match.

They could not see directly into the red door. Dane stared at its pock-
marked inner side, the red paint crudely slopped over the edge. He forgot
Charles, laying on his side, face down, bleeding, praying. Sidi he ignored. The
red, the red, he could not look away. It was red on both sides, the paint fresh,
the color intentional. Sidi – he hated Sidi. He wanted to paint him red with

that switch. He wanted to leave *him* bright and freshly colored on both sides. His hatred was visceral as the welts, the swollen limbs, the dry, pasty thickness of his mouth.

Placidly, the monster sipped his cup. A cold wind spit at him from across the river. He hunched down into his jacket playing at the scarf. Dane leaned, slightly, carefully. Pain zig-zagged through all the courses of his body. He spasmed, froze, then moved again. Rolling his eyes off the door he looked at the red checkered fabric around his captor's neck.

The tiny man living in Dane's skull poked at his side. He was a bit angry, though there was little he could do about it. As he could take his frustration out on no one else, he took it out on whom he could.

"Red. Red. Red," he said in Dane's head. "Look at the beast, the beast with the pretty scarf. Red. Red! RED!" The little man laughed. "Red lines on the beast, red drips from Charles's mouth, red is the light by which we are beaten, and red is the color on the door. Red, Red RED!"

Dane burned with anger. A futile, empty, heatless flame. He looked at the strip of fabric around Sidi's neck. He would twist the stupid thing. Twist it until Sidi's face turned red, until red was the color under which *he* suffered, and death had its way with him, violated him, made his freakish, boyish, stupid head turn red. The little man gleefully said that even his eyes would crimson, and his scalp would blush.

Red.

But the little man, sitting in the cavity of his soul could not press the levers, could not make the beaten shell move. The limbs, the torso hurt to touch, to move. They were stiff, they were tired, they were numb.

Sidi nodded to one of the guards standing at the black door. He was the one who kicked Charles. Did Dane hate him more than stick-and-rope-man, more than the four men who passed the red door? He hated them all. And he HATED Sidi.

The guard poked his head in and gave a command. In a few minutes they came out, slaked, satisfied, smirking. A limp, naked thing bounced along behind two of them. They dragged it over across from Dane. Not three feet away it lay parallel to him, facing him.

Sidi sipped. He crossed his legs low, observing.

Over the slumped, bare shoulder of the figure Dane saw a slice of Charles, desperately turning his head towards them. Trying to speak he rolled out a slobber of spit, teeth, and congealed blood. A low, groaning tone sounded from his throat.

He looked at the remnants of the woman – soiled, stained, with blood seeping from unthought of places. Sad. Dane felt a little again. He watched her carefully. Something thawed. One eye opened. The other was swollen. It reminded him of an old scar left on a tree when a branch is cut off at the trunk. The eye looked at him. Dane looked away. She saw him and he had to look away. Both of *his* eyes were good.

It occurred to him then that his tormentor hadn't directed the men to hit his face. In all that he inflicted so far, he had left the face, and the pit of the abdomen alone. Dane knew, or rather he guessed that Sidi wanted his "pet", his "dog" to eat, to speak, to prolong the game.

"Kill me," he whispered to himself. "Kill me, kill me."

Rolling his eyes up he spotted Sidi. The psycho looked like a Middle Eastern author waiting to do an interview, daintily holding his cup. The monster looked at the woman and smiled that enraging smirk.

"Stupid Sinbad Seedy!" Dane almost giggled aloud at the childish name, at this whole idiotic situation.

A thin, feminine noise escaped the body.

Dane looked back. It was watching him, pleading with him - that eye. But he was helpless. What could *he* do?

He was alone.

So was she.

Did she say goodbye to her man just now? Did she tell him how much she cared for him yesterday? Were they still in love? Do they have kids? Did they want to kill Sidi too?

Dane wanted to kill Sidi.

The little man plinking his ribs wanted to kill him. Badly.

"Stupid Sinbad." Dane smiled at the little man who spoke in his head. See, he could hide this from Sidi. He would never know. The eye - she would never know. Meat and Head would never beat it out. This delicious, hidden kinship was to be relished. Dane clung to the little voice. He reveled in its rebellion toward Sidi, toward the entire camp.

"Stupid girl's scarf," the little man said. "It would all be red, no more pattern crossed with white. It could all be red, and Sidi dead." Dane nearly giggled aloud with glee. The marionette lay damaged, half its strings severed, several joints displaced. But it could hide behind the painted face and laugh at the puppeteer, sneer at him, hate him.

She whimpered. He forced himself to look at the eye. Obviously, this broken thing had once been a beautiful woman. They were never going to let her be. She would never be beautiful again. Even if she lived, they would mar her, maim her, inside and out, up and down, back and forth. Charles would never be Charles. This broken thing would never be her. She would transmute into something, somewhere else, anywhere but here. Bitterly, this shade would haunt the shadows, laughing and calling the men crossing the red threshold names, mocking Sidi with words cutting and emasculating.

But it would never be her again. Never.

Why didn't they ask *her* to confess? Perhaps they didn't want her faith, just her suffering. Dane looked at the eye. It was brown, unbloodied, attractive in its own right. Charles, sad dude, must have fallen into that liquid pool in better days. Did he still love her? Would he, could he love her after this? He might still love the good one, the pretty one. What about the swollen one, broken and puffy as it was? She would never be the same. And now the eye floated in solitude midst the wreckage, the carnage of human cruelty.

The eye began to melt. Dane looked at her. He saw her. His heart melted too. The little man dejectedly sat down in his psyche and began to weep. He was alone. She was alone. Across the three-foot chasm they flicked signal lights. They could do nothing more.

He hated this. He hated himself. He hated Sidi, the meatheads, the four doors, and this island, all the way back to the stupid French colonists that held the dainty hand of Madame Cadillac as she gingerly stepped ashore. He swore and cursed Detroit for being, the world which gave it context, and even a god he did not believe in.

Sidi nodded. Two guards grabbed Charles and held him just outside the black door. Dane involuntarily shivered. It was cold. Everything was cold. Life was cold. His eyes roved from one point of pain to the next – black door, red door, the scarf, settling on the body across from him.

There was no throne to be captured, no romantic or epic aspiration to this drama. This was no hero's journey. It was the story of a broken, useless coward who rode no steed to the rescue, brandished no lance, nor bravely took to ship and sea. No quests or golden halls flowing with mead awaited him. His life was no more relevant than a cigarette stubbed out on the ground, snuffed under tread into dirt and gravel. To the lonely, battered man this whole play and its insipid acts were nothing more than a sick fantasy, a twisting of primal, human flesh against force, a perverse bloody game of gods and swords.

Chapter 43

"**D**id you observe, Al Kalb? Were the dynamics not engrossing? A man, his wife, her safety, his impotence. He could do nothing to stop it. She could do nothing but surrender to it." Sidi sipped. "And you, you sluggard, is there no chivalrous bone in your body? So coolly you lay there watching. But, ah," he soothed, "I have upbraided too severely. A character defect, I'm afraid."

The man sighed, took a drink, and thoughtfully viewed his beaten pet. "You, Al Kalb have your own...what to say?" Sidi paused a moment. "Ah, your own grass to cut. Yes, I like that." The man laughed and re-crossed his legs. "That metaphor would never have worked in my village, but I'm sure it does for you. You know, I never had a lawn as a child. What grass there was, was for the goats." He washed down a mouthful of tea and looked dolefully into the blue. "Perhaps that explains some of my eccentricities."

Dane shifted his view to the babbling madman. "On and on the Devil sawed upon his fiddle gold." He almost laughed aloud as the random doodle tripped across his thoughts. The core of him was coming back to life. With that life came attachment to the now, and to his wounds.

The eye caught him again, ethereal, disembodied. Looking past it, he saw the husband. Sidi stopped his mouth for half a second and nodded to the men. Charles, poor man, dead man, was toast. "Toast?" wondered Dane curiously. Where had he heard that word before?

This dithered, confessing body hadn't heard it. He was sure. No, not this broken rib stupidity – it only vaguely remembered the young man, the boy that lived in it before. No, that was another time, another life. He looked again at the woman's eye. The mote in it glared like a candle wick, liquid wax pouring out on to the gravel. Shame suddenly came over him.

Trying to see beyond the dark, slender arm, he noticed the tear. Where a smooth, rounded shoulder had been he saw a flap of skin that hung over, a limp fold of body cloth, tattered along the edge. It was deep, thick, and stuck to her collar bone by a paste of clotted blood. He was fascinated by the dark red strand of muscle terminating in threads of pink and white anchored to the bone. The line was too torn to be a knife cut. Maybe they threw her down too hard on the floor, or against a wall, or tossed her around a bit.

"I love you," deep in the throat the man's cry filled the yard. Dane's eyes were pulled from the wound.

"How tender," Sidi sat back, wiggling his foot. "How gallant."

Charles could little resist the men. They pulled him into the black room.

"Black room, room of doom, room of gloom," Dane muttered. He dare not smile, or grin, or smirk again. The eye watched him. She was a good woman. Dane would hate for her to see him come unhinged.

"Seedy's a schmuck, Chuck, and you outta luck," the little man shouted and danced around in his skull. Dane really focused on not laughing. Not just for the eye, the sad, dripping, brown lens, but for himself. There was still fight in him. Insanity would not win today. Dane hissed out his breath slowly through clenched teeth.

They took Charles into the building and left the door open. Dane could not see things by the strokes of realism. He saw this portal of suffering through shades and subtle scraps of a bastardized impressionism; through a glass, a cracked lens, smeared with grease and blood, dirt and forsaken hopes. There traced a semblance, a murky outline of a man hung across a beam, arms spread wide. Staring intently past the skin tear, the gravel yard, the black door frame he wrinkled his brow curiously at the figure of a glowing tree, floating in the darkness. It danced and bobbed at the end of a stick, gleaming a fiery orange white at the center, red to grey at the edge. The man – poor Charles, toast Charles, hung with head on chest. The symbol darted toward his midsection.

It was not one noise that rattled him loose. Two came together – a crisp, hissing, steaming sound, like the moment a steak hits a hot grill, and a scream, a long, wet-in-the-throat howl of excruciation.

"Oh, Lord," the mouth spoke beside the eye.

Dane had heard his own screams, but this scared him, reminded him. It was a portend, a foreshadowing of his own immediate future.

Sidi babbled.

The eye melted.

Charles threw his head back at a pain so intense it bleached everything to white crumbs of glass in his eyes. The shriek punctuated the yard, with the one meritorious effect of finally shutting Sidi up, if only for a moment.

"Oh, my," the tormentor sat forward, looking at Dane with raised brows. "I wonder what pain face that was on the scale."

Dane cursed this demon, this incubus. He hated him.

HATED him.

He was Mengele, methodically tearing apart the limbs and organs of the living. Like Kremer, he could eat without conscience of his wicked occupation, dishing heartily into his "one half chicken with potatoes and red cabbage." At least the Nazi doc used phenol for some of his captives. Dane had read about the sophisticated sickos of this world. He never thought he'd be autographed by one.

A little witch of wind blew by, cold and vindictive. The sky cleared to a pale blue. Red, twitchy in its movements a male cardinal landed over near his cage. Dane heard it and moved his neck to look. Pain – did that chirping thing understand what was going on? Oh, to be a bird, the sky, the wind, carefree, oblivious. Animals never did these things to each other. What they did they did for survival, not for the fun of cruelty. He saw the beauty of the Spring life midst all the human ugliness around him. Out of nowhere lines from Wordsworth came to him –

"If this belief from heaven be sent,

If such be Nature's holy plan,
Have I not reason to lament
What man has made of man?"

And, if there was a god, Dane wondered why he didn't just eradicate humanity completely, like one virulent strain of disease. He could turn the Earth into his personal golf course. Would the universe be any worse off?

Charles screamed and groaned. The eye ran, the mouth prayed, and Dane dropped his head again to the ground. A constant in the background was Sinbad laughing in his cup over the general stupidity of America, and the "insuperable" advancement of Islam. He praised Allah *this*, extolled the virtue of Sharia *that*, and polished it all off with a rousing exposition of the glorious end of all things.

When done, the Middle Eastern doctrinaire stood and signaled to the guards. They said something to the men inside. In about five minutes time one of them pitched something out. It rolled until it bumped into the back of the torn-up figure across from Dane. They eye could not see it, the mouth could not say it, but somehow down inside the cracked whorl of bone and skin, the young woman crouched in a quivering ball knew. She knew and wept with great bitterness.

Dane looked over the limp arm and across the yard. From the black door out into the limestone chips he saw a skipping trail of bloody prints, like paint on one side of a ball. Then he knew what she knew, what they all knew – Charles was dead.

Without any ceremony Sidi walked over to the young woman, pulling a pistol from his jacket. The report was sharp, heavy, bouncing off the buildings with a dull, ringing sound. Dane flinched. With a spasm the whole body flinched and settled. He watched the eye widen, snap shut, then slowly open. It stared.

Sidi said something to his men, and they dragged both bodies, and a head, out of the square between the black and red doors.

Chapter 44

Yusef sat in his darkened apartment trying to enjoy the gas fireplace and a tumbler of scotch. He was not so good a Muslim – not as far as dietary and bodily restrictions were concerned. Come to think of it, what he was *really*, perhaps only, good at was deceiving those he needed to deceive. That was his function. It was his job. Others preached Sharia, hadith, caliphates, and mysterious, end-time imams. He, quite honestly, didn't care.

There was no creed but money that he followed. And, he loved the game, the hustle, of getting it. He wanted the luxuries, the perks that came with cash. But he was culturally tied to Islam, to people who practiced it, to people who believed it. And every plane must have its runway. He took off a Muslim. He landed a Muslim. But he loaded his cargo hold with almost anything, for almost anyone – as long as they paid.

Sipping the cold, fiery liquid, he took pleasure in the tinkling of ice against the thick, clear glass. The news was on. It was in part interesting, in part the quiet, humming noise of the evening wind down.

Weapons, now that was his theology. That catechism he understood. His job was not a side passion, it was his all-passion. Yes, he was generally friendly with his clients. But he only sympathized with their causes so far as it increased his bottom line. Regardless of their ideology, what he saw in them was power – a power he both feared and respected. But he did not covet that kind of power. It was too much of a pain for him. Too messy dealing with people. He did love, however, the intricacies of acquiring weapons, the technicalities of it, the rush of the deal. No one could negotiate like he could, no one could sew up the loose ends with such finesse.

The dealer procured for his comrades all the niceties and necessities for waging their holy wars. Almost always he got ahold of more than they required and even secured things they didn't know they needed. As he so frequently came through even the purists, the sanctified turned their faces away from his money grabbing and licentious intrigues. It was the privilege of being their "master sword maker." Provided he continued as a pipeline, they would leave him to his own devices. Just as Yusef did not worry about the apocalyptic details, so they did not worry about him. They believed Allah would sort him out in the end, or simply use them to do so.

Yusef's day job was also rewarding. He dealt with leading edge tech. His numbers and knowledge were both high. The corporation loved him. They pampered their eloquent, handsome workhorse and Yusef ate up every minute of it.

He poured more scotch and stared at the TV. Something grabbed him. Sitting forward he pointed the remote and turned up the volume. A female news anchor was speaking.

"Today, at approximately three PM, a small watercraft containing two bodies was found among the boats at a marina on the Detroit River shoreline. Mike Kennedy is on site." The view switched to the reporter in the field.

"Thank you, Cheryl. What a sad, gruesome scene. The victims were identified as Charles and Anita Johnson, husband and wife. The police have yet to give us more information or verify the details, but a few eyewitnesses stated that they were laid side by side, unclothed. A source close to the investigation stated that the man, Mr. Johnson, had been beheaded, and also branded on his abdomen with some sort of tree icon."

"Does that symbol indicate some form of terrorist group?"

"Cheryl, with all the turmoil and violence that has recently occurred in the city, I would hate to read too much into it until there are further investigations. Apparently, there was also some kind of literature in the boat, and speculations have been circulating that this would be a key to understanding the meaning of their deaths. But all this information has yet to be confirmed."

"Thank you, Mike. Keep us updated."

"Will do, Cheryl."

The remote feed cut off and the news shifted to the weather.

"Idiots," Yusef shook his head. "If it were plastered on a billboard, they still wouldn't see it. What does an honest terrorist group have to do to get a little attention nowadays?" he mused, playfully.

"Sidi," he said aloud, "this has your signature all over it." Yusef's mouth tightened. He crunched an ice cube, slurping the burning frost through his teeth. He knew Sidi's work well, quite well, in fact. *And*, he always found him to be a total head case. But the man was amusing, not to mention very effective.

Sidi's brother Asan – now that was a different matter altogether. It always felt like he was dancing with Iblis when he dealt with him. That smile, and those stupid eyes: corpse eyes, dead eyes. There was not even a teaspoon of like ever lost between them. Yusef pressed a hand into his abdomen. He threw back the last of the drink and set it on a small table to his right. Shuddering slightly he got out of the recliner and turned up the heat.

"And what am I to do about Sharkface?" Yusef wondered aloud. His first plan to get rid of Asan hadn't worked. Should he try again or just hit the eject button? For all the cash, and all the pleasure this organization took in their arms dealer's handiwork, he carried a constant dread of his impending demise. Asan was that threat personified. Did he suspect that Yusef tipped the authorities off? Would he find out?

If he did, Yusef didn't need to ask what Asan would do. Before he ever got to around to cutting his throat, he would hurt those he cared for. Yusef pressed his stomach. "Don't let him get inside your head," he said to himself. "Chill out, play your hand. You were careful. You know how the game works."

These words did little to comfort him. All he could see was Asan's fingers stroking that black colored weapon at his hip.

Walking over to the expensive, bullet-proof window, he looked through the muted reflection of his fireplace, his lamp. It was a broad, upscale thing giving a sweeping view of the city, the river, the darkened neighborhoods beyond the all too slender arc of the moneyed district.

The drapes were never opened wide. Careful is the man of secrets to view through slits. Exposure was never a prudent tact. He laughed. He sipped.

Everything that was going on in this town, the chaos, murder, robbery, and the burning, he knew it all. Generally, he stayed out of the granular details of the plotting and planning. He didn't need their minutiae; he had his own.

But not caring for their planning didn't mean he wasn't informed of their plans. There were always eyes on him. Always. But he had his eyes too, searching, seeing, ears for learning, well-paid lips that whispered well-earned flutters in the dark.

Yusef knew that very soon he may offend one too many of the staunch leaders. He was working on putting the last pieces of his escape plan into action. Before these fanatics decided to blow a dirty bomb at the RenCen, or release a deadly toxic agent into the air, he wanted to be far, far away. Yes, now, more than ever it was best to keep an eye on things.

Pausing for a moment the arms dealer did something he would seldom ever do – think of someone else's well-being. "What about my sister?" he said softly against the window. Even if she was in no immediate danger, would she and her children survive whatever was to come? Would they pull his brother-in-law Aalam out? Collateral damage didn't seem to bother these radicals in the least. What was one poor cleric and his family to trouble them? Should he arrange for them to come with him? Yusef exhaled, leaving a spot of steam on the cool pane.

Raising the drink, he took another swig. Clinking against the glass the ice floated outside his mouth, bumping against the teeth. He sucked air, felt the warming vapors and watched the ant farm of life below.

"They have no clue," he said, a faint blush of remorse in his voice. "No clue."

Yusef was a cat. And the thing with cats is they could pad in on soundless feet, sit unnoticed and watch everything through half-closed, dozing eyes. Most often no one paid them attention. The licked their paws casually, contentedly, yet never missed a thing in the room. Yusef sat. Yusef watched. Yusef did his thing detached, yet very much in tune with the currents burning through the conduits of death, ideology, and power. He was no fool, though he oft played at one through slit lids.

Chapter 45

Dane was sitting in his crate. The crude door had not been shut. It was at best four feet in each dimension. He had been placed here, chain on neck, with unbearable pain firing all over his body. What he could see of his torso was red, with large, puffy, purple patches. His whole body felt like a charley horse. He spit and swore. He cursed Sidi's ancestors and spit again. Groaning, he rolled over. The fat, swollen feet felt marginally better, or perhaps he thought so because the rest of his body felt incomparably worse.

Sidi and two men came over. He put down a table. They brought platters filled with hot food and the ubiquitous tea.

"Welllll..." rubbing his hands together, "we have had a fun-filled morning. Say, that reminds me." He fished in his pocket and pulled out a brochure and began to read. "Welcome to Camp Misery," he said whimsically, "kindly take the time to complete this survey and tell us about your experience. Remember to be honest, because," pointing his finger into the air, " 'we aim to please.' "

His men repeated the phrase clumsily, their tongues not quite forming the words. Dane doubted they even knew what it meant. The paper was ignored. He turned his face and hurled a name at Sidi.

"Oh, Al Kalb! That is so hurtful *and* untrue – I know my father, and my parents *were* married. But do be sure to note such feelings in the 'Additional Comments' section. He smiled grandly and tossed the paper into the cage. It bounced off Dane's side and fell aimlessly to the slat floor.

A third guard came with a folding chair and an empty serving tray.

"Al Kalb," he said cheerily, "let us have a magnificent feast." Sidi stopped a moment and said what Dane assumed was a prayer. He then proceeded to wash his hands and load the tray up with hot, steaming food.

A feast it was. The tray sat on Dane's lap, and, despite his pain and thrumming rage, he truly enjoyed the meal. Savory foods, spicy dishes, meat, fruit, vegetables, bread, and sweet things, most of which he could not name, were eaten by the famished man. He washed down gulping cupsful of hot, pungent tea and felt some warmth and strength return. Food was a currency in this game and with it he must line his pockets as oft as possible.

If he stopped to think, he knew Sidi was keeping him supplied with sufficient calories to better endure the rigors he had planned for him. Dane shuddered. He shrugged. If he was to be a calf for slaughter, better to be a fatted
one.

"You are wondering," leaning back in the chair, using a toothpick, "what
became of the lovely couple we interacted with this morning."

Dane stared blankly. "I guess," knowing the inquisitor would chatter like
a monkey until he answered.

"Oh, indeed you do." Sidi shifted, brushing the tousle of hair from his
brow. "It was a tragically romantic scene," he began wistfully. "We laid them
side by side in a raft and launched them out upon the cold, grey waters. The
little electric propeller pushed them toward the shore with the slow, pathetic
pulse of life at its end." He sniffled, wiping his nose and one eye with the back
of his hand. Thoughtfully he sipped his tea, staring thousands of yards away
into the milky sky.

Dane shook his head, mouth open in wonder. "Are you sure you knew
your father? I'm thinkin' you're Dahmer's kid."

Sidi soberly recovered himself. He blinked twice at Dane, sipped his tea,
and blew up in rolling tides of laughter. It all ended with a cough, another
swipe at the nose, and a blissful silence. The cardinal sang behind them, entirely ignoring the stupid, human drama.

"Of course, this begs the question 'why?' " Sidi stated. "That is under-
standable. Well, there was a certain cinematic scope to the whole affair, but
let us refrain from aesthetic commentary, shall we?"

"Uh, by all means." Dane bit into a cake.

"You see, my pet, we have said nothing – nothing to the authorities. We
have so befuddled their communications and infrastructure that they scarcely know what has happened. I thought I would send them a message."

"Two dead people?" Dane pulled his head back, puzzled. "In a boat?"

"Should I have tried FedEx?" Raising his eyebrows. "Yes, dead people –
well, one relatively whole woman, one headless man, and...a head. You know,"
twitching his mouth around, "one of my assistants had the brilliant idea
of sending someone else's head along. That would certainly have confused
things on the other end. Despite their brutish ways," he nodded toward the

guards, "they can be quite creative at times. Perhaps my capering has rubbed off on them." He said this with an almost paternal pride.

"So, that's how you plan on telling them what you're up to here?" Dane asked.

"I sent their driver's licenses, and a pamphlet from the religious rally they were attending at the Park across the river." His tone was incidental like one talking about the barometric pressure or the local price of cabbage. "Oh!" hastily fumbling with an inner fold of his jacket. "And I sent along one of these." He showed Dane an oversized post card from a popular amusement park. "Wish You Were Here," was printed in large font across the top. On it was a glossy, full color photo of Sidi standing next to a well-known costumed character. Both figures were giving a double thumbs-up. Sidi wore tan shorts, sandals, sunglasses, and a pink polo shirt.

"You're misleading them to make them think you're in Florida?"

"Oh, no, I put 'Belle Isle' in the 'from' space. And I put a death pledge to Allah as the message. Al Kalb, tell me honestly, do you think I communicated clearly enough?"

The beaten man's head dropped. He exhaled. Despite every rotten, miserable thing that happened to him he couldn't help but chuckle. Nothing made sense down the rabbit hole of Sidi's mind. "Sure."

"Besides, it is not important that the FBI or Homeland Security or The Parks and Recreation Department knows *why* we are doing this right now. The pieces will quickly fall into place. We have created chaos across the U.S. And everywhere we go we proudly leave our label." He sat forward and held up an index finger. " 'This act of terror proudly brought to you by Bay'at Ashshajarrah.' Ha! It will become our reoccurring symbol, our leitmotif. Picture it," fanning his hands outwards -

"Boom!" an explosion rocks their world.

" 'Ah, there is Siegfried,' they will say. "

" 'Allahu Akbar!' he will shout."

" 'Now, whatever does Siggy mean by that?' They will respond in their politically simpering way."

"I ask you, Al Kalb, what is to be done with such a people? We have stuck hundreds of sticks into the beehive all at once and then most of our compatriots have simply melted away. By the time they figure out whom to sting we will already have accomplished our goal."

"Which is?"

"To begin doing to America what I am doing to you."

Chapter 46

The eyes stared. They faced out into a room of disorder, upset tables, books and papers scattered on the floor. Floating on a white scleral field, the glassy disc of dark cornea reflected the rectangular shape of the window. Despite the cold, diffused patch of light coming through the pane, the pupils never contracted. The irises were fixed, the lids unblinking.

They stared, vacant and hollow, mirroring in the wet lacrimal gloss the sash, the trashed room, and the man lying in the midst of it all. Aalam was, and had always been the center of her world, her heart, her home. His family lived in the apartment next door to hers for as long as she could remember. They had been sandwiched into their tiny living spaces in the middle of a poor section in a large, noisy Syrian city.

Aalam was her childhood playmate, sweetheart, and, thanks to parental machinations, her promised husband. She would have it no other way. That he would be in her life was never a question. Always remaining a tender, fawn-eyed girl toward him she could not even conceive of anything different.

Slowly the eyes began to rotate. More precisely the body, and by inference the head began to turn, slightly skewing the fixed orbs away from the center of the room in favor of the window. When the heater kicked on the slight vibrations worked their way up through the floor and into the door-frame. From the wood outlining the doorway energy was transferred to the hook that was screwed into the top face of the casing. The hooked piece of metal hardware sent movement down the short length of piano wire which was wrapped around her ankles. In time the body, hanging like a pear in the wind began a slow rotation back toward Aalam.

Somewhere in the background, indistinct and locked in a closet were small, snuffling sounds punctuated by the occasional cry. A boy and a girl were spared. The man on the floor was injured, yet alive. But the woman, the wife, the mother hung like a calf in the slaughterhouse.

She had loved her brother Yusef. However he was to anyone else, he was always kind to her. Yet his ways made her nervous. That his loose living, and dealings with dangerous people would one day catch up to him was a regular theme in her thoughts toward him. Part of her loved to see him when he visited. Mother and Father were gone, so Yusef was the only one left of her family. The other part of her nearly developed an ulcer every time he came around. She feared not only for his life, but also for Aalam and her children. It never crossed her mind that she might be the target one day.

That day was today.

Asan had found her.

The lifeless eyes began to turn slowly toward the window as the body rotated. Silently it hung above the thickening pool spread out like crimson ink on the floor. Aalam woke from his stupor and began to weep.

Chapter 47

The pain was unbelievable. His bladder and the incredible knifing rakes up and down his ribs pulled him awake by the hair. In he sucked. Out he wheezed. Pressing at his lower abdomen he tried to ignore the tightness, the waves of discomfort.

In the late afternoon Sidi had allowed him to use a hole with a five-gallon bucket in it as a bathroom. The meal was so good. Everything else was two steps shy of his own personal Hell.

There was no counting how long it took to drag over to the hole, how long to adjust his clothes, how long to try and clean up. Every move was done in gasps. If he turned or bent the wrong way his one rib made a small, snicking sound like a cracking peanut shell. That stabbed him, making him grunt long through tightened teeth.

He was closed up tightly in his little box when the sky began to nod its head. The guards did not help him. Crawling sidestroke to the crate he twisted, pulled, and turned until he lay on his side, fetal and exhausted. The sleeping bag was there. At least a fitful hour of starts and stops it took him to work the smooth, nylon fabric around him. Another twenty and he had it zipped up. He cried out often, clenched his body, cursed Sidi's stupid face, and wept along the way. His head pounded. There was a little Sinbad on top of his skull, with jeweled turban, scimitar and silk pantaloons, talking, always running its idiot mouth. The bearded toad merrily danced about in its pointed slippers, dinging his blade against the thick plate of cranium. Dane felt every thump.

"Al-ka-leeeeb," the irritating sing-song. "Al-ka-leeeeeeeb...you, my pet, have a headache. Oh, and it is a bad headache. You should take up safer hobbies."

He hated Sidi.

He hated his voice.

His face.

His faith.

Hate.

This was only natural. Who, in their own resources could help but struggle this way? Who wouldn't feel these things?

Like a shivering rodent he stiffly curled up into the bag, covering his head, fighting off the bitter, nighttime weather. The woven dream of sleep fed all night off the loom, a tattered cloth, blood-blotched, stained with urine, and thread-worn. It did him little good. Cold, the harpy screeched constantly outside the slats. Spasms of irritation taunted him. Physical and emotional exhaustion rolled on him, laying Dane down with desperation.

He awoke. There was nothing to see. Spotting a tiny, orange-red glow he knew it couldn't be a lightening bug – way too early. The guards were over there by the green door. The light flared again – a Phillip Morris firefly. He couldn't see faces. There were no voices.

Rolling over he unzipped the sleeping bag. He relieved himself into the corner.

"This is worse than some stupid book," groaning with exhaustion. "You never read about the star doing this." He cursed the world in general and set about the long, irritating process of getting back into the bag. Somewhere in the ink he fell back into the artificial sweetener he called "sleepartame." How he held on to the vestiges of a sense of humor he couldn't say.

The first clink echoed in the gravel yard. Dane's eyes flipped open. He swore. Another rap of glass on glass. Not this again, he groaned to himself. Today he was Sidi's dog, drooling fear at the bell.

"Al-ka-leeeeb...I have a surprise for you. Al Kalb, wakey, wakey. Are we a sleepy head this morning? It is no wonder, the way you ate." Sidi hunched into his coat and rubbed his arms. Three small bottles rolled in the dirt.

"It is cold today, Al Kalb. But I have a treat for your eyes only." He stopped and looked curiously around. "Oh, and my men, I suppose. And our special guest. Ah," with mild irritation, "technicalities, all technicalities." He waved these impediments off. "Yes, your eyes only."

Motioning toward the black and red he summoned a guard who came pushing an older man in front of him. Long and flowing, the simple, white garment he wore was stained. Two soft, blue slippers shuffled underneath him, kicking the hem out in small billows. Sadness painted his face, darkened his eyes. A chunk of his thick, greying beard had been torn out.

"Al Kalb," Sidi gestured, "this is Nasri. Nasri," pointing at Dane, "Al Kalb."

"Al Kalb?" the man said softly, stirred from his pensive sorrow.

"Al Kalb, Nasri is a devout Muslim, a cleric. Oh, that is like a...a pastor, a holy man, a teacher, you know," nodding encouragingly.

Dane's eyes were thick and bleary. His head was better by a few degrees, but it felt dopey, leaden. He gave a sort of crooked nod at the man. Pain would not allow him to sit up. Pity gripped his guts and twisted them in a bunch. He didn't know this man, but he knew something bad was coming up for him. The cleric looked like a nice man, a kind man. He resembled a Saint-Gaudens, a memorial of sadness, or peace, depending on the beholder's perspective. To Dane, it really looked like resignation. He knew, the man knew, what Sidi knew – Nasri was also toast.

"Well," Sidi rubbed his hands and blew into them, "let us begin." Turning sharply to the man he raised a finger at him. "Nasri, you have betrayed your faith."

"I have not. I am Muslim. I am a man of faith and peace," looking at Dane.

"No!" Sidi said sharply. "It was bad enough that you failed to join us, to support us, but you warned that Christian – who, by the way, is here and anxiously waiting his turn."

"Turn?" thought Dane. He glanced at the black door and shuddered.

"He has done nothing," Nasri, quietly stated.

"He *is* nothing," snapped Sidi. "But you – you, Nasri *are*. Oh, yes," wagging his finger he circled him, "*you* are a traitor, to Allah, to your brethren."

"Traitor?"

"Yes, yes – not only helping the Christian, but worse, you were going to turn us in to the police. The police!" Sidi stamped his foot and moved around to face Nasri. "You might have ruined all my work here!" he whined. "Do you know how inconvenient that would have been? How many energy drinks would have been utterly wasted, not to mention the paint, the wire, the strobe lights-"

"What?" It was the first and only time Nasri moved his eyes away from Dane.

"Yeah, he's nuts," the caged man almost said aloud.

"Do not try to get me off track, Nasri," Sidi scolded.

"I do not kill innocent people," the older man said, facing Sidi. "We are not at war, we are at peace here."

"PEACE!" Sidi, bursting capillaries. "Islam will not rest until, praise Allah, it has overtaken the world and then the end comes."

"Cowards! You attack unarmed women and children!" Nasri fired back.

"Okay, Nasri, next time I'll give them all swords first – just for you."

"Yep, nuts," Dane mused.

Nasri shook his head and spoke. "Our faith does not-"

Sidi moved violently toward him, finger in face. "Do not," heated, "speak to me about *our* faith. Islam demands obedience. How can you be a Muslim and repudiate the very words and life of the Prophet? For he is the most beautiful pattern, the greatest example for mankind to follow. He is the exalted standard of character."

"The Prophet, yes, may he be honored." Nasri bowed his head. "But you do not speak as a Muslim. You speak as an Islamist, not for Islam."

"Lies!" Sidi shrieked. "You cannot hide behind some genteel hadith to put off the raw truth. Just because you are squeamish as to the harsher side, the reality, the history and founding of our faith, does not mean all of us are, or must be. I will follow it from the bedrock, unfiltered, unmediated, until the wicked are slain and all the world bows the knee."

"Did he tell you to slay the innocent?" Nasri's voice was strangely even.

"Innocent?!" Sidi said something sharp Dane did not understand.

" 'I have been commanded to fight against people 'til they

testify that there is no god but Allah, and that Muhammad is the messenger of

Allah.' Muslim one, thirty-three. Does that not seem clear to you Nasri?"

" 'To you, your beliefs, to me, mine.' " Nasri said, looking straight ahead.

"Ah, so you *do* know the Quran." Sidi twirled around, hands in the air.

"You take it too far," the man looked more intensely into Dane's eyes.

"Is this far enough –

'O, you who believe! Fight those of the unbelievers who are near to You and let them find in you hardness.' Quran nine, one twenty-three. Or this –

'Fight them until there is no more persecution and religion is only for Al-lah.'

Quran eight, thirty-nine. Do I need to go on, eh, Nasri? Those with your view will join us or be put out of the way." Sidi was an inch from his face.

"I will not join you. I worship Allah, not you, your movement, or your deluded leader."

Sidi absorbed this, nostrils flaring, chin jutted out. "Then I will finish with a *final* admonition:

'He who fights that Allah's word should be superior fights in Allah's cause.' This I will follow Nasri, even against such as you!"

The accuser motioned. Men came forward bearing things Dane couldn't see. He only saw Nasri's eyes – tired, sad, and resolute. They closed once, the lids pressing hard together. The mouth of the man condemned moved in silent prayer. Dane had no regard for any god, but he saw this man. This one could be his neighbor, his co-worker, maybe even his friend.

Now he was his fellow sufferer.

They forced Nasri to his knees and tore his garment to his waist. Gentle, brown eyes, moist with fear looked up at Dane. The man's mouth was set, un-wavering.

Behind him two men were filling something on the ground. Dane caught the fumes of gasoline. Two other guards drove a heavy iron stake into the hard ground behind him. The one man grunted as he brought the sledge down again and again on the mushrooming metal end. When done, the long spike stood about a foot below Nasri's head.

Pulling him back they bound him at the wrists and ankles to the shaft. He looked at Dane, into Dane, through Dane. The eyes became unfocused, long staring, swimming in the distant, hurried memories of life and loves, of soft hands, and kisses upon little foreheads in the deepening eve.

Sidi made some sort of proclamation to Nasri, to his men. It rolled out of his mouth, native and final. As Dane didn't know Arabic from Pashto, he guessed this was the "*say yer prayers*" speech.

Two guards lifted a black ring carefully and placed it over Nasri's head. It immediately began to slosh a liquid.

"What the-" Dane was stunned.

It was a car tire, old, winter tread, and full of fluid. The top of Nasri's eyes poked over the edge. He looked directly at Dane. When he tipped forward it flowed down his chest. His arms, being bound tight and low behind, would not allow him to fall. Closing his eyes, he began a prayer, a lament to his god.

In the timeless ooze of the surreal a flame, a blow torch came up behind him. Like the small, blue finger of death it stretched forward to touch the kneeling man, to deliver a final cut to the strand of life. With a "whump" the vapors caught, and the tire ignited. His skull was engulfed in flame. Instantly his beard singed, glowed, turning white, then ash, then black.

Nasri screamed.

And screamed.

Dane cried out. He A to F to Z bombed Sidi, the guards, their mothers, their children – whole countries under the interdict.

The gas flared on Nasri's chest. Writhing in spasms the body shook wreaths of fuel down his torso setting the clothes ablaze. His voice broke into a long, high wail then ceased. Small choking sounds erupted. Searing heat and suffocation stuffed an unconscious rag into the gentle man's mouth. He slumped over to one side. More flames poured out onto his blackened rags and the ground. He was a ball of sick, sizzling char, engulfed in tongues of yellow, red, and sickly teal.

The black necklace smoked, belching up thick ropes of nauseating plumes. The odor, the odor, oh, if there was a god, Dane begged him to take it away. It clogged his eyes and filled his nose. He tasted it. He never stopped tasting it. Cloying, laced with burning hair and accelerant, it stank like boiling tar. It never left him, it never forgave him his impotence. It hung on him the chains of immortal bitterness. No matter what they did to him, no matter what they broke, regardless of what they forced on him, or took away, this would never be excised from his memory. It was burned forever into his mind – the smell of rubber.

Chapter 48

They dragged him by the wrists. He lay on his back watching the wispy white curls dance off the corpse. Nails of pain scratched down his ribs as they hauled him toward the door, black and angry. It wanted him. This horror was the odd kind, the perverse kind, the one where you survive by dreaming to fall asleep, fearing because you're awake. This black, hungry monster ate the ones under the bed. That's where you try and hide – with them, away, underneath, anywhere but here.

A stone struck his spine and grated along his back. He grimaced and arched. He watched the smoke. He hated. Like prey sucked into a hungry throat he went through the hole.

What was done to him was unspeakable. It was the kind of thing heard through squinting eyes and curling toes; too cruel to be believed, too crushing to brush aside.

He screamed 'til blood broke through the lining of his throat, his voice box a ragged bag of swollen pipes. There was no limit, no bounds, no fixed point or moral stay to hold them. Only his face was protected for now. Every joint, every orifice, every surface was plied in the pain trade.

The sadist sat and read aloud Koranic verses, old copies of National Geographic, then The Saturday Evening Post. He quipped from Maxim about masculinity, then from an old, stained copy of Redbook on tips for juggling mealtimes, family activities, sports, homework, and marriage.

"It must be sheer torment," Sidi said, smiling, "to be a soccer mom."

Dane dreamed of running Sidi over with a minivan, backing up on his head, then running him over again. And again. He fantasized about popping open the back hatch and watching the sports equipment tumble to the ground on top of his broken body. He imagined doing things to the running mouth with softballs and cleats that had never entered his thoughts before.

"And now," the tormentor said with great delight, "on to the feeding habits of the African Dung Beetle."

Sidi was the water torture – his voice, the inane, disassociated topics, the happy lilt of his tone and snappy verbiage. Dane knew the bearded gremlin was sticking a blender into the soft, grey tissue of his mind. Whirring at variable speeds, Sidi strived for a pourable liquid meeting his own malicious ends.

Here Dane moved a step closer to the unretractable realms of mental glass. He was losing reason and began the redefinition, the perverse revenant of a new psyche. It was a deformed birth, a squalling, sniveling alien child whose sole point of existence was base survival.

The wall of his soul was being assailed and whole sections of brick and mortar began to shift and crumble. Some gave way entirely. Soon he no longer recognized the cruelly calculated methodologies of Sidi. He no longer cared. He was tired, beyond weariness. The tormentor's OCD adherence to his efficacious system found no relevance in Dane's mind. He simply wanted the agony to stop. He craved cessation. Dane wanted death.

He yearned for the stroke of mercy from sleep's darker brother. Under his hand he would not dream, he would not fear, nor love, nor laugh, nor weep. Nothing would suck and pull. The beeping would stop. Falling like a ragdoll he would tumble until inertia became the law, and he, the body at rest. And Sidi would *finally* be quiet.

"SHUT UP!" he screamed.

"Oh, Al Kalb," Sidi looked up from a magazine, "how *are* you holding up?" Dane hung by the ankles, gnawing maggots crawling along each nerve ending wherever he had any feeling left. Blood dripped here, body matter dripped there, Sidi dripped his devil's smile.

"Pain," he began yet another exposition, "is a tremendous cleansing agent. In all its forms it tends to be a great clarifier. Right about now, I guess," he tilted his head and looked Dane over, "that you have come down to the most practical and sensible desires. You see, no more cellphone bills to worry about. No more alarm clock or work, or friends, or family – not even your girlfriend or your social causes are on the radar."

Dane moaned pathetically.

Sidi stood and walked towards him.

"Oh, no, no," he patted a smeared shoulder. "Do not overexert yourself. This is a very rough patch of transition. On the other side is a Jungian waste-land of utterly no dimensions. You will simply be by not being at all. Fasci-nating. At some point you might actually thank me for freeing you from the surly bonds of this Earth." He briskly rubbed her hands together. "Oh, I simply bust with anticipation."

He turned away, walking like a schoolmaster having pierced through to a student at the very apex of a teachable moment.

"Continue," he said absently. Sitting down he indulged in tea and a reading on the principles of hydraulic mechanisms.

Dane no longer heard.

He yearned for it to end.

He wanted himself to end.

But he still had hatred for this piece of filth. Holding to this burning ember he lived and endured by its light.

Chapter 49

"Cat and mouse, Miss Banks." Aimes walked slowly across the empty room, hands clasped behind his back.

"They couldn't have left here more than a day ago." She flailed her arms out. "Every lead brought us to this place. Every piece of evidence and-"

"And we're a day late," her partner said, nodding his head. "It would appear so, my dear. I risk sounding like a field manual, but you know that our success relies on good intel, solid investigation, and unyielding perseverance."

"And timing," Tamari said.

"Yes," he turned.

"And luck?" She faced him, her mouth hooked up on one side.

He smirked, nodding back and forth.

She sighed.

"Do not despair, Miss Banks. We've all been in a whirlwind. The gap is closing. Our mysterious, arms transporting protagonist fleeing in the back of the boat has not entirely disappeared from the screenplay. He is yet only twenty-four hours ahead."

"It might as well be a year. I mean, look!" She motioned to the empty space. "They totally wiped it clean, all of it."

"Even the windows...impressive." Aimes looked out onto the street. He wore a pair of latex gloves. Running a finger on the sash he turned it over and examined it. "Most impressive."

Forensics had already swept through the place. Nothing. The escape boat was dredged up. It was stolen. Untraceable to any relevant suspects. It was empty – a big fat zero.

Tamari circled around the barren living room. Slowly, carefully she walked to the kitchen. There had to be something. Something. The sun pushed in through the curtainless panes, flowing in a swirl of dust motes. A dark line of shade fell across the floor from the countertop. She leaned against the sink, putting her hand to the back of her neck.

"Think, girl, think," she urged herself. "There has to be something." Mentally she went over the process. The OIS had excellent teams, top rated labs, everything that could be done was done. Neighbors gave some information

– but only some. It was mostly fear and silence, with a little apathy thrown in for good measure.

A small spike of light strayed through a hole in the window frame. It fell down into the bottom corner where a stove once was. In contrast to the grime, the dirty greyness of old floor tiles and greasy wall something white glinted. Tamari focused her eyes. It was the smallest little triangle, like the point of a piece of paper. She shifted off the edge of the counter and moved toward the spot. It stuck out from between the cabinet and the plaster wall. Squatting down she deftly fished it out. It was a white, plastic bag with Arabic and English writing on it.

"TACHI HALWA – Orange Flavored Gelatin Confection," it said in bold, red letters.

She sniffed the bag. Sweet. It reminded her of Jolly Ranchers. "Were they gummy bears?" Looking over the details she made mental notes: 453.6 grams, made in Pakistan, contains nuts.

Standing she carefully placed it in an envelope. It didn't seem like much, but it might just be everything she needed.

Chapter 50

Dane lay in a heap. Not a ball, curled for warmth and protection: a heap. He lay in his box where they threw him. Nothing worked. Everything hurt. Opening an eye, he blinked away a crusty scum of film. The yard was bustling with people.

The shoulder joint of his left arm having been pulled back and away, was now stiffly trapped beneath him, a purple hand extruding out behind the opposite hip. Though burned up and down with small, cigarette-sized craters, his right arm - wrist, elbow, and shoulder could bend. Affliction, like a heavy man lay over his lessened frame. Smothered, he wheezed, his ribs felt constricted, squeezed to pulp. Slowly he pulled up his good arm. It shook. Wobbling unsteadily about it was like playing some odd, disjointed POV. Why wouldn't it just listen?

Like a long-expected friend that finally showed up the quaking palm slapped lightly down on his cheek bone. The index and middle finger twitched. Forcing in breath he winced. He must breathe. He must blow on the one pathetic coal he had left. The two fingers began to drum on the side of his head – a slow, unsteady tattoo, over and over, tap, tap...tap.

Two men had been beaten to death that morning. Both bodies lay face down. Dane hadn't heard. He hadn't noticed. He peered beyond the slats of his cage and saw women in and out of the red door, men in the black, scraped off like bugs and thrown back out.

Opening quickly a man thrust out of the grey door, punching things into a tablet. Dane saw electronics, fluttering LEDs, server arrays, and some monitors. He noticed for the first time the constant hum of an engine running on the far side of the building. Men were talking and listening in the grey. They were clamping down on veins across the river, feeling the pulse, measuring the rapidity of beat and blood.

A thumping sound came from a distance. Dane couldn't see anything. He viewed the world through one eye and two-inch gaps. It became more distinct. Men in the camp looked up. Some raised weapons. An order was barked. The muzzles went back down.

Roaring overhead, a helicopter shot low and fast, just above the soft-budded trees. Hope brushed its sparkly painted fingers across Dane's face. Could he be rescued? The thought made him salivate. Visions of bullets danced in his head, several of them pirouetting through Sidi's brain pan. But his cynicism, his pain told him this kind of hope, with her long nails, full lips, and promising eyes was little more than a harlot. She blew kisses of short-lived pleasure but never pledged her fidelity.

"May she interest him in a day unfettered?" He declined. The tramp must've never met Sidi. He was a hope-sucker.

Still, a high-powered round passing swiftly, fatally through that bearded fruit head - now that was a downright wedding ring. That kind of hope he could believe in. His optimism butted in and gave a quick sales pitch involving night ops, Navy SEALs, and a boat ride home.

He saw Sidi cross the compound.

An old crow fluttered down and sat on Dane's skull, beginning to pick at his mind. It dug into his scalp and gave little, mewling caws at each strip of happy expectancy it tore away. Hope, the emotional tart, had left him and was walking with Sinbad.

"Maybe she likes his scarf." He closed his eye.

Someone came and threw him a chunk of bread. "What, no tea?" he mentally protested. He would certainly mention this to the manager. Maybe he *would* fill out his stupid survey. No smile, no laugh, his humor was too bitter, to sarcastic, but at least it was something.

He wretched. A gob of blood and phlegm rolled out the corner of his mouth and splattered to the ground. Pain squirmed head to toe and he shuddered. Rolling over he lay face up, his left arm free. It was numb. That made him glad, strangely glad; one less thing to worry about, one more thing to feed the crow.

Hot tears leaked from his eyes. He couldn't remember his mother, her voice, her face. Jia, Rick, Micka, Mama Mata – they were fading, like ghosts in the morning graveyard. Sidi's work was stripping every beautiful, precious thing out of his life. The past was being torn wholesale from him. But this moment, the dreadful now – he knew *its* face, clearly, and in detail.

More than a lifetime of barbarous hurt had been shoved into his thinning frame. It ate him, squirming in his soul, a pumpkin gut pile of maggots.

They writhed and turned, bored and gnawed. He was now partially unmade. Never the same, he could never be normal, or even a new normal. Twisted, misshapen, his inner man was even more traumatized than the newly scarred and battered flesh. It despised this weakened shell. It revolted against its insistent demands, its painful groaning and complaining.

The day was a blur of screams. He had never heard such desperate begging. Never had he encountered such terror, such pleading, such futile attempts of the broken to escape. It was an odd occurrence at this littered, human intersection, a once in a lifetime batch of misery piled up in a quivering, blood pudding mess. Where would one experience this in the everyday life? Movies and books, twisted stories - these were all abstractions. Pain was real, here, now.

Strange, with everything he had forgotten, he did remember hitting a deer once out in the country. In late Autumn they were skittish, pushed by mating drives, hunters, and hunger. One flew out of the dark, out of the blind. The beater car shook at the impact. He watched in horror as it tumbled over and over. Pulling off the road he watched in the headlights. Tense knuckles wrung the steering wheel. What should he do? What could he do? Its side swelled and relaxed, over and over. Streams of breath blew out in the cool, wet evening. Dane leaned forward, mouth on hands. He forgot to breathe.

Then the deer did the impossible. It struggled to rise. It must go. It must flee. Broken, the back half dragged at a bad angle. Still it fought to the other side and tumbled into the thicket over a hill. *Run, live, survive.*

Dane panicked. Wasn't he supposed to do something? He wasn't driving that fast. The old car still ran. What was another dent? He told himself it was just wounded but would make it. He told himself the convenient lie. He put the car in drive and left.

Sidi didn't let his deer go. He slowly licked the bite marks, savoring, enjoying the warm throbs of life.

Dane wasn't looking at a doe. It was a woman. She had been violated in the red. Having lost all real sense of time he counted not in minutes, but in lives. He saw at least six go in and out. She screamed, then cried, then she begged - again and again she begged. Then there was silence. They dragged her out, stripped, violated, blood oozing from a cut in the forehead. She was flopped on to her belly. Dane could see her face. He wanted to close his eye, but nothing would obey. Gripping the wheel of his heart, his conscience, he saw her lay in the gloomy headlamp of a sun too clouded to warm, too distant to care.

She began to crawl. A crying spit, exploding with mist escaped her. One hand over the other she dug into the unforgiving, unyielding ground and headed for some unseen growth in which to plunge.

Dane hated himself. He couldn't help. He couldn't breathe. Wasn't there something he was supposed to do? Staring, gripping, holding everything in he watched her go a costly fifteen feet and collapse.

The men laughed.

They said cruel, taunting things. One need not know the language to syntax evil.

He cursed them all.

A guard kicked her foot. There was no motion but her rising rib cage. She lay still, facing towards Dane, eyes closed in pitiful exhaustion. Dane lay watching her a while. The diffuse shadows began to grow long, stretching away into the East.

Something sounded like an animal. It was a long, loud wailing. He heard a baby once at a hospital, a tiny newborn. Red-faced and quivering it screeched with a cry that was shockingly painful. As he knew nothing about babies it freaked him out. Was it dying? How could you let it suffer like that? It was amazing to him how beet-colored, kicking and violent the hoarse, little thing was. The scream came again, across the yard, through the black door. Deep and booming it tore the ear, rising to a higher pitch, white-hot with exploding nerve endings.

Melting away the light fell to a clamped reminder of daytime. Dane saw the woman again. He peered through the crust, through the slats, through the dusk and watched one finger twitch. Was she like a grasshopper? Squash it flat and at least one leg will wriggle and spasm. The pinky finger went up and down, twice. Slowly, achingly her head came up. She moaned.

A body suddenly hit the ground in front of his crate like a bundle of sopping rags. Was it the screamer?

"I'd scream too, if I looked like him." Dane said. A smile teased the left corner of his mouth. He didn't want to know what he looked like himself, not after the way *he* screamed. But he was glad, truly glad that today wasn't his day to enjoy Sidi's company. Cringing he had thoughts of tomorrow, of the dawn, of his own red-faced, squirming form screeching on the bed.

A bloody, broken man lay congealing on the ground so close Dane could hear him whispering. He was praying, moaning, crying. A man with a weapon walked over. He strung a chain from a post under the shelter where the dog box was. The end was snapped to the bleeding man's foot. At this, he groaned and rolled over. Walking away the guard went towards the woman and savagely kicked her.

"Lord, have mercy. Forgive them, Father, forgive them." Michael Pearce exhaled and lay silent in the coming dark.

Chapter 51

In his more lucid moments, Dane remembered a man in a long robe singing something at times. Half of the guards would leave, others would come, always watchful, always wary. He saw one of the exiting men carrying a rug. A general ignorance chalked all this to "Muslim stuff." It didn't matter. It would only matter if they *all* left. But then what of his cage, of his collar, and his chain?

Nightshade fell over everything except the wash of light outside the gray room. He watched the traffic in and out of the doors. Red and black were gender select torments, gray communications, and green, some kind of storage or break room. Men ate something in there, sometimes. They had to live, even while crushing others. These doors were the portals of life in the yard, the flow and ebb of existence and death, of replenishment and deprivation.

For these men and their masters, this was just, this was righteous. It was divine judgment. They were the theocratic tools through which the deity executed his wrath. Upon the soles of their jackboots they engraved the word "holiness." With the boldness of this sanction they ground blood and matter from the skulls of captives. Dane wondered how many ounces of guts assured them safe passage to their Heaven.

Bitterness crept into his bones. The cold, the hate, the wounds seeped down from the upper bunks of sorrow into frigid, empty night. There was always a breeze off the water. It penetrated even to the cluster of leafless trunks and brown brush. He tried to pull the stained sleeping bag over him, or under him. Everything, every joint was stiff and sore and bruised.

The man wheezed. He groaned.

"Shhhhh," softly from Dane's lips. "You'll wake her," he croaked.

Pearce didn't hear him. His teeth were chattering, exposed as he was to the air. He groaned again. The woman moved and made a faint noise. Honestly, Dane thought she would be dead by now.

Morning reminded the caged man how close to death he felt, or wanted to feel. In an odd relativity he thought himself fortunate. His face wasn't busted up, he had some shelter, crude as is it was, *and* he had this luxurious, nylon sleeping bag, though mostly useless to him at present. But at least he could lay on it.

Bruised knuckles knocked against a wooden slat. How stupid it was - a piece of cellulose stood between him and freedom. And what would he do with his liberty? Freedom, like time, seemed spent so cheaply until you are out of it. What *would* he do? Start a website: A Man Called Dog? Or maybe inthetigersteeth.com? Perhaps he could lend himself out to PTSD research at a university. "A novel," the momentary thought bloomed, "now I can write what I *know*."

He saw a burgeoning career, a "making the most of every opportunity," situation in the works. Dane wanted to host a freak show podcast. "Good morning world, I'm 'The Boy in the Box.'" Hobbling on to Oprah's set he saw himself nervously taking his seat and bringing the audience to pitiful tears, showing them his filthy collar.

News reporters would frantically jam microphones and cameras in his face, chasing like a school of tiny fish the crumb of his life dropped into the pond. One politician would come and ask him to say how kind he considered his captives to be, dispelling all the evil, right-wing conspiracies of Islamist as anything less than ideological paragons of peace. Another would contact him and request that Dane denounce the leftists for coddling those radicals and making it easy for them to wreak havoc.

Maybe now he would finally have his slice of fame. Perhaps society would find him entertaining enough to look up and see his point of light against the darkness. Was suffering sufficient fusion to birth his bright, ascendant star?

Laughing a little he wondered if these thoughts meant he was coping, or on his way to losing it.

Dane could scarcely move. He was as inflexible as the blood-crusted rags he wore. The hand drifted back, *tap-tap-tap*, against the temple. Alone, beaten, a stepped-on beetle, rolled over on his back, flailing, too punctured, too leaky to flip over and crawl away.

The man moaned. The woman was silent. He lay odds she would freeze through the night, that the sands of freedom and time had quietly drained away on her. There might be a few grains stuck on the upper curve of glass, but the guards would be sure to knock them down.

Echoing across the sky, far away, yet distinct, another helicopter pounded out its rotor call. Dane tapped. The copter beat the air. Would anyone come? They must know there were hostages. How could they storm the place? Given his circumstance it seemed a frivolous fear that he didn't want to be shot when rescue came. He thought some of his gears must be slipping, that his mind was beginning to go soft. The first fingers of a forced insanity played upon his mind. He giggled.

No, he didn't want to be shot. That would hurt.

Hurt.

He giggled again.

He was branded now, marked. He was Sidi's plaything, his experimental hobby, his perverse, little, shrinking creature. When would the day come that his tormentor was satiated? When would the little, demented "Sid" be done torturing his toy?

All he really wanted to do was disappear. To hide in some small box of his own, away from life, away from Sidi, the blood, the hurt, and death. Then maybe he could lay down quietly and molt from this dead shell of what used to be Dane, emerging as a new visionary, a motivational speaker or something. That would be sweet. That would be *massive*.

Or maybe he could just lay there and die.

Chapter 52

"Reverend Pearce." Fearful and hurried the whispers fluttered in the night air. "I'm Ginny. I was at the rally. Here." Dane heard a sloshing sound, something in a bottle. "Here's some water. Reverend Pearce," insistent, "hurry, please drink some." The man couldn't open his eyes. They were gummed shut. He was curled tightly, instinctively against the night. It was cold. Like prison bars the press of the freezing air bound him in place.

Dane reached out with his ears sculpting the picture, gaining understanding from the noises, the inflections, the fear. He heard a bottle tip up, liquid slosh into something, then sputter in sloppy fits to the ground.

"Where will the water go?" Dane wondered. "It was too cold to help a seed yet. The ground was too hard to just soak it in." He kept thinking how stupid it was to think of these little things, the minutiae of every occurrence. Then again, who cared? If they kept him engaged, who really cared? He was still human. He was no listless animal.

"Would Flatus Malodorus care?" the thin whisper fluttered through Dane's dry, numb teeth. It was the very Latin sounding name he began to call Sidi, for every wretched villain needs a proper, Latin sounding name that simultaneously lampoons his existence. "Al Kalb," was it? Fine! Flatus it is, and Flatus it shall ever be. Dane swore with his usual punctuation terminating any sentence regarding Sidi.

"Reverend Pearce," the girl's ethereal whisper cut the silence like a boom. "Please drink. Don't let them kill you. Don't let them win." Water sluiced to the mouth, to the ground. "We are praying for you."

Dane listened to the fine, subtle detail, the minor shifts in sound. The man was struggling, sucking, gasping through swollen tongue and broken lips to pull into his body the precious resource. Without water we die quickly. Water was a form of hope, tangible hope, real hope. It wasn't a helicopter, or a full metal jacket through Emperor Flatus' gourd, but it might buy you another day.

Dane groaned.

Another day?

"Just let him die, girl!" he wanted to shout. His stupid mouth wouldn't work right. King Dane was troubled, for his temporal subjects were in open rebellion. Nothing would obey but his right hand. He attempted a chuckle at the allusion. An acoustic laugh could not be formed for the treason in that corner. But a monarch always had a right-hand who would remain loyal.

Dane called his left Brutus. The recalcitrant tongue he named Caligula, for the many, witty victories of his short, verbal life, now driven utterly mad by adversity.

"I am alone," Dane thought sadly, "even my stupid body has abandoned me. I can't even tell someone to die, let alone kill myself."

Truly, he was on an island, in a box, entombed in a warm-blooded coffin, and he simply could not escape. There was nowhere to transcend to as he had no God, Nirvana, Valhalla, or interdimensional plateau to which he could retreat. He could not ascend into reincarnation for his suffering, or a punishment of the damned, whether frozen, or flame-and-devil tormented at Dante's pleasure. He could only make the lateral moves from the troubled, yet socially acceptable and productive computer twenty-something, to the squished, yet resistant captive, to the drooling patron of Sheogorath's virtual realm. Madness. Insanity. Retreat. Oblivion. What else was left him? He moved and tried to turn.

The soft shuffle of feet came towards the cage.

"I can't see you," the girl's voice whispered. "Here's some water." She dragged hand and bottle around on the boards, feeling the slats, looking for a big enough opening. Something slipped through and bumped into Dane's head.

"Here," she urged. "Be careful. It's open. Don't spill it."

Slowly, the loyal, but bruised right hand reached up and found it. With clumsy effort he grasped the cold glass. It felt like a Pepsi bottle. He cursed. Pepsi would taste *so* good right now. Anything would taste so good right now. But water was what he needed. "Besides," he reasoned to himself, "all those empty calories would just live on my thighs." He laughed where he presently lived - in the head.

The bottles opening somehow found a way to his mouth. It was instinct, the infantile nursing reflex - find life, get food, survive. Most of the water found his throat. Some slipped to the bottom slats. "Where would this go?"

he wondered. "Maybe it would find an acorn, and that acorn would sprout into a sapling, then a tree lifting him into the sky and away-"

He was nuts. He knew he was nuts.

Holding the molded glass against his skull the hand rested. It was tired...so tired. What he just drank, was it Sidi's agent? Did it help in the effort to keep him alive, only to further the plans of the grinning gargoyle sitting with tea in his recliner? He could try to die by thirst and starvation. But did he have the strength and courage? Would he die before help came?

Lifting the bottle back up toward her hand was a feat of engineering. He had to concentrate, to work by stages. Pain rolled in crests and troughs of nausea. His maneuvers nearly caused him to spit up what he had just washed down.

"I'm sorry I can't do more," Ginny said sadly.

If only she knew how much she had done.

The girl shuffled away.

"Reverend Pearce," the whispers shouted again. "Drink some more, please. Lord, help him, give him strength."

He groaned and picked up his head to receive the liquid life. This time less was spilled and more of the slender thread secured him to the precarious toehold on the cliff.

"I'll try and come back," the little one promised, "tomorrow night, if I can." She stopped a moment. "I tried to wake her up," emotions puddled the words. "She wouldn't move. She was really cold." Her footsteps disappeared into the blackness.

Dane lay for some time in a sort of stupor. The water had mildly revived him. His head was still thick and sluggish. He was exhausted. Drifting in and out he thought he heard a sharp noise, a young scream in the distance, then silence. He went out.

It was still night, still dark, still frigid. Murmuring came to Dane's ears. Startled, he snapped out of heavy slumber to a fuzzy consciousness. The man – it was the man on the ground. He was speaking softly, but loud enough for Dane to make out the words. There was no wind. The yard was quiet.

Pearce began to talk clearly.

" 'In you, O Lord, I put my trust; let me never be put to shame.

Deliver me in your righteousness and cause me to escape;

incline your ear to me, and save me.' "

The sound broke off as Pearce took a long, heavy breath and wet his thick tongue. Dane listened with interest.

" 'Deliver me, O my God, out of the hand of the wicked.

Out of the hand of the unrighteous and cruel man.

For you are my hope, O Lord God; you are my trust from my youth.

By you I have been upheld from my birth;

you are he who took me out of my mother's womb.

My praise shall be continually of you.' "

He exhaled and lay panting from the effort, like a man struggling to the top of a tall hill. The rhythm of the breathing continued apace then slowed, then settled. Pearce fell into a jerking, un-restful sleep.

Fragments, thoughts, rolled around Dane's mind. There was a certain hunger, a desire for something to anchor to. This storm he found himself in tossed him about in ways he had never known. He clung as a man at sea to a slippery rock. Where could he go? What hope was this? Everything seemed dark, futile. Where was this strength he couldn't grasp? In the words? In the voice? Wounded and groping, his inner man stretched out for something, for anything.

"Oh, God," it was the first, albeit sarcastic prayer he had ever prayed, "if you're stopping to pick him up, can I hitch a ride?"

There was no sound now but thready breath, and the occasional word or cough from the guards at the grey door. Dane's troubled mind wandered away again into the unconscious mist.

Chapter 53

Dane couldn't wake up. Like swimming in a deep tank, he pressed toward the top, the faint light above the water. Air, he needed air. Straining he rose higher, blowing out a stream of breath. Everything was garbled. He heard something. It was distorted, muted, all through liquid and bubbles. There were shouts, begging, pleading, a young voice, full of fear, hysteria, and panic. Commands in a foreign tongue barked out, heavy things were thrown to the ground, punctuated with the simultaneous pounding of a hammer and a wrenching, unbridled scream of agony.

One eyelid cracked. Daylight. He saw the indistinct form of a man. Pearce, he thought. Beyond him, about fifteen yards, something was rising up into the air, some structure - someone. The right hand was deployed. It pulled at the other eye, nearly glued shut. He met a finger with his tongue, rubbing and lifting until it opened.

Something dropped into a hole. The young voice screeched then wailed long and hard.

"Oh, God, help me!" it sobbed. "Oh, God, please."

Pearce didn't move. He breathed, but lay still, completely out.

Dane's eyes focused. "What in the-" pulse and heart quickened, pounding with disbelief and shock.

"A crucifix?" The only word that came to mind. The voice, he never heard it so loud, but he *had* heard it before.

She was a black girl. Her pretty, round, dimpled face was languishing below a head of thick, yarn-like curls. He felt so sorry for her. Ginny. It was her. She gave him water. He couldn't do a thing. They had nailed her hands at the wrists to a crossbeam, her feet, spiked through the ankles to the center post.

They crucified her.

She hung naked, defenseless, bleeding and exposed.

"She gave both of us water," he hissed to Pearce, the truculent mouth finally complying. "And what...we do for her?" He cursed himself, his weakness - he was a dog, a chained, worthless, former human being. He was in Hell and all around him danced the pitch-forked demons.

"Oh, God!" Ginny cried in excruciation. "Forgive them. Oh, God!" She pushed herself up rotating pierced ankle bones on the metal shaft. At the apex she exhaled. Thrusting her chin out she heaved in and fell back on the pins.

Dane was sick in his bowels. His toes involuntarily flexed, his eyes half shut, wincing as from shared pain. He squinted. It was too terrible. This was impossible, unreal. Couldn't God destroy Sidi? Couldn't he burn him with flame, or drop an airplane on his head, or throw him in the river? Dane dreamed of spinning projectiles dancing through Sinbad's head.

"Al Kalb," Sidi's happy smiling face broke into view. "Al Kalb," snapping his fingers, "are you in there?"

Dane raised his fingers at the girl, shredding the yard with her laments.

"Oh, her?" Sidi thumbed at her casually. "She was bad, wandering around. Al Kalb, she was a threat to my men. What would I say to their parents if harm came to them? Think of their wives and children. You have no idea, Al Kalb, the amount of responsibilities a camp coordinator such as I must carry."

"From a little girl?! You b-"

"Ah, this again. Al Kalb, I insist that you cease calling me that. I have always known my father. If you persist, I will begin to take it personally. But, listen, I know seeing the girl in the early bud of puberty treated in such a fashion is a bit unsettling. But you must understand, I had no choice. I gave her the chance to convert, even offered her the honor of marrying one of our brave, young men. Yet," his voice taking a sad, regretful tone, "she refused. However, you may be happy to know she would not renounce her Christianity. I genuinely tried to persuade her, oh, in earnest, Al Kalb. I truly did. But, alas, what is to be done with this younger generation?"

Sidi turned wistfully toward the girl, hanging helpless and bloody. "Myself, I appreciated her zeal - martyrdom is admirable in any form."

"Why don't you blow yourself up, then?" Dane hissed.

"Ahhh," Sidi turned slowly back to Dane, smiling wide. "There is my young American. I knew I hadn't beaten the wit completely out of you. And this one," he gave Pearce's head a stiff push with his foot. "This one refuses to listen as well. No matter how reasonable I was, he would not convert. I even offered him a wife," his tone evincing a certain disbelief at the refusal of such an honest bargain. "What the heck, I told him he could have one for every person he convinced to join us. I am all about upsell and bonuses. But, nooo," nudging Pearce again, who moaned heavily, "all he would say is 'Jesus is Lord,' over and over again." Sidi spat something rather impolite the Dane didn't catch. "I tell you Al Kalb, mine is thirsty work."

Danes eyes watched a cup tip and pour something warm past the tormentor's lips. Through the space below Sidi's chin to the crook of his elbow he briefly saw Ginny. She gasped in short, lurching breaths. It was as though she could breathe in but couldn't get it out. Tears mingled with bloody wounds and ran down her face. She grimaced with pain, pulling torturously on the bolts through her wrists pushing up on her bloody feet. She exhaled, cried out, and fell back down again with a wet, slapping sound.

Though her head was bowed Dane could see her mouth moved. He assumed it was prayer.

"Father," Pearce whispered, "forgive them. Have mercy."

"Hey, hey," Sidi chided, "wait in line, you! You'll get your turn up there soon," facing back to Dane, "if he doesn't freeze to death first." He said this behind his hand, comically wagging his eyebrows.

Dane didn't laugh, couldn't laugh. "Everything but the clown suit," muttered to self.

Chapter 54

Victor set the package down.

"Find anything?" Tamari stood behind him.

It was late. Normally he would have left for his apartment around six or seven. In the morning one of the specialists would have taken the piece of evidence and started their inductive dance. Tamari couldn't wait. Vic couldn't keep a lady waiting.

"Find anything?" Orville strolled up behind them, tea in hand.

Vic turned in his chair. "Tag teaming me, eh?" Tamari liked his little Canadian inflections. He was born in the US but spent some time under the maple leaf working with the Canadian Security Intelligence Service.

"Take off, eh?" She tried the accent.

"Funny...in my father's day," Vic held up a finger.

"Aw, I'd never fit in with your northern friends," kicking her toe on the floor. "I'd feel left out."

"The cool CSIS kids would love you, Tamari - *if* you were with me." He looked at her sideways. "They might even let you sit at the same lunch table."

"Youth," Aimes dismissed. "As much as I hate to cut across the *sportive* banter" he motioned to the envelope, "perhaps we should focus on working."

"Curmudgeon," Tamari said, rolling her eyes.

"At times I am astounded at your expanding vocabulary." He sipped his tea and tilted his head. "Emulation is the highest form of-"

"Proceed!" She bumped Vic's chair. "And it's imitation, Lord Fossil."

Aimes raised his brows and shrugged dismissively.

Pressing his thumb into a small pad Victor logged in to the system. He started two cameras recording, tapped his headset mic and slipped on a pair of blue, nitrile gloves. Carefully opening the package, he lay its contents on a clean, white examination square attached to a long, stainless table. Mounted next to the square was a movable arm with a bright rectangular light bar surrounding an extremely high resolution, three-dimensional camera rig.

"Inventory number 404-23-001. Removing from sealed evidence pouch at nine-oh-three PM, Eastern Standard Time." He methodically listed the date, agent, her ID, location found, time, and other items necessary to protect the chain of evidence. The video units faithfully digitized a record of the proceedings.

"White, polymer bag, approximately five inches wide by seven inches tall." He indicated all the writing found on the bag, then swung the 3D rig over the package. A green matrix shot down onto the square. Vic aligned it and snapped a shot. He flipped the item over and took another pic. The grid disappeared but he kept the bright light floating above it. He reached over to a squeeze bottle of ethanol, doused a sterile wipe and cleaned up the handle on a bar code scanner.

"Uhhh," he was a little tired. "I should have cleaned this *before* I started." He began whistling a fragment of Mozart, then the Grateful Dead.

"A bit like ice cream and motor oil," Aimes commenting on his musical medley.

Vic chuckled. "Perhaps a little Vivaldi."

"Sprinkles on top," Aimes said casually and sipped his drink.

"You two are duds." Tamari shook her head. "What, no funk?"

The two men stopped and looked at her.

"Fine," holding up her hands, "tweedledee your snobby dum all you want. Stiffest bunch of collars I ever worked with."

Vic chuckled.

Aimes preened his shirt at the neck.

Taking up the device, Victor pointed it at the small set of lines in the back corner. A spray of red laser washed over the code. Something beeped. Data popped up on the screen.

Vic studied the information. "TACHI HALWA," he read aloud. This is basically a dense, sweet candy sold by the TACHI Confectionery Company, located in Raipur, India."

"Candy?" Tamari said, leaning in.

"Yeah, they call it halwa," Victor clarified, "but it's also known as halva, or a number of different variations, depending on the region. This one's flour-based, gelatinous, cube shaped, like orange flavored gummy bears with almond pieces. It's typically distributed across Western Asia and the Middle East - from India to Turkey. According to the reported data not a whole lot of this particular brand and type comes into the US. And," he paused, searching the screen. "Hang on." He made a few movements with the mouse and typed something into the keyboard. "Shocker – what little is sold to North American markets comes via Amazon."

"The world comes through Amazon," Aimes added.

"Well, all your little knives do," Tamari, playfully sarcastic.

"Quite so." Sniffing, Aimes raised his chin.

"And," Vic tapped in a few more parameters, "only three shipments of this specific product have been made to the Detroit area in the last six months."

"Now *that's* what I'm talkin' about." Tamari snapped her fingers.

Vic turned to face them. "I'd say you've got something solid to work with here, at least a start." Facing the monitor again he spoke what they were all thinking. "It may be that one of the suspects has a very specific sweet tooth. If you can trace the purchases online, you may be able to tie some threads together."

Tamari snorted. "It'd be easier to get Apple to give up a pass code."

"Patience, my dear acolyte. There are ways," Aimes smiled knowingly, "there *always* are."

A chime sounded on the monitor. Vic swiveled back to it.

"Hot diggity," he said.

"Whaaaat?" Tamari sung long and slow. "Diggity?"

"Okay, cool, then. The 3D scan is flagging us with a little extra bonus –a fingerprint."

All three of them leaned closer to the display. Aimes looked at Tamari. Tamari bunched her brows, made a face and looked back at her partner.

"Busted," they said together.

"You two are *so* cute." Vic hunched his shoulders and snickered.

"And so are you." Tamari put her hand on the top of his well-built arm. Vic quit scrolling the information. He slowly turned his head, looking sideways at her hand, then at her, grinning. Their faces were an inch apart.

She straightened and pulled her hand off. "Sorry. I got excited."

Vic slowly turned his head back.

"Quit smiling." Tamari pushed his chair.

Aimes sipped his cup, ignoring them both.

"How long before the results are in?" He asked Vic.

Victor looked at the count on the screen. The system was grinding through hundreds of thousands of comparisons with other prints searching for a match. "It could be a couple of hours yet-"

The monitor beeped.

POISTIVE MATCH.

The three of them leaned in again. They stared at the screen.

"Get out." Banks' mouth hung open in disbelief.

"Astonishing," Aimes chimed in.

"Dude..." Vic didn't know what else to say. "You two are not going to believe this." He picked up his pad and swiped, throwing an image onto a fifty-four-inch display. On it was a man in shorts and shades, standing next to a cartoon character in a fabric suit. They both gave thumbs up. A mark-up showed where a technician had dusted and found a print – right over one of the man's thumbs in the photo.

"Where is that from again?" Tamari asked.

"Belle Isle." Aimes said.

"The one that came with the bodies in the boat." Vic sent pictures to other monitors. Crime scene photos showed two bodies, one decapitated, the post card pinned to its chest.

"What stupid moron puts his own print on a card and sends it?" Tamari asked.

"One with tremendous cheek." Aimes, dryly. "He is overconfident, arrogant, and...*very* good at what he does. He isn't afraid of being identified, because he assumes he will never be caught." Aimes stood upright and set his jaw. His voice became a menacing whisper. "But *I* don't live by never."

Tamari looked at him. It was at times like this her partner sort of made her hair stand up a little. He wasn't pretty, but he was as solid and strong as a slab of granite. Something in his eyes, something that floated up from his past made her glad he was on her side; even more that he wasn't hunting *her*. There was so much she didn't know about him. Whatever it was that came viciously out of his closet, she knew it was from long experience, painful exposure to danger, and born in blood.

She looked at man on the card. "Now you've done it."

Chapter 55

Little patches of sunshine punctured the clouds on occasion, like errant angels who woke and made smoky holes in the vapor to peer down on the suffering of mortals. The happy, dancing smiles of golden rays did not comfort Dane. He had been fed, more or less dragged out to urinate, then hauled back in.

Pearce had been given water and an old piece of canvas to cover him. Those who helped him were prisoners. It seemed the guards, other than to inflict pain, did not deign to touch him.

Dane saw women in burqas, and unarmed men running around doing various odd jobs and chores. They never went into the doors, and the women never walked about alone.

"Where had they come from?" he wondered. "Did Sidi keep them stored in a crate until needed? Who were they?" Suddenly, it came to him.

Converts.

Willing or unwilling they caved, like him. There was obviously some kind of holding area, a building or tent, down the path between the red and gray doors.

An undefinable sense of hollowness and shame plied his conscience. Dane stared at the dirt. He kept his eyes there. A heaviness hung on his neck so that he could not, would not look up. There was no sound from the dying girl, not since the early reaches of sunset. It had gone on all afternoon, slowing by pitiful degrees, until finally ceasing. Now, there was nothing, not even a whimper.

Dane told himself he didn't *have* to look. What would it help? Would it change anything? He didn't even need to turn away as his face was already down. "Once down, stay down," he told himself. If you looked, you cared. If you cared you had to do something, or face the stinging truth that you were too useless to do anything at all. Dane saw nothing but the cold, stiff dirt and felt in it a comforting kinship.

At dawn even a strangely burning curiosity couldn't compel him to look. His eyes stayed down. Hadn't he seen enough yesterday? Wasn't the pit of his stomach knotted enough? Didn't he close his eyes and blot it out for a reason? Why should he look now? What would he see? Pearce groaned. Raising his eyes, he saw past the man.

Dane looked.

He stared.

It couldn't be helped.

Or changed.

Ginny hung. The skin on her delicate body was a hazy, grayish hue all over, with darker patches where blood had stained and thickened.

Her eyes.

Shouldn't her head be hanging down too? At the cessation of life, shouldn't all go limp? It seemed like her shoulder joints had given way, bunching just enough to support the head. It was like she kept her face up until she froze that way - staring, accusing, condemning. Like one of those creepy portraits that followed you around the room she gazed in his direction, not at him, but wherever he was. Her eyes were taking him in, the whole world, every soul in it.

Too, like those oil masterpieces the subject held its viewers in contempt. "Who are you to look at me?" the figure on the canvas would accuse. "Are you the artist, and now the judge, or perhaps just the ignorant admirer? Do you know what this cost? Do you know the toil? Who are you to have a thought, or make comment, being untutored, barbarous, to that side the cultivated?"

Surveying the cold, broken world and its wretched inhabitants, the poor, little, dead thing raised a voice of prosecution. Dane could not bear it, could not stop hearing the pain of it, could not pull his eyes away.

"Judged!" The smooth skinned husk declared. "Judged, you Islamists for your actions, butchers of men and women, tormentor of children. Judged you soft, lily-handed captains of the American ship who sat in their safe, expensive chairs of power, coddled their feelings, and refused to call evil 'evil'. You who had no stomach for despising political correctness and doing instead what was right. Liars!" Her unclosing eyelids raised a scathing rebuke. "I was young, compassionate, innocent and brave - and who will answer for my blood?! This world, this society thought nothing of me! Judged, for you could have chosen better! Judged, because you turned a blind eye. Judged!"

"Because we could have stopped it." Dane said with a thready whisper. He began to weep. What torment awaits those, wholly stretched out on their bed of comfort, watching the world burn; those who won't lift a finger for it costs them little to blow it off? Those who suckled the sweet, refusing to believe the bitter until it lays in their mouth? How were his tender, multi-cultural feelings now? He heard Sidi laugh and laugh until it rang in his ears like the Newgate Bell.

"Fools!" Dane hissed, spittle falling from his mouth. Angry thoughts burned on through the dry forest of his cultural assumptions. "We, the whiners of the digital age. We, the wiki scholars - are *we* the next leaders? Are we played so well by our emotions that we can't think anything through? Do we trust in our political and social leaders only to find them utterly corrupt? Lies!"

He rummaged around in his mind. He tried to remember the verses from Niemöller. Un-ending tears streamed down his face. He rasped out with great feeling, "then they came for me - and there was no one left to speak for me."

Dane was alone, except for Pearce. But he was just another dead man waiting his turn to realize it.

The man on the ground in front of him moaned. Dane's eyes focused on the crumpled mound in front of him.

Ginny had called him Reverend.

"Dude," he said to Michael, "I bet they *really* hate you."

Pearce looked out from one eye. "What's your name?" he asked.

Dane froze. The sound of Michael's voice startled him. He didn't answer right away.

The misshapen tarp covering Michael looked like a shell. His head poked out of the roadkill, smashed, brown and red and covered with dirt.

"Aren't you turtley enough for their turtle club?" Dane began to giggle.

Pearce looked at him with pity, believing he had lost his mind. "Poor man," he thought, "what did they do to him?"

"My...my name is Dane." He hadn't been called that in a while.

"Dane," Pearce replied. "My name is Michael." The reverend dropped his head. "Father, give Dane strength. Help him to endure. Open his eyes, Lord

Jesus, that he may know You, for You are the way, the truth, and the life." His breathing fell into labored rags.

"Life?" Dane swore. "What kind of life is this?!" The words hissed through his teeth.

"This life is only a vapor...a mist in the morning, gone by noon," Pearce strained.

"Looks like ours is on the eight AM departure," sounding oddly like the old Dane.

Despite all the pain and gravity of their circumstance, Pearce began a mumbling laugh, more of a short barking chuckle, resembling a cough.

"Dude, you all right?" Dane's right-hand gripped the slat below his line of sight. He couldn't help, but he could ask.

"Laugh," he coughed for real, "just laughing."

"That *was* kinda funny." Dane let out a little laugh himself. He was still Dane, not a dog, still a human, and for the moment, befriended.

"Why do you pray?" Dane asked.

"Why do you breathe?" Michael returned.

"Uh, because I need to, I guess," Dane answered.

"Yes. But it's *because* you're alive." This response started a coughing fit in the Reverend. It took him a moment to bring it under control.

"Well," Dane mumbled, "if it floats your boat."

Pearce chuckled. "My boats probably gonna sink soon. It's where I sail too after this 'eight AM' that counts." He laughed and coughed a little more.

Chapter 56

It was about mid-morning when they pulled Ginny down. They jammed a crowbar under the heads of the spikes, crunching down on her still, little limbs as they pried the fasteners out.

Her body was taken off the beams and heaved against the side of the red door building without respect or ceremony. She was a carcass. A thing. In a short time, they took her out like trash. Dane never saw Ginny again.

Momentarily bored with other toys, the monsters come for him again. Dane tried to resist. It was vain. He was too feeble. They were feeding him less and less. Sidi, head sicko, had him in a controlled burn. This was no wildfire, no erratic arsonist. One plot after another in his psyche was being torched and blackened. Dragging him across the yard they threw him again to the flames. Into the black he went.

"Ah, Al Kalb," Sidi spoke with jubilance, as though a long-lost friend had arrived? "You have come again. What a spectacle that Ginny made, no? Can you believe the eyes – spooky, huh? She was looking your way. 'Maybe that little dog in the crate will rescue me,'" his voice falsetto. "Oh, the thoughts she must have had!" The head psycho clicked his tongue and stood, mug in hand.

"But, enough of old news," Sidi snapped his fingers, "the morning is fresh and ripe with new discoveries."

"You sick freak," Dane, looking up at him from the floor.

"Yes!" triumphantly. "I was hoping you still had some fight left in you. Though I must say your self-preservation *has* been on the low ebb." He pinched his bearded chin, eyebrows bunched. "But see, I gave you a chance to rest, a little nourishment and now there you are fat and sassy. Like a good parent, of sorts, I have seen to it that you have had a multitude of meaningful experiences. It's a way of teasing out all the real elements of a mind past the more superficial facets of personality. Ahhh," Sidi clasped his hands together, "you *are* a well-rounded child. 'Spread your wings,' I always say."

Dane slumped his head to the ground and sighed. This was like talking to a mental patient. Only, this one was systematic, wicked, smart, and presently had him firmly by the throat.

"What you are doing is wrong. It's," he searched for the word, "it's evil."

"Back to this again? Fascinating." Sidi pursed his lips and pulled over a chair. He sat. "What a word for a young American to use. 'Evil?' Really?! That very word denotes judgment based on a universal, moral law. And if so, there must be a universal, moral lawgiver. But you have thrust God out of every corner of your culture, trampled and ridiculed every principled behavior, believe in nothing, and yet you pronounce an absolute, summary judgment on *my* cultural tenets – mine?!

Al Kalb, what right do you have? If you have looked to man to grant your freedoms to you, why are you shocked when man takes them away? You are not on the level plain of rights, my young pleasurist, you are under the top-weighted reality of power. True, this is but a small realm over which I reign but is it not a microcosm of a fast-changing world. For me, and mine, we embrace a divine prerogative to do what we are doing. By pen or by sword we will capture the nations for Allah. Personally," cocking his head to one side, "I prefer the sword – but, everyone has their tastes." Sighing with resignation he stood and began to pace, hands clasped behind his back.

"You have cast off your constitution, your leaders are weak, calculating, corrupt, your people are divided, your military often reduced or hindered by aforementioned politicians, and your enemies are breathing down your neck." Sidi stopped, turned, and looked down at Dane. "And you turn to *me* with a newfound moral certitude and say 'evil'?! It only matters now because it is happening to you." Sidi stood over him, a berating headmaster, assuming his lecture will affect reform. He suddenly straightened, pivoting on his heel.

"Now," flourishing his hand, "on with the show." Two men came and pulled Dane up into a chair. Every inch of movement hurt the mistreated man. Holding up a syringe a third man came and stabbed it into Dane's neck. It shot into his blood stream, through his brain, down the stem and out into his abdomen and limbs. Every nerve ending screamed awake with an electric fire.

His body went stiff, every muscle contracting at once. Sliding to the floor he shuddered, unable to move, unable to respirate. Then it broke loose, a thousand wasp stings all over his body, fire ants crawling in his nose, mouth, and throat, happily injecting alkaloid venom. He screamed and tore at his flesh, digging the ragged, dirty nails across his face, his chest, down his legs.

Deep, bloody gouges formed on every inch of skin he could reach. The shirt and sweats tore away as he pulled and kicked out of them. He was in flames.

For a half hour Sidi stood observing Dane, mental clipboard in hand. He watched clinically, a knowing smile on his face. The clock chimed. Two of his soldiers sprang at Dane, binding him wrist and foot. With involuntary tremors the damaged man jerked about on the ground.

"Now, Al Kalb," Sidi said without emotion, "we begin the rapid descent into darkness."

A hood, a thick, black dirty thing was thrown over his head. By some device at the neck it was locked on even tighter than the others. Panic swept over Dane. He began to hyperventilate. He choked.

Was this it? Was it over? Was he going out as he came in, hooded and bound?

They dragged him on the floor. He heard a hissing sound, like steam in a pan. Constricting, his windpipe clenched, his chest hammered in an emotional attack. A chain rattled down as on a pulley. They hooked his hands and feet then hosted him in the air. It was the cranking sound, the metal clicks of gears turning, lifting and mocking him. How strange he should think of a roller coaster. That jerking of the car, the clack-clack-clack as the ride is pulled up the first, big hill. Then the hesitation at the top, followed by the booming roll downhill.

Then the screams.

Chapter 57

For two days.

Two days of man-made Hell.

Forty-eight hours of The Devil himself as obliging host.

They dropped him in scalding hot water, hauled him up, then swung him to another tub. Down into an icy bath, the bitterest cold he had ever known. Up, over, and into the heat he went; back again into the cold.

He passed out. They shot him up with adrenaline, anti-biotics, stimulants, and a fair amount of psychedelics. Flashes of light through the hood, pain in a multitude of forms, degradations – every species of manipulation was applied that ever sprouted from the soulless pit of man. Yet Sidi made sure to stay within calculated bounds: never enough to kill, yet sufficient to achieve his ends.

Round the clock, men in shifts never let him rest, never let him sleep. With the precision of Aryan science, Dane was subjected to a vicious array of psychological, physical, and mental rigors that liquefied his resistance, his identity, his inner man. Sidi was the master, the fascist dictator of the little domain of Dane, now no bigger than the tormentor's teapot.

This was all approaching the climax, the great hour of his transformation, and it would not end until he became the "worm formerly known as."

Chapter 58

Even the one retreat, the mindless refuge of sleep was taken from him now. He stepped out of one den of Hades into the torment of another. Over and over the nightmare replayed in his tattered mind. Dane couldn't tell any longer if he was awake and suffering, or asleep and being scorched alive. It no longer registered that his eyes were open or closed. Reality was tearing away from him in wholesale chunks, leaving him wandering listlessly through an endless tract of burnt and smoldering badlands.

One by one they brought a string of weeping, begging, screaming bodies before him, each one strapped to the metal stake. Dane stared at them blankly. Were they real? Were they shadows, or regrets come to plague him? Did he have anything left to care for the anguish of their flames?

Licking upwards the fire spasmed below a thick, boiling smoke. The smoke went up, the flames went on, and tiny, black bits floated to him. They covered him like wicked snowflakes. He was upright, but curled into a cumbersome, semi-fetal posture as though warding off the world, its cruelty, its anger, its pain with the only ally he had – his skin. His right hand constantly tapped at a thick, scarry ooze on his temple, his left tenderly cradled the right jaw just below the ear.

Elbows in, knees drawn up he rocked back and forth, forth and back. It was never side to side, nor truly front to back, but a sort of mindless north by north-east diagonal. Filth was his only clothing. Feces, urine, dirt, and old, dried blood were his bedfellows; hunger his companion, misery his most ardent suitor. But the cold he no longer felt. Fear, remorse, regret, these were utterly beaten from him. He was a thing made inhuman, cast upon the littered shore.

Vacant eyes stared through the crude slats. He didn't see the humans or their doings, nor the smoke or flame. The yells, screams, threats, the conversation or its language – nothing found him. All the horrible sizzles, cracks, and sputtering pops were lost on him. This was not the first time. It was not the first victim. He knew none of them. He no longer saw them.

The smoke reached to him, wrapping around him, breathing and constricting, filling up his little world. He sat and rocked. He stroked and tapped. The undulating flicker danced before him. He smelled it all.

Chapter 59

"Ladies and Gentlemen, we now have a substantial number of helicopter surveillance and satellite images of the Belle Isle situation," Meredith Dobbs, Director of the FBI Detroit Office said. She fielded various questions around the large conference room at her headquarters.

OIS Director Marz remained silent. He was teleconferencing in and felt he had little to contribute at this moment. While a rescue attempt of this sort wasn't what his agency was geared for, he still wanted to be kept in the loop. Looking over the various participants he realized he knew about half of them. The rest were too young, or too new to their respective organization to have crossed his path. Detroit Police, State Police, National Guard, FBI, NSA, Homeland, SWAT teams – the whole range of alphabet roulette was spinning around the table.

"Surprisingly," Dobbs continued, "there has been next to nothing regarding chatter. Despite the overall tone of discipline and well-planned execution, some of the messaging we have received speaks of hubris bordering on lunacy." She pulled a picture of the now famous postcard and bodies-in-a-boat communique from Sidi. After a lot of raised eyebrows, and not a few curses, a man spoke up.

"Director Dobbs?" he motioned with his pen.

"Yes, Special Agent Michaels," she recognized him.

"Do we know who this mastermind is?" he asked.

"This is also his picture." Dobbs pulled up a high-resolution photograph in black and white. "It was taken by an operative who infiltrated the island two nights ago. This," she clicked, and a grainier photo sprang up, "was taken from security footage at Detroit Metro Airport three months ago." With all three pictures side-by-side it was plain to see they were of the same man. He was thin, handsome, and had a full but well-trimmed beard.

"Despite the fact," Dobbs continued, "that we have all of this, *and* two clear thumbprints, we have no idea who this man is. What we do know is that according to our boots on the ground, this man is sadistic, well organized, and the undisputed leader of the compound."

The FBI Director opened yet another file. "This picture started as thermal imaging but was clarified and enhanced by compiling all of the data we have. You will note the guarded area is approximately one hundred and fifty feet by two hundred thirty. It consists of four main buildings, oriented in a rectangle running roughly north to south, a carport off the building in the southwest corner, and a large pole building about one hundred feet to the east."

On the picture, all of the aforementioned structures were defined in a ghostly grey against an almost black background. Different figures were color coded for identification. "By our count there are twenty-one guards. These are colored red. The thirty-eight captives are marked as green with most clustered in the pole building, one or two scattered in the yard, and one curiously chained to a box by the carport. At the last, our mystery villain is highlighted purple."

"Ma'am, what is happening to the captives?" A man in a military uniform asked.

Dobbs put her hands palm down on the table and dropped her head. "Torture, slavery, persecution, rape, mutilation, beheading, crucifixion."

"What?!" a woman in a police dress blues said.

"For real?" another man asked.

A few curses blew up around the table.

Suddenly a flurry of talking and exclamations broke out.

"People," Dobbs raised her voice and motioned for silence, "please. We must talk this through. Please!"

The room quieted, but not a few were stung with anger and disbelief.

"We had to know what we were getting in to. Though there were no demands made we still had hope that some form of communication might open up for the hostages. But there has been *nothing*." Her chest heaved up once and fell with frustration. "Now that we know the basic players of the game, we can move forward. If we were worried about them killing captives because of our rescue attempt, we are far beyond that now. We must act swiftly before they end up killing or permanently maiming these citizens."

Marz nodded his head, pleased that they were going to do something. He listened in while Dobbs appointed three people from various institutions to put together a rescue plan to be launched in no more than twenty-four hours. The great hope was that they could save at least some of the lives, kill or capture the enemy combatants, and maybe, just maybe apprehend the elusive figure colored purple.

Chapter 60

G rey fingers stroked the scalp of sky.

 Morning again.

Life, light, the great eyelid of the world opened to a new day.

Still death was the sweeter option.

Dane held on by the slenderest of threads. The strand was weak, frayed in the fibers, slowly unspinning, the gathering of a twenty-something mental distaff being deliberately, adroitly unwound.

They hauled him out of his box and stretched him on his side in the roadway between the red and black. He lay like some dried out slug, a salted leech, curled and shriveled, exposed.

"Good morning, Al Kalb." Sidi squatted down and patted him affectionately. "Ah, you have been put through the paces, haven't you?" He sipped his tea. "Very cold this morning, Al Kalb. And you are, no doubt, very hungry, and, I imagine, quite thirsty."

It was true. It was intentional. Sidi carefully measured every calorie and squeezed down just the right amount of dehydration to create, amongst all the other torments, a swollen tongue and burning thirst. At a signal one of the guards came forward and shot Dane up. It was a cocktail of amphetamines, adrenal hormones, and pain killers. It stimulated his beaten, tormented body just enough to rouse consciousness, and the barest ability for movement.

Like a flame under a pan of cold water he felt some return of his awareness and senses, a slow rise in the heat of pain and deprivation. Dane shuddered convulsively. It was far better to disappear into the numb, unfeeling depths. His mind screamed in panic as they forced him to float.

"Look, Al Kalb, look." Sidi motioned down the lane towards the green and grey doors. There, but five feet away, was a steaming tray of food, fresh water, and hot tea. Its wisps rose lazily in the cool of dawn. "All you need do is crawl and take it. Yes, my pet, you have but to reach for it, to grasp it. Think of how you will be relieved to drink, to eat, to take a civil cup of oolong at the beginning of this brisk, beautiful day. And here you thought I was insensitive to your needs. Oh, Al Kalb, if only you knew how I favored you." Sidi's voice was smooth and consoling.

Dane's eyelid fluttered open. They still hadn't touched his face. He smelled the food. He saw the wisps, rising with promise. Churning awake, a hunger, a desire to satisfy surged up in him. The injected juice coursed through his body. The shaking right hand reached forward.

"But, wait," Sidi stood. "There is a catch, of sorts."

He dragged Dane around like a carcass until he faced the red door. A child stood there, pale, small, clutching a ragged, stuffed animal. Her curly locks were matted, a purple-blue bruise on her round, soft cheek. The door, red and blistered, surrounded her. It seemed in Dane's view to swallow her. He started rapidly sucking in breath. A small tear rolled, pulled violently from his meager reserve of physical and emotional fluid.

"Mummy," she said softly, imploringly.

"Ah," Sidi stood by Dane's head, hands on hips," here is an ethical Gordian Knot. You, my sensitive, compassionate young man – you have a choice. Think about it, and choose carefully, my Al Kalb. Simply put, you may save her, or satisfy yourself. Your thirst is maddening, and who could blame you? You are starving. All your body is screaming for sustenance, for life. But what a pathetic man it would take to let her go through that door." He leaned down to Dane almost whispering. "And you *know* what will happen." Straightening up he slowly paced like a prosecutor delivering closing arguments.

"She will never live as this child again. As a professional, educated in such matters, I can assure you of that. So, what will it be? It's you or her, Al Kalb. Her," he pointed to the little figure, tears etching dirty pathways down her filthy cheeks, "or you. I will give you one full minute to decide."

Sidi said something to his men, and they passed money amidst laughs and gestures.

Dane loathed himself. Bile spit up into his mouth. The thirst was maddening. What little was left of the man he was longed to help the small child. She was so innocent. This was not her fight. It was not her fault. Hunger and want urged him to save himself. Self-preservation inhaled the faint odor of the food. The thoughts of tea, water, a meal – if he was able to salivate his mouth would be full of juices.

Hating himself, hating Sidi, hating God and the world together he clenched his teeth in the bitterness of this life. Though he couldn't now recall their names, he knew he had failed others, and now even this little one. Scum – that was the only word for him. He despised everything he was, and even more the terrible truth of what he wasn't: He wasn't good, or noble, or strong. He wasn't a man.

Trying to weep left him gagging. Small sucking and grunting sounds escaped his mouth. Back and forth he pulled between sensibility and satiation, between sacrifice and shame.

As its master wavered so also did the right hand. Where would it point? What would it seek? Dane looked at the brown-haired doll, terrified, sad, and completely by herself in the world. Her large, beautiful eyes would melt anyone's heart. What they would do to her! How they would crush her like a plump, little ball of flesh until she was a withered skin of dried pulp and seed.

There was still a small, guttering flame of humanity in his breast. It flickered tenuously, keeping a precarious hold on some hazy notion of what was right. The struggling lumen cast but a feeble, timorous light on the plight of the little girl.

He looked at her. Like the rich arterial lining of a shark's mouth, the red door yawned behind the delicate, soft-chinned frame, ready to engulf her, to tear her apart in the thrashing teeth. The eyes – why did they always look at him, look *to* him? How was he supposed to help? He couldn't stop them. They were all caught, buzzing helplessly on the same web.

"Yes," he reasoned with the last shard of conscience, "I can't help her. They will rape her another day, if not today. What did today matter, or tomorrow, or a week from now? All the captives were dead – Charles, his wife, Ginny, soon Dane, and soon the soft little flower would be decimated by the wretched ogre.

He looked at her shining eyes. Ignoring their pleading he raised his right hand in a feeble gesture of apology.

Towards the tray he turned. The shaking hand obeyed. It was decreed in the ravaged manse of Dane that survival would triumph, condemning the poor waif to her doom. Still pumped up on the chemicals, the broken body put its best efforts into obtaining the food, the oasis in its desert of need.

"Al Kalb, I am not surprised, but I am so very disappointed. Oh, how I would have loved a heroic ending to the story, however futile. But this – oh, I am ashamed of you. What will the neighbors say?" Sidi colored his words with a chiding sadness, continuing the play of his perverse game.

He spoke and two men moved forward. One turned Dane's face towards the tray. The other kicked the teapot, water jug, and plate of food across the gravel yard. It was all lost. Dane was lost. Yanking his right arm, they took him back into the black.

Sidi pulled the girl's hair from behind. She cried out, disappearing through the blood colored door.

Chapter 61

They had broken him. Pale, grey and indifferent, the sky had no pity. The bitter fingers of morning had no sympathy. Even the earliest of robins utterly ignored him and his human exigencies.

They had broken him, and he was no one; not Dane, not Al Kalb, not even human. A vicious, militant Zen of nothingness was forced upon him. He wasn't anything to anyone – not son, or brother, love, nor friend.

They had shattered him and propped the mass of poorly glued pieces upright in the back of the pallet prison. No chain was on his neck, the door was open. He was tethered by the nothingness, caged by the useless meat sack and the lack of motor to drive it.

He stared into a world that wouldn't look his way. Eyes, once warm, inviting, were two shells of coconut, thready, dull, and hard. There was nothing on him, but he felt no cold. The sun had increased in strength, but it meant nothing to him. Its beams were oddly happy, the gentle blush of warmth in pale yellow white. But the creature could feel no heat. The thing that sat there was unoccupied. Having vacated, the previous tenant was far away, running wildly across fields of flowers, down dunes, across a rugged shoreline, bathed in glorious, summer light, awash with roaring surf.

The husk, the dry, molted cicada skin still clung to the approximation of life. There was but one, pathetic sign of existence. *Tap-tap-tap*, his right hand beat out a time against the temple. *Tap-tap-tap*, it drummed to an unknown music, unheard of by fellow creatures. The cob, stripped of its golden kernels lay discarded, unwanted by the ever-hungry teeth of the world. He had nothing more to give, there was nothing more to take.

They came then for Pearce. Dark shadows, unafraid of the daylight, crept from the blackest corners of humanity. Michael knew his end. They had done what they would, and he would not yield to their demands. The monsters sought him, found him, and took him.

As they stripped off his cover and clothes Pearce thought of the early Christians dying in the Roman Colosseum or dipped in tar and set on fire to light Nero's garden.

When they laid him on the wood, he thought of Justin Martyr, Huss, and all those who stood and did not yield – paying for it with their lives. As they nailed his hands and feet he cried out and remembered those who suffered the Inquisition, the fleeing Puritans, The Huguenots, those lost to humanity in the prisons of Soviet Russia and the correction camps of China.

While raising him up he was reminded of those Christians in the Middle East who had lost their lives at the hands of Islamists, crying out "Jesus" before beheaded.

Hauling him up in place made him think of the sufferings of his Lord Jesus Christ who came not to be served, but to serve and give His life as a ransom for many. That in dying Christ was reconciling the fallen, sinful world to God.

"Have mercy on them, Father," he cried out in terrible agony.

As he hung the long, slow hours of torment he thought of the great cloud of witnesses from God's Word – how they were tortured, judged unjustly, imprisoned, stoned, and wandered about in caves and dens of the Earth. These gave testimony to the Glory of God, urging him to run the race without wavering.

He knew that he would have given in, converted, denied Christ were it not for the Grace of God, for the sustaining presence of the Holy Spirit. Through this strength his soul found the endurance to never surrender, to fight the good fight of faith to the end. He knew in Whom he believed. Christ was the author and finisher of his faith – He would never leave him, nor forsake him.

As they day grew long and Michael slipped away from this world to the Glorious Kingdom, he remembered those who lived under the banner of Christ, faithful through all suffering, those of whom the world was not worthy.

Chapter 62

Three bursts echoed through the dark. They were answered. Back and forth, distant then closer, shots rang, and muzzles flashed.

"Al Kalb! Al Kalb!" Sidi spoke cheerfully while knocking on the cage. Dane didn't answer. "Oh, come now, Al Kalb – don't be so hard-hearted towards me. What is a little hurt between friends?"

No response.

Sidi waved off the silence.

"At any rate...isn't this exciting? We have been prepared for this since day one." Sidi put a finger to his mouth. "Okay, since day two, technically? But who is keeping track? Certainly not you, Al Kalb. Yes, we have been ready and knew they were coming almost twenty-four hours ago. We have mice in many places, you see." He gently patted the mottled, swollen leg. "Say, I hate to trouble you, but I am afraid I must. I know you have had so much on your mind, wherever it presently is, but now is not the time for reflection, but action."

He signaled and guards quickly pulled the broken wretch out of the pallet box, laying him on a stretcher.

"Come, Al Kalb," Sidi said with heroic resolve, "our work here is done, and it is time to leave."

The tormentor said something in Arabic and the men lifted the captive up. They moved swiftly from the camp. Sidi walked beside the silent, tapping form, chatting happily away.

"Al Kalb, you may wonder why we are leaving, why do we not stay and fight? Oh, most of the men are. They will sacrifice for Allah and be eternally rewarded. We were not here to hold a territory, my curious pupil, no, we were here to inflict a wound, one deep enough to keep them distracted. This is but one of many such made on the body of your country."

"And now, Al Kalb, I will move on to greater things. There is something *awesome* coming. You see!" slapping Dane's arm playfully, "I am incorporating your trendy sayings into my speech."

The carriers bumped and hustled along. Though the night was black, the sky was clear, and their path well known.

Serious gunfire erupted to the west of them. A helicopter flew by two hundred yards away. Down to the shore they trucked, setting him on the ground next to the midnight water, lapping thickly against the brown soil. Dancing lazily side to side a small boat was tethered to some leafless bushes. Sidi whispered something briefly. The men opened their packs helping him to don a wet suit, fins, and scuba gear.

Like the shadow of death, a thick, muscular man rose from the water. His mask shimmered and dripped, a strange, alien eye.

"Asan!" joy in Sidi's voice. When the man waded ashore, they embraced.

"Come, come, Asan," Sidi, ever chipper. "You must meet someone."

"Another project?" Asan replied with humor, switching to the dialect of their childhood village.

"You know me too well," in native tones.

Sidi turned on a pale, blue light, illuminating the battered form with a funereal glow.

"Al Kalb." Sidi swept his hand out.

Asan snorted.

"Al Kalb," tapping a bare, emaciated arm. "This is my brother, Asan. We are going to leave now. Oh, the fireworks are just beginning. But," curling down his bottom lip he began to nod his head, "it is wise for us to be on our merry way." He patted his arm again. "Ciao!"

The brothers turned toward the water. Sidi slipped a tight, black hood over his head, tucked it into the suit and put a face mask on his head.

"Brother," in the home tongue, "you should just kill the infidel."

"Asan, what sort of man do you take me for? That would be very, very immoral."

Asan began to laugh, then laughed more. "My brother," shaking his head, "my brother."

They checked all the equipment and disappeared like ghosts into the murky river.

Chapter 63

He floated serenely. Little slaps against the hull knocked inquisitively like curious water nymphs wondering who this stranger to the river was. Claws in the dark had grabbed him and put him in the little boat. Muttering something at him, something they found humorous, they turned on a small, electric, trolling motor fixed in place, and launched the craft off the eastern shore of Belle Isle. The buoyant dinghy swam silently into the stretch between Detroit and Windsor.

At a perversely charitable order a blanket had been thrown on him. He never noticed. His heartbeat, his body functioned, his eyes were open. But he was gone, far away on a distant shore thundering with the roar of breakers, the Earth alive and turning with the vibrations of life.

She raced in front of him, sprinting on her long, shapely legs, a gazelle in the earth-bound stretches of flight.

He was mad. She had driven him there.

In a final burst of speed, he grabbed at her fluttering, summer dress. With a squeal she turned to him. They both tumbled in the sand. Laughing, they sat up together. He had caught her. She had let him.

It was not who he expected, yet more than he could have dreamed. She, with the green, living eyes and her unearthly smile was a refuge, a dream, a place of retreat when most needed. And now that he had her, he knew. He finally understood. This winsome lass was desired by billions, pursued by hundreds of millions, embraced only by a comparative, but fortunate handful.

She was life, she was liberty, she was freedom.

For himself and his world, for his culture, peers, and future he feared more than anything that she would slip away. He pulled her close, yearning to hold her, to keep her. But with a toss of her head she was gone.

Sitting alone, arms empty, his face fell, and he began to weep. How tenuous had his hold been? How easily she slipped from his grasp! *"Why?"* the man wondered. *"What more could I have done?"*

In that state of brokenness, he finally saw the truth of his own heart: he desired to use her for his selfish passions, but was never willing to pay the cost for loving her. It was the thing she had known all along; the reason she had fled, and the monsters had come.

The man stood, reaching, yearning for the sky, dreaming of a chance to escape, if but momentarily from the sad isolation of his soul.

Hazel brown eyes came alive for the briefest of moments. They pushed up, away from the light, the shelter of an inner world, the safe escape into which he had retreated. Through the conscious membrane, out and into the dark, lonely night he emerged from this ameliorating cocoon. Upwards to the celestial sweep they focused and searched. There, in the midst of the flowing Lethe, from the bottom of a dirty boat a crushed man lay dreaming, looking, hoping.

Dane saw the stars.

As cities in clouds, and dancers in flames, the eye will see what it desires, yearning to capture the sweeping dream, the romantic, ethereal swell within the benign elements before it.

Tracing out their brilliant fires against the endless abyss, he formed a dragon.

His beloved filled all the sky for a moment then erased. The vision fell back from its apex in the fatal plunge to Earth. Down the tunnel, back to the shore, away from the pain he plummeted. This broken mind would never surface again. It would never be unbroken. And on the downward slope he prayed his first and last earnest petition.

"God....help us."

Chapter 64

They both wore shades. The sun was brilliant.

"It feels deliciously warm, doesn't it?" Aimes said as they walked slowly along the graveled path.

"That's one way to put it." Tamari agreed. "I'm just glad it's not freezing anymore. I'm tired of being cold."

Laughing a little, Aimes chided her, "then why ever do you live this far north?"

"Ok, I'll quit complaining." She looked around the area and noted the four buildings. Everywhere was carnage. Death. Suffering. What drives mankind to this? How crazy do you have to be to spend this much effort just to destroy, to hurt?

Yellow tape cordoned off large sections around the four buildings, and an ugly little crate under a carport. There was a chain, a collar, a bowl. Scores of forensic investigators and military personnel combed over every inch, documenting, sampling, trying to piece it all together. Survivors were cared for and questioned. Bodies, or parts of them, were sent to the morgue.

"I don't think Bell Isle will ever be the same." Aimes lowered his shades. "As a child I was here on holiday in the mid-seventies. We fed deer from our car. And now, the soil is soaked with blood."

"Only right around here, Aimes. I'm sure people will forget in time. They'll pack their lunches and ride their bikes right on through, past whatever memorial plaques they might install someday."

"I should think they would put something, Miss Banks. All that happened here is just part of the continuing indictment against humanity. If God is there, he will surely weigh us wanting in the balance."

Tamari nodded her head. She looked around at the brokenness, the death that humans wreak on each other. Despite the daylight a strange fog seemed to lie in the hidden corners of the island. Though her emotions begged for it to be different, she knew blood lay ahead, and tears. Scenarios began running through her head - tracking down the killers, unraveling the plans of those terrorizing this city, bringing them to justice. Pressing her eyes closed she turned toward Aimes.

"Here." Tamari handed her partner a dossier locked in a thin briefcase. "This is everything I could piece together on the graphic from that picture."

"Ah, the one on our resident rock thrower's bandana," Aimes said, taking the attaché.

"Yep," Agent Banks nodded her head. "And what's more it was found on the headless body that came from this island."

Aimes looked at Tamari, his brows together in thought. "That man and his wife?"

"Yeah," she said quietly, her head down. "The more I found out, the more troubled I became." She took in a deep breath and looked toward the choppy water.

"I will certainly read it over," Aimes said. He opened his mouth to say more but curiously spotted an object and stopped. A small, stuffed animal hung upside down in a leafless bush. The object seemed both incongruous and sickening at the same time. Gathering his thoughts, he stirred Tamari up from her silence.

"Anything you can clue me in on now?" he said softly.

Tamari cleared her throat and spoke. "The word in Arabic is *bay'ah*. It translates to 'pledge' or 'oath of allegiance.' It comes from *bay'at ash-shajarah*, meaning Pledge of the Tree. Short and sweet, in 628 AD, Mohammed set out on a pilgrimage to Mecca. The Quraysh, a group non-Muslim Arabs that controlled the city wouldn't let him in. He sent an envoy named Uthman in to see if he could work out something. The dude stayed longer than he should have, and they wouldn't tell the Muslims where he was. So, they assumed he was killed."

"Most irritating, I assume," Aimes answered casually.

"Right you are. Muhammed gathered about fourteen-hundred of his followers under a tree, and made them pledge to fight to the death and avenge Uthman."

"Ah, I see it now." Aimes nodded his head curiously. "How clever – a tree with bay'ah on it. And?"

"And from what I gather these guys are nuts! They currently follow some murky leader that's supposed to usher in the end of the world." Tamari said this with exhaustion in her voice. "On that note, I'm guessing it's a bad time to put in for vacation and hope that this is all over." She glanced at the building with the red door and shuddered.

"Quite so," Aimes tightly squeezed his lips and watched two men zipping up a body bag. "One must not hope such a thing." He turned and faced her squarely. "I fear, my dear, that it has all just begun."

Endnotes:

i *Pirates of the Caribbean, at World's End*. Dir. Gore Verbinski. Prod. Jerry Bruckheimer. By Ted Elliott and Terry Rossio. Perf. Johnny Depp, Geoffrey Rush, and Orlando Bloom. Buena Vista Pictures, 2007.

Don't miss out!

Visit the website below and you can sign up to receive emails whenever David T LaDuke publishes a new book. There's no charge and no obligation.

https://books2read.com/r/B-A-OEGE-YMSX

BOOKS 2 READ

Connecting independent readers to independent writers.

Did you love *The Smell of Rubber*? Then you should read *Eyes Wide* by David T LaDuke!

Like high definition snapshots capturing crisp images of a powerful woman's life, each chapter of EYES WIDE tells a piece of the Tamari Banks story. A glimpse of happy, quirky childhood, hard challenge and success in military training, and a plunge into the dark world of terrorism reveals not only what she has done, but *who* she really is. This novella is a potent mix of action and emotion, nostalgia and intrigue. Prequel to the Tamari Banks Thriller Series, it lays an insightful backstory out of which the beautiful, young hero emerges, determined to make a difference in this world. Read it now, meet Tamari, and buckle in for the series ahead.

Read more at https://dladuke.com.

About the Author

Born 1967 in Detroit, Michigan I was raised by loving parents who impressed in the clay of my childhood a belief in God's existence. Around eight years old we moved farther north to a town called Hartland. I graduated from Hartland High School in 1986. In December of 1986 by God's Grace I became a follower of Jesus Christ.

After a couple years at University of Michigan - Flint I moved to Pennsylvania and was married to my beautiful wife, Julie in 1989. Five children, multiple grandchildren, and various houses and pets later I now reside in Beaver County, Pennsylvania.

Learn more about me at www.dladuke.com

Read more at https://dladuke.com.

About the Publisher

Founded in 2018 by David T LaDuke, LaDuke Communications focuses on in-house, Christian publications.

www.ingramcontent.com/pod-product-compliance
Lightning Source LLC
Chambersburg PA
CBHW060535260626
47161CB00003B/912